FOREVER DIAMOND

GILLIAN GODDEN

Boldwood

First published in Great Britain in 2023 by Boldwood Books Ltd.

Copyright © Gillian Godden, 2023

Cover Design by Colin Thomas

Cover Photography: Shutterstock

Every effort has been made to obtain the necessary permissions with reference to copyright material, both illustrative and quoted. We apologise for any omissions in this respect and will be pleased to make the appropriate acknowledgements in any future edition.

A CIP catalogue record for this book is available from the British Library.

Paperback ISBN 978-1-80280-097-5

Large Print ISBN 978-1-80280-096-8

Hardback ISBN 978-1-80280-095-1

Ebook ISBN 978-1-80280-099-9

Kindle ISBN 978-1-80280-098-2

Audio CD ISBN 978-1-80280-090-6

MP3 CD ISBN 978-1-80280-091-3

Digital audio download ISBN 978-1-80280-094-4

Boldwood Books Ltd
23 Bowerdean Street
London SW6 3TN
www.boldwoodbooks.com

For my son Robert and his fiancée Ellie on their forthcoming wedding x

1

THE SPIDER'S WEB

'Where are we going? You've taken the wrong turn at the roundabout.' Patsy Diamond sat in the back of the police car and looked out of the window as the sign for Glasgow sped past her. Knots churned in her stomach. She'd just been arrested at the airport by two detectives supposedly taking her to the police station and now they were driving in the opposite direction. Confused, Patsy said, 'I demand to know where you're taking me!'

The man in the passenger seat grinned as he turned to face her and held out a cigarette he'd lit for her. 'Hold out your arms, Mrs Diamond.'

Patsy leant forward and put the cigarette in her mouth, while tentatively holding out her arms. The man in the passenger seat leaned towards her and unlocked the handcuffs he'd put on her earlier. 'Isn't that better?' He smiled.

Taking the cigarette out of her mouth, Patsy exhaled into the air, forcing the man in the passenger seat to open the window. Rubbing her wrists, panic began to rise inside of her. Taking another drag of her cigarette, she stared at the back of the heads of the two supposed detectives.

'If you don't tell me where we're going, I'll scream and pull that bloody driver's hair out by the roots,' she shouted at them both and kicked the back of the seat, hurting her own foot in the process.

The man in the passenger seat looked over his shoulder and smiled again. 'We're going to the airport Mrs Diamond; that's where we're taking you.'

A frown crossed Patsy's brow. She didn't understand. 'Where's Larry? And why to the airport? We've just come from there. Just who are you exactly?' Her face flushed and anger rose inside of her, and she could feel a stickiness on her palms. The back seat of the car felt claustrophobic. There was no escape and all she could do was sit and wait, although her nerves were frayed.

'Calm down, Mrs Diamond, you're safe and so is Larry. It's not him we want, it's you. You've driven us to this. You refused to come when you were politely asked and now we've had to go to extremes to prove our point. Just sit back and smoke your cigarette, we'll be there in a minute. Personally, I found it very strange when we arrested you that you came with us so easily. Is that who you are, Mrs Diamond? A drug dealer, a madam and a money launderer?' The man laughed and turned to his friend in the driver's seat. 'You're going to have to be a better liar than that.'

Patsy's mind was racing; she couldn't understand what was happening. What had she refused to do? She was supposed to be going on a long holiday to the Maldives with her boyfriend Larry but had been arrested and handcuffed at the airport before they could board their flight. Larry, being a lawyer, had protested and told her to say anything to the detectives, but she had been marched through the airport in handcuffs, red-faced with shame, leaving Larry to follow in another car. It was all a mystery, and now she was driving along with two strange men who seemed to know her, but she didn't know them. Their accents weren't Albanian. She'd had a lot of turf wars over drug dealings with the Albanians and could only assume it was something to do with them. But no, they weren't clever enough to set up such a charade and they didn't have that kind of power or authority.

The car pulled up outside the airport again and getting out, they opened the back door for her. Patsy looked up at them both, trying to compose herself, all the while her stomach was in knots and she didn't know what to expect.

'You'd better put that cigarette out; they don't allow them in airports.' The man took the cigarette out of her mouth and stubbed it out with his shoe. 'Come along now; we haven't much time.'

'None of this makes sense. This is kidnapping, you know that, don't you? Is it money you want?' Patsy could hear herself babbling on but couldn't stop.

The man was starting to become irritated by her constant questioning. 'Come on, we need to see you safely on the aeroplane. Your flight is in fifteen minutes.'

Patsy's jaw dropped. 'You're letting me go on my holiday? Have you told Larry? Is he here?' Patsy looked around, but she couldn't see him. The two men pushed her forward but said nothing. One of them linked his arm through hers and marched her towards a check-in desk. As he took the ticket out of the inside of his pocket, Patsy's heart sank when she heard him speak in French.

Now the penny had finally dropped. They were sending her to France. She wanted to say something to the woman at the desk, but her mouth was dry and she was finding it hard to swallow. Her knees felt weak, and she could hardly put one foot in front of the other as they pushed her forward to board her plane. 'I have no luggage. What about Larry? What are you going to do with him?'

'Mrs Diamond, I told you he's safe. Now, we have to be quick. You don't have much time.'

Patsy walked ahead, nervously turning backwards to look at them as she did. She thought about making a run for it, but could see they weren't going to leave until they knew she was safely on the plane. There was nothing she could do but follow their instructions. They were working for the Milieu – the feared gangland bosses of France. She thought she had appeased them with their joint business venture and paid them what Karen Duret had owed. But apparently they weren't finished with her yet.

Karen Duret had been the thorn in her side from the very beginning. Her initial dealings had been with Patsy's late husband Nick. She had sold his drugs and done his bidding and even faked her own death to be free of him. She'd escaped to France, where she'd got up to her neck in debt and was in trouble with the French gangland bosses who wanted her home and her business off her. Once she'd found out that Nick had died, she'd hatched a plan to waltz into Patsy's life and claim Nick's drug money and empire for herself. It had become a battle between them, and Patsy had finally rid herself of Karen, but not without consequences and a near prison sentence. She'd been blackmailed and put through the mill and the Milieu had saved her skin! They were on good business terms and they'd shared the booty since Karen's demise.

As far as Patsy was concerned, there weren't any problems between them, even though the thought of them and their sadistic ways sent chills down her spine. She had seen what they were capable of and it frightened her. It seemed to her that they had spies around every corner of the world and even their closest associates weren't safe if they crossed them. What did they want from her now?

As far as she knew, everything was okay out there. She had sent Greek Paul to oversee the running of a restaurant on the land she owned in France, and reports from him had been promising.

He had become a loyal worker for her after Nick had blackmailed him into selling drugs for him at his one of many shops. Patsy had suggested Paul go to France to start afresh and oversee her restaurant and the truffle farm at the chateau. A sweeping thought crossed her mind, that maybe he had done something stupid in her absence.

As she climbed the steps up to the plane, sweat appeared on her brow as she remembered the last time she had seen the Milieu in the cellar of a bistro in France, where she had witnessed them murdering Karen Duret's brother. She felt sick to her stomach and bile rose in her throat as she wondered if that was to be her fate, too.

Once on board, she ordered a large gin and tonic, almost gulping it down in one when it arrived. She must have looked pale because the flight attendant asked if she was okay and assured her the flight would be okay. Patsy just smiled at her. She felt frightened, lost and alone. No one apart from Larry knew she had been supposedly arrested; everyone would think she was flying off to her romantic destination, drinking champagne. How wrong they were.

Agitated and nervous, she couldn't wait for the flight to be over so she could ring her best friend Sheila. Holding on to the arms of her seat, she could see her knuckles were almost white from squeezing them so tightly. Smacking her lips together, she cocked her head to one side to grab the attention of the air hostess. 'Another gin and tonic please.'

Patsy ran her hands through her hair in despair as the male passenger beside her nudged her with his elbow. 'It's a short flight, Mrs Diamond; better not have too many of those.' He grinned, his French accent disturbing her. Not only had she been safely put on the aeroplane, but they had organised an escort in case she tried to make a run for it. Her heart sank. These people had gone to a lot of trouble to make sure she arrived to face their wrath or whatever it was. She could feel the sweat between her breasts, and her back felt wet against the seat. She wanted to cry as fear gripped her but fought back the tears. What was the point? she asked herself. The sick feeling in the pit of her stomach wasn't going to go away until she knew what they wanted. There was no point in fighting it, she had willingly gone into business with these people and now for whatever reason, she had annoyed them.

The air hostess stood beside her and proffered the drink she'd ordered. 'Would you like anything else, madam?'

Taking the glass, Patsy shook her head, when all the time she felt like screaming out, 'I need help!' But what good would it do? Taking a sip of the cool drink soothed her parched throat. She tried casting a furtive glance at the man beside her, but didn't want to interact with him. It was clear to her that he had just been making his presence known.

The two police officers parked outside the police station. One of them got out of the front seat and opened the back door. 'You may as well get out here, Mr Kavanagh; we're just parking the car around the back. You know the way.'

Angry and red faced, Larry had continuously threatened and shouted at them for their wrongful arrest of Patsy and ranted about how he was going to drag them through the courts and make sure they lost their jobs. His threats, although annoying, hadn't bothered them. They'd sat in the front and said nothing, until now.

Surprised, Larry got out of the car. 'Aren't you going to escort me into the police station? That's the normal procedure, isn't it?'

'You're not under arrest, Mr Kavanagh. So go ahead; I'm sure you're anxious to find Mrs Diamond.'

The mention of Patsy spurred Larry on. 'Too bloody right I am. God knows what she's going through.' Larry ran up the steps to the police station. Flustered and annoyed, Larry stood in front of the desk sergeant. 'Where is she? Where is Mrs Diamond?'

The desk sergeant, who knew Larry as the local duty solicitor, looked up at him through the Perspex window. 'Who are you looking for?'

'Diamond... Mrs Patsy Diamond,' Larry shouted. 'I demand to see her now and those two police officers who brought me here will wish they never had. I want their jobs for this!' The Perspex glass steamed up from his hot breath.

Furrowing his brows, the elderly desk sergeant scratched his balding head and tapped on his computer. Looking up at Larry, he shook his head. 'We don't have a Mrs Diamond in custody, Mr Kavanagh. And who were the police officers who brought you here? There's nothing here to say anything was called in regarding bringing you to the police station today.'

Stunned at the question, Larry looked around the room, trying hard to think. 'Check your computer again; they've just arrested Mrs Diamond at the airport in front of everyone, accusing her of all kinds of things.'

The desk sergeant raised an eyebrow. 'Did you see their warrant cards? Surely an experienced solicitor like yourself would want to see their identity cards?'

Larry felt the red flush of embarrassment creep up from his neck into his cheeks. He hadn't followed any of the normal procedure in his blind panic. 'I'll go and check,' he answered sheepishly. Opening the doors, he looked outside. There were police officers milling around, but none he recognised. A thought crossed his mind and he walked back into the police station.

'They could have taken Mrs Diamond to another police station. The one in Edinburgh maybe...' he stammered. 'Check your computer again.'

Sighing, the desk sergeant tapped into his computer once more. 'No Mrs Diamond has been taken to any police station Mr Kavanagh. I don't know what you saw, but it definitely wasn't police officers from this region.'

Sheepishly, Larry cursed himself. 'If that is the case, then Mrs Diamond is a missing person. God knows where she is or who she's with, but it sounds like kidnap to me. I have no idea who brought me here, but they were in uniform, I swear.'

'You can't report her as a missing person for twenty-four hours, Mr Kavanagh. How long has she been missing?'

Larry felt a sinking feeling in the pit of his stomach. 'About an hour now, I suppose,' he muttered.

'Well, I suggest you go home. She could be there wondering where you are.' A queue had started to build up behind Larry and he could sense their impatience.

Turning, Larry pushed his way past the other people behind him and flung the doors open wide, nearly knocking them off the hinges. Standing outside, he looked around and breathed in the fresh air. His mind was racing. He couldn't understand what had happened. Confused and angry, he hailed a taxi. If anyone would know what had happened to Patsy, Sheila would. A glimmer of hope crept up inside of him. He would go to Sheila's, he decided. She would know something.

Arriving at Sheila's, Larry hammered on her door. When she opened it, the look of surprise on her face showed Larry that she didn't know anything about Patsy either.

'What are you doing here, Larry? Shouldn't you be flying off into the sunset by now?' She laughed and opened the door wider to let him in.

Pushing past her and running into the lounge, he ran his hands through his hair and stood with his hands on his hips. 'Where is she, Sheila? Where the hell is Patsy? Has she called you? You two are like sisters and she wouldn't disappear anywhere without telling you.' He pointed his finger accusingly at her.

Sheila stood there, stunned, but quickly regained her composure. 'Now listen to me laddie. Do not come into my house shouting. Either tell me what's going on or fuck off out!'

Tears brimmed in Larry's eyes and fell down his cheeks. 'I'm sorry Sheila. I was hoping she would be here. She's disappeared. Two men pretended to arrest her at the airport and now she's disappeared!'

A sense of foreboding washed over Sheila and she could feel the hairs rise on her neck. 'Sit down Larry, I'll get us a drink. You certainly look like you could do with one.'

As she poured them both a drink, all kinds of things went through her mind; she was glad that Angus was at work and her girls were at school. 'Tell me what happened, Larry. Have you tried calling her?'

Larry shook his head; he'd been so distraught he'd checked his mobile for calls from Patsy but never thought to call her. Sheila got her own mobile and rang Patsy's number, but there was no answer.

Larry sat on the sofa, looking down at the floor as his tears fell. 'Someone has kidnapped her. I should never have let her out of my sight.'

'What did they say when they arrested her? What were they arresting her for?' Sheila was curious but didn't want to reveal too much for Larry's sake.

'Racketeering, money laundering, drug dealing. For Christ's sake Sheila, we know her husband was up to all kind of things, but not Patsy. She's spent all this time trying to clear his mess up.

Do you think it has something to do with Nick?' Larry asked, while wiping his tears and nose on the back of his sleeve.

Sheila's hollow laughter filled the lounge. 'Patsy drug dealing and money laundering? My God, whoever it was had a vivid imagination. She's a bloody hairdresser laddie.' She didn't quite meet Larry's eyes when she said this. 'If it was a kidnapping Larry, surely they'll be in touch with their demands.'

Giving a weak smile she hoped was reassuring, Sheila turned her head and looked at the wall, all the while wondering what had happened to Patsy. Only time would tell.

2

DEMONS

As the plane landed, Patsy gave a sigh of relief and a sideways glance to the man beside her. 'Will you be joining me on the rest of the journey?'

The man shook his head.

Shrugging, Patsy unfastened her belt and stood up to join everyone else in the aisle to get off. She had no luggage, so once she had shown her passport, she walked out of the airport. A car pulled up in front of her and a man got out and opened the back door. 'Welcome to France, Mrs Diamond.'

She nodded and got into the back of the car. Instantly she reached in her handbag and took out her cigarettes. Lighting one, she tapped the driver on the shoulder. 'Where are we heading?'

The man looked up into the rear-view mirror and caught her eye. 'My instructions are to take you to the bistro, madam.'

Patsy sat back in her seat and let out a deep sigh. That was what she had feared most. The bistro. Now she knew she was in trouble. They could kill her and bury her and no one would ever know. The very thought of this chilled her to the bone. As she held the cigarette to her lips, she could see her hands visibly shaking. She was terrified.

The driver didn't say another word on the long journey and Patsy looked out of the window, watching the world go by. People milled around going about their everyday business, ignorant of the fact that she had been kidnapped and was about to meet her maker. Patsy reached into her handbag on the seat beside her to get her mobile phone. Her heart was pounding in her chest, and she didn't want to raise suspicion. The driver was busy shouting in French at a cyclist through the open window. Sliding her hand into her bag, she pressed WhatsApp and Sheila's name popped up. As quickly as possible, she texted the word Milieu, and then took her hand away. Once Sheila got that message she would know where Patsy was and that she was still alive, even if it wasn't for much longer.

Frightened, but feeling a little calmer now Sheila knew where she was, Patsy yawned and moved on her seat to get comfortable. She tapped the driver again. 'Any chance of stopping for a drink and a toilet break, mister?'

Opening the glove compartment, the driver took out a bottle of water and held it over his shoulder without taking his eyes off the road. Taking it off him, Patsy sighed. The driver then passed her a plastic mixing bowl from the front passenger seat. Looking at it oddly, Patsy reached out for it. Then it dawned on her what it was for. 'Oh my God, is this my portable toilet?'

'Yes, madam. Use it.'

Gobsmacked, Patsy put it on the seat beside her and looked at it with disdain. Although she took a sip from the bottle of water, she decided to not overdo it. After all, she didn't want to degrade herself by using the plastic bowl!

Patsy how no idea where she was; all the roads looked the

same and now the driver had veered off onto a country lane with nothing but hedgerows on either side.

Out of the blue, the driver started shouting in French and when Patsy followed his line of sight, she saw a farm truck heading towards them. The driver was flashing his lights and blowing his horn.

'Pull over you idiot; he's almost wider than the road!' But instead, her driver wound down the window and made abusive hand signals towards the truck. Fear gripped Patsy, and her heart pounded. She felt herself bounce around the car and pain seized her. Screaming out, her instinct was to cover her face as the truck ploughed into them. Suddenly, she felt an impact and the car was rolling along the hedgerows. With each roll, she felt herself bounce around the car, not knowing which way was up. She tried holding on to the seat, but a black veiled curtain overwhelmed her and she passed out.

She could hear banging and shouting, as she slowly opened the slits of her eyes, drifting in and out of consciousness. As she looked up, she saw a man jump off a white horse and run towards her, frantically pulling open the car door. His shouts seemed distant in her head, and she couldn't understand a word he said, but she could feel his presence nearby. Moans of pain escaped her body as she felt strong arms dragging her out of the car to safety. She could barely see and her head ached, but she could feel herself being dragged out into the road. The hedgerow tore at her body, and branches scratched her face.

The man lowered his head towards her mouth to see if she was breathing. Once he had seen that she was alive, he spoke to her. Patsy stirred and through the slits of her eyes, she saw him get back onto his horse and gallop away. Weak and helpless, she laid her head on the roadside and drifted back into unconsciousness, abandoned and alone.

Opening her eyes again, she blinked and could barely make out her surroundings, until a nurse leaned over her and smiled. 'Welcome back to the land of the living, Mrs Diamond.'

Still drowsy and with blurred vision, Patsy looked around and realised she was in hospital. Her head ached and her neck felt stiff. Reaching her hand up, she felt a neck brace and winced. Her mouth was dry and she could barely speak.

'Where am I?' she whispered.

'Drink this.' Holding the straw to Patsy's mouth, the nurse smiled again. The cool water quenched her thirst, making her cough.

Half dazed, she looked towards the foot of the bed.

'Maggie?' she muttered through swollen lips.

Walking around the side of the bed, Maggie held her hand. 'I'm here lassie.'

The sight of Maggie's familiar black cardigan comforted her. 'Don't you fret now Patsy, you're in good hands and everything is going to be okay.'

Maggie stepped back so that a doctor could examine Patsy. Although his accent was French, he spoke very good English. 'Do you know where you are, Mrs Diamond? Do you remember what happened?' he asked while flashing a pen light into her eyes.

'The car, I was in a car, it crashed. I'm not sure,' she whispered. She felt weak and was trying hard to remember what had happened through her foggy brain.

'There was no car crash Patsy. There isn't a sign of a car and nothing has been reported. The gendarme has not been here.' The doctor smiled and said something in French to the nurse.

Slowly, Patsy asked, 'Gendarme? What's that?'

'The French police, Mrs Diamond. No one has reported a car accident otherwise they would have been here. The ambulance that brought you said they received an anonymous call that a woman was on the road. Possibly reported by another car passing by.' The doctor looked concerned and frowned. 'There are no other casualties here, Mrs Diamond.'

'How do you know my name?' Patsy asked.

'Your passport was in your bag. We telephoned your next of kin; Sheila, is it? She said she would be here soon. Your friend here came as quickly as possible. You have good friends, Mrs Diamond. I am not so sure someone would come to my rescue as quickly.'

'I was in a car, doctor. I remember the driver; he drove towards a truck. What has happened to him and the driver of the truck?' Tears ran down her cheeks but she didn't know why.

Maggie reached forward with a handkerchief and wiped her face. 'It's okay lassie, probably just the shock. It's been a long two days.'

'Mrs Diamond, I assure you, there are no signs of any drivers. You have had a nasty bang on the head and sometimes it can take a while to recall such things. Take it easy and rest.' The doctor and the nurse left the room, much to Patsy's despair.

Although Patsy's head ached, and she felt like she was floating on air, Maggie's words seeped into her brain.

'I've been here for two days?' she muttered under her breath. 'I was in a car Maggie, I swear! It happened just like I said!'

Maggie leaned forward and whispered, 'Everything is okay. Don't worry. Don't upset yourself; you will make yourself feel worse.' Maggie looked up at the blank painted wall of the hospital room then gave Patsy a weak smile.

'Why hasn't Sheila come?'

'Because of Larry, Patsy. Do you remember? You were supposed to be going on holiday with him, but then you disappeared. He's been frantic.'

Slowly Patsy nodded. Suddenly it all came back to her and she remembered being arrested at the airport. Frowning, she shook her head. 'Where's my bag and mobile?'

'Lay still Patsy, I'll get them.' Maggie bent down and opened the little wooden locker at the side of Patsy's bed. Putting Patsy's handbag, scuffed with mud, on the blanket, she unzipped it and brought out Patsy's phone.

Flashbacks and jumbled up memories popped into her brain. Patsy remembered messaging Sheila in the back of the car. She searched through her messages. She was right, she had sent one to Sheila, but there was also one to Larry. She didn't recall sending it. She felt tired and weepy as she read the short message.

Larry, everything is okay. I need time to think on my own. I'll be in touch soon, P.D. x

Maggie nodded and looked around furtively before leaning in closer to Patsy's ear. 'Sheila will explain everything when she gets here. She's told Larry they are visiting Angus's mam. Get some rest; she should be on her way anytime.'

Patsy nodded, but her eyes felt heavy and closing them, she drifted off to sleep.

* * *

Maggie heard the clatter of feet and then the door burst open. 'Sheila! Oh my God, are you a sight for sore eyes. I am so pleased to see you.' Maggie put her arms around Sheila and hugged her.

Sheila turned towards the hospital bed. 'How is she, Maggie?'

'She's been asleep most of the day. Woke up this morning, a bit out of sorts. I told her you would tell her everything once you got here. What did you tell Angus?'

'Never mind Angus, it's that bloody Larry. Now he is seriously getting on my nerves. Every day he has been around my house banging on the door like a bloody bailiff asking me if I've heard anything. She needs to speak to him. I don't know all of the details Maggie, but it's not good and now he's bloody angry thinking she's dumped him and just wandered off without telling anyone.' Hearing a noise, Sheila turned towards Patsy. She could see she was stirring and walked over to her bedside.

'Now then lassie, how you feeling?' Sheila stroked Patsy's hair back from her face and smiled as Patsy opened her eyes.

'Sheila, is that really you?' Patsy asked, almost believing she was still dreaming.

'Aye lassie, it's me and I've come to take you home, but in the meantime, I've brought you some things.' Glancing towards Maggie, Sheila smiled. 'Do you fancy getting us all some coffee, Maggie? Do you have any money?' Sheila opened her handbag to get her purse out, but Maggie stopped her.

'It's okay, I have some Sheila.' Maggie nodded and left the room.

'Wake up Patsy, properly I mean. We have a lot of catching up to do. I got your message about the Milieu and then I got a strange phone call. But that can wait. Why were you arrested and why didn't they take you to the police station? What the hell is going on?' Sheila wagged a warning finger in Patsy's face. 'And I mean all of it.'

More alert now, Patsy shook her head. 'I messed up Sheila. That Jules telephoned me the night before our holiday. He said they wanted me in France and had things to discuss. I was tired and being a smart arse, said I would come after my holiday...' Patsy let out a huge sigh. 'I can't believe they set up that performance for my benefit. It scared the hell out of me though. You should have heard the charges they said they were arresting me for Sheila, and Larry heard all of it. How is he?'

'Larry's pissed off. He looked a real dickhead going to the police station expecting you to be there, only to be told you had never been taken there. He thought you'd been kidnapped. He wanted to report you as a missing person, but that text stopped it all.'

Patsy looked up at Sheila. 'I never sent that text Sheila.'

Patsy noticed Sheila's sheepish look as she looked down at her feet and pouted. 'Well, truth be told, I had a phone call too. It was a man and he had a French accent and he asked me if I knew you and what was our relationship. Once I heard the accent, I said we were family. That was when he informed me that you had been in an accident and that I should come to France. By the time I got the call, Larry had already been to my house demanding to know your whereabouts. I knew he was going to kick up a stink, so I told the man on the phone that everyone else knew you were going away, but your fiancé Larry would be reporting your absence to the police. The man on the other side of the phone, said he could sort that out Patsy...I'm sorry, I thought it was for the best.'

Shocked and disbelieving, Patsy sat upright. 'They've been here? They must have searched through my bag while I was asleep. My God Sheila, they could have cut my throat!'

'Well, at least we know they don't want you dead Patsy, because if they did you would be by now.' Sheila shrugged.

Letting out a deep sigh, Patsy grabbed Sheila's hand. 'You're right. But this is a warning not to fuck with these people. They pulled one hell of a scam at short notice, didn't they? These people don't take no for an answer. I should have delayed my flight for a couple of days, never mind what Larry said. He'd have sulked but, he seems to be doing a lot of that lately.'

'You don't speak very highly of a man you're engaged to? Is everything okay in paradise?'

'I'm just not looking forward to going home to face the music. What the hell can I say?'

'Well lassie, thankfully, Victoria is a better liar than you.'

'Victoria knows I'm here? Who else knows?' Startled at this revelation, Patsy felt weak and helpless. 'I need to go home Sheila.'

'Not yet you don't. Nancy and your parents think you haven't been in contact yet, because it's a long flight and you would be tired when you landed. That covers the last two days. You make sure you call them tonight. As for Victoria, she said your best excuse is to say you got cold feet and wanted some space to yourself. All that's happened recently suddenly overwhelmed you and you needed time to think. As for the wrongful arrest, all the police wanted to do was question you about Nick again. Fin said there is another police station down the road from the airport which doesn't come under Glasgow or Edinburgh jurisdiction, and he should know.' Sheila tailed off.

'Fin knows as well?' gasped Patsy; she couldn't believe what she was hearing. Her heart sank and all she wanted to do was lie back and go to sleep again, preferably forever!

'Of course he does. Now, the main thing is to find out what's so important to that gang of thieves to stir up all of this trouble. Do you know there's nothing in the news about this accident of yours?'

It was the first time in all of the conversation that Patsy smiled. 'Since when did you start reading French news, Sheila?'

'Since Google Translate, you cheeky bugger! I've searched the internet; there's nothing. They haven't reported a woman lying in the middle of the road abandoned! That's bollocks, Patsy. Do you remember much about it?'

'The driver was angry, and went crazy at this truck driver.'

Patsy shrugged. 'I don't remember much else, apart from the man on the white horse...'

'What man on a white horse? Where did that come from?' Sheila burst out laughing. 'Crikey lassie, if I had a road accident I would have Angus in his mobile rescue uniform and truck, but you get a knight in shining armour on a white horse! What the fuck are you talking about?'

Patsy couldn't help but laugh. 'Don't make me laugh Sheila; my head hurts.' She grinned. 'I don't know. Vaguely, I remember opening my eyes and there was a man on a white horse. Then I felt myself being dragged out of the car. And then I remember nothing until I woke up here.'

Sheila gave her a knowing look and a wink. 'That was one crazy bang on the head you had Patsy, but a nice fantasy knowing Sir Lancelot was on hand when you needed him. At least you didn't see a bright light into heaven!'

They both burst out laughing and suddenly Patsy felt the heavy weight lifting from her shoulders. She knew she could always rely on Sheila when needed; she had proved herself a good friend and loyal ally.

'Well, this sounds better,' said Maggie as she walked through the door, trying to juggle three plastic cups of hot coffee.

'Hey, Maggie, listen to this,' Sheila shouted towards her, 'Patsy's last memory is of a knight in shining armour on a white horse saving her. Now that's a vivid memory I could cope with. Much better than seeing Angus in his boxer shorts scratching his arse in a morning.' Sheila winced and they all laughed, thinking about Angus in his underwear.

'Right, you two, how soon can I get out of here? Fetch that doctor and let's see what the damage is.' Now wide awake, Patsy was eager to leave. She wanted to see the Milieu and then go home and face the music with Larry.

'I'll go and find someone,' said Maggie, leaving the room again.

Sheila frowned. 'Don't you think you should give yourself a couple of days? You've only just come around and as much as we're laughing, you're talking dribble lassie. Although, I suppose' – Sheila drummed her fingers on her chin and pondered on Patsy's words – 'you should strike while the iron's hot. I wouldn't tell anyone else about your memory flashbacks or fantasies though, Patsy or they'll end up locking you up!' Sheila laughed.

Patsy turned serious again. 'What do I look like Sheila? My lips feel swollen and my face hurts. Get me a mirror please.'

Sheila looked down at the floor and then back at Patsy. 'Are you sure you want to do that lassie? It doesn't look good.' Sheila opened her handbag and took a small compact mirror out. Passing Patsy the mirror, she shrugged. 'It's all cosmetic; you will look better soon.'

As she held up the mirror, Patsy's heart sank. She hardly recognised the reflection looking back at her. Wincing, she moved the small mirror around, inspecting each side of her face. The awful truth was, she looked battered and bruised. Her eyes were black and puffy. There was a white plaster over the bridge of her nose. There were stitches in her eyebrows and her lips were thick and swollen. 'Oh my God Sheila, I don't recognise myself. What happened to me?' Passing the mirror back to Sheila, she sniffed. 'Take it away, I've seen enough. I'm going to be scarred for life. Look at me, Sheila, look at me!' Distraught and full of despair, Patsy laid her aching head back on the pillows. 'I look hideous.'

Sheila held her hand. 'Patsy love, it will heal.'

The doctor entered the room and gave a slight cough to make his presence known. 'Well, Mrs Diamond, the ultrasound is fine, but you will have quite a headache. You're battered and bruised, but luckily all you have is a sprained wrist. The neck support is so that you didn't move your head in case of injury, but otherwise you're fine, although I think you should stay in another night. After all, you have only woken up today.'

Sheila and Maggie agreed with the doctor, so Patsy reluctantly decided to stay a little while longer. Although she didn't admit it, she was little relieved because her head ached and she felt as weak as a kitten.

When the doctor nodded his approval and left, Patsy said, 'Sheila, do you think you can contact our mutual friends and organise an appointment?'

'I'll see what I can do, and don't you forget to ring your parents and Nancy and tell them you've decided not to go on holiday with Larry. You never know, he might contact them. God knows he's been everywhere else.'

Drowsiness enveloped Patsy while Sheila was still talking. She was worn out and her eyelids felt heavy. 'Tomorrow, Sheila,' she muttered and drifted back off to sleep.

'Come on, Maggie, let's leave her to it. There is no way she could leave this place tonight and you look like you could also do with a good night's rest and a decent meal.' Linking her arm through Maggie's, Sheila kissed her on the cheek. 'Come on, a wee dram is in order. I'm bushed.'

3

COLD LIGHT OF DAY

Although Sheila had wanted to get Patsy home as soon as she was discharged, Patsy was adamant that they go to the chateau first to see how things were there.

Patsy sat in the kitchen of the cottage built on the chateau's land. It was surrounded by acres and acres of farmland, where they grew their vegetables and truffles. Truthfully, Patsy had no idea what was there. She had only seen it once and hadn't paid much attention to it, given that she'd had other pressing matters on her mind. Karen Duret had almost held them captive there, and she had certainly kept Patsy's young daughter, Nancy, there after Karen's brother had kidnapped the young girl along with Patsy's parents.

Once her family were safe, Patsy had appreciated the beauty of the place and was determined to have it, by whatever means. Although she was a born and bred city girl and the closest she had ever got to a vegetable was in the supermarket.

'It's cosy in here, isn't it?' Patsy remarked, looking around the cottage. 'I don't remember seeing much of this place the last time, but it really is nice. You would book something like this for a holiday.' Patsy sipped her mug of coffee at the large wooden table. The cottage had that farmhouse appeal, with its aga and its farmhouse kitchen. The light blue floral sofas in the lounge, opposite a huge fireplace with logs at the side, made it look homely. The fire itself was all clean and ready with its twists of paper and firelighters to light if the weather turned cooler.

'This place is gorgeous, Patsy, but it's full of mystery and history. Are you really sure you want to get involved with it?' Sheila sighed and took a sip of her cup of steaming coffee.

'This whole place will be a gold mine in the right hands Sheila, you can see that for yourself. But it needs a proper inspection now we have the chance. I'm sure Paul and his brothers have all of this in hand. He doesn't suffer fools gladly, but I think we have to tread carefully though.' Patsy winked at Sheila and Maggie. 'I get the feeling that now he has his newfound freedom, this place will become his empire. A place he can express himself without fear hanging over him like the grim reaper.'

Frowning, Maggie felt it was time to butt in; something had bothered her but she hadn't wanted to point it out when they'd arrived. 'Don't you think it strange though, that all the flood lights were on when we got here? It was as though someone expected us to stay here. I never called Paul in advance to let him know we were coming, did you?'

Sheila and Patsy put their mugs down together. They had all been so tired after Sheila had driven them to the chateau, it hadn't crossed their minds. Sheila looked at Patsy. 'I know your head's still not in the right place, but Maggie's right. Even the beds were made with fresh linen. The only reason I followed this path, was because I saw the lights on in the front windows.'

Cocking her head to one side, Maggie pondered Sheila's words. 'Well, someone knew we were coming; there's fresh milk and things in the fridge too,' she commented.

Drumming her fingers on her chin, Patsy realised they were being watched. 'This place is probably bugged or something, so be careful what you say. Someone knows our every movement!'

Putting fresh mugs of coffee on the table, Maggie nodded. 'That had crossed my mind too. I think your friends are watching you.' Maggie shrugged and gave them both a knowing look. 'The sooner you do whatever business it is you have to do, the sooner we can go home and all feel better. I know I definitely will.' Pursing her lips and shaking her head, Maggie held her hands up to stop their protests. 'I know I can go home any time I like; I've done my bit and I'm not a prisoner, but I'm not leaving you both just yet. I wouldn't settle anyway.'

Patsy reached her hand across the table and put it on top of Maggie's. 'Thank you, Maggie, for everything. You're right, let's all go home together.' She smiled.

Changing the subject, Sheila asked, 'Did you ring your parents and Nancy?'

'Yes, I haven't told them anything other than that I got cold feet about Larry and wanted some time to myself. My dad understood; he said since Nick's death, I haven't had time to breathe, always having to sort things out for everyone, and then I jumped into the first pair of arms that offered me comfort and sympathy. Not the best way I'd describe it, but maybe he has a point,' Patsy mused.

'But I thought you loved Larry?' asked Maggie. 'He's a nice enough laddie, good job prospects and he cares about you... isn't that enough?'

'I think after this little stunt I've pulled, he won't care about me too much.' Patsy sighed. She felt drained and tired. 'And I can't tell him much, more for his own reputation than mine. He's a respected lawyer and I'm running around like the Godfather! Not really what Larry wants for a wife, is it? He could be struck off or disbarred, or whatever happens to lawyers for having a criminal for a wife, and let's face it ladies, that's what I've become.'

'You're just feeling down lassie; the last few days haven't been easy.' Maggie patted her hand. 'Maybe you could change; marriage is compromise. Although, I get the feeling your feelings aren't that strong for Larry, otherwise you wouldn't be doubting it. If so, why did you agree to get married?' Maggie paused and waited for Patsy's answer.

'Oh, I don't know. With hindsight, do I really want another Scottish lawyer? Been there, done that, got the T-shirt. I've been given a taste of freedom, and although it hasn't all been good...' Patsy threw her hands up in despair. 'Do I really want to have dinner on the table when he comes home?' Patsy put her still aching head in her hands. 'I really don't know. The truth is, at this moment in time, I don't know anything.' Unexpected tears fell down her cheeks and she sniffed and wiped them away. 'These bruises are going to be hard to disguise from him, so I could tell him the truth about a stupid car accident which is why I haven't been in touch. The best lies are the ones you shrouded in truth.' Patsy smiled, and sipped her coffee through her still swollen lips and winced.

'Or,' Sheila laughed, 'you could tell him you came to Paris for your Botox injection; you look like a pouting goldfish!'

Although it was hard for Patsy to laugh, they all chuckled at Sheila's comments. She always saw the humorous side of things and turned the worst possible situations into something more bearable. Patsy looked at Sheila and Maggie and held both her hands out to reach theirs. 'What would I do without you both?' She smiled.

'Oh, I can't be doing with all this female bonding. Cheer up Patsy, and put your best mask on. You have an appointment today.' Sheila gave her a knowing look. 'Are you up to it?'

Pensively, Patsy nodded. 'Yes, I want those bastards to see me like this and explain that charade. There was no need for it, Sheila. What time do we have to be there?'

'Two this afternoon at that bistro place...' Sheila trailed off. She could already feel the bile rising in her throat when she remembered her last visit there.

Putting her hand to her mouth, Patsy stared wide eyed at them both. 'Oh my God, I don't have anything to wear!' Patsy suddenly remembered her luggage. It would be somewhere in the Maldives by now! 'We need to find a shop; if nothing else, I need clean knickers!'

'Oh lassie, we can wash those under the tap for you, but didn't you look in your wardrobe? I did. Why do you think I'm wearing this posh jumper.' Sheila pulled at the crew necked cashmere jumper she was wearing. 'I definitely didn't buy it.'

Patsy stood up, scraping her chair back on the slate flooring as she dashed upstairs to her bedroom. Sure enough, as Patsy opened her wardrobe, dresses and suits all in her usual style were hanging up inside. Frantically, she pulled open the chest of drawers where inside were lots of small boxes. Quickly she opened them, and silk underwear fell out. They all gasped in surprise. Stunned, she turned around to Maggie. 'Let's see what's in yours.'

Marching through, they opened Maggie's. Her wardrobe was a little plainer, but there was underwear, a selection of blouses and tops and trousers. 'For Christ's sake, what is this? This is seriously giving me the creeps. How do they know our sizes?' Maggie let her hand roam across the hangers in her wardrobe. She had never seen anything like it. Dreamily, she picked out a pink floral satin blouse. 'I might try this on for size,' she muttered, almost embarrassed.

Sheila linked her arm through Patsy's. 'Come and see mine.

Father Christmas has been!' Sheila ran into her bedroom and opened the wardrobe doors. Sure enough, it was full of clothes. 'Whether we stay or not Patsy, I'm taking these home with me. Whoever bought them has bloody good taste.'

Patsy walked back to her own room and opened the white wardrobe door again. Unlike Sheila, she didn't feel excited. If anything, it frightened her. She knew this was the doing of the Milieu, but being spied on like this made her feel out of control.

'I'll use the knickers Sheila, but I will not attend this meeting wearing any of this lot. Can I borrow some jeans and a T-shirt? I presume you brought something like that with you.'

Maggie and Sheila both stopped what they were doing. 'Why Patsy, what's the problem?' Sheila stared at her in wonderment.

'Because I'm not playing their manipulative games.' Patsy pointed at her chest. 'I am Patsy Diamond and I will wear my own clothing, not their shrouds to murder me in!'

Sheila and Maggie sobered up from their excitement and nodded. They could see the flush of anger under Patsy's bruises and that fiery look in her eyes. Instantly, they realised their mistake. 'Sorry Patsy, we just got a little carried away with it all.' Maggie was still holding the hanger with the blouse she had picked out. 'I'll go and put this back,' she muttered apologetically.

'No, don't do that Maggie. It's not about you, it's about me and any future business plans we have, if any. But I have to start as I mean to go on and sing my own tune. You wear what you want, but it is a real cheek to do this to me after everything else they have put me through. Do they seriously think a few dresses are going to make us kiss and make up? No, definitely not. It's time they realised I don't play games. Time to show these people who they're dealing with.'

4

BUSINESS AS USUAL

Patsy let the hot shower rain down over her battered body for what seemed like forever. The last few days passed through her mind; it had been a whirlwind and this afternoon would answer all her questions.

Going into her bedroom, she saw that Sheila had left a pair of jeans and a lemon-coloured T-shirt on the bed for her. She found a belt in one of the drawers and tightly fitted it around the jeans. Downstairs, the smell of bacon, eggs and fresh coffee greeted her and made her realise that she hadn't eaten properly in an age.

Walking into the kitchen, she saw Maggie at the stove working her magic. 'Here you are, get something solid inside you.'

As they sat down there was only the sound of their eating and drinking. Eventually, Maggie spoke. 'How did your drive up to the chateau go, Sheila? Did you see Paul?'

Sheila nodded in between mouthfuls. 'Mmm, yes, he's really busy. Did you know he had builders in Patsy?'

'No, he never said.' Patsy ripped off a piece of baguette and stuffed it in her mouth. 'I'll go up there to see him, I need to know how he's getting on anyway. Maggie that was delicious. Christ, I can't remember the last time I ate. Thank you.'

'Aren't you going to put any make-up on your face and bruises, Patsy? I have some but I did notice there's all kinds of things on the dressing table if you're interested.'

'No, I'm not.' Patsy shrugged indignantly. 'I'm going like this, warts and all. Besides, they're the reason I look like this anyway. What time is it?'

Sheila looked up at the clock on the wall. 'Nearly twelve; we should be leaving soon. Are you sure you want to go out into the world without any make-up Patsy?'

'I am, indeed; in fact, it feels quite liberating. Anyway, what make-up could help this face? I'll just take a quick look in on Paul and then we'll go.'

Maggie looked down at the table. 'If you don't mind lassies, I don't want to come on your trip with you. I'm a little tired, and I'd rather stay here and put my feet up if you don't mind.'

'Of course not Maggie. Me and Sheila have got this, you rest up. Is there anything you need while we're out?'

Patsy could see the relief wash over Maggie as she shook her head. She was tired, of course she was, and there was no point in dragging her to a meeting she knew nothing about. Over her mug of coffee, Sheila gave Patsy a wink.

As Sheila drove the hire car up to the chateau, Patsy looked out of the windows. It truly was a magical place and the land around it seemed to go on forever. Everything was different shades of green meeting the blue skies. The long, gravelled driveway seemed newly laid and neater than Patsy remembered, and she smiled when the chateau finally came into view. It stood like a castle in the middle of all this beauty.

As Patsy looked more intensely as they drove up, she saw there were builders and decorators painting the outside of the chateau and workmen darting in and out with what looked like new work-tops and kitchen equipment.

Patsy took off her sunglasses. 'What the bloody hell is going on Sheila? I never gave permission for this.'

Parking up, Sheila laughed. 'Apparently you did Patsy. You told Paul to sort everything out and make it into a restaurant and that is exactly what he's doing. The wee laddie is in his element; he loves this place. He is up at the crack of dawn with the farm labourers and personally goes and looks at the truffles they pick. He looks like a new man; that grimace he wore has nearly turned into a smile.'

As Patsy walked in, she hardly recognised the place. The whole interior had been gutted. Long gone were the memories of Karen Duret. It had warmth, which had been seriously lacking the last time she had been there.

'Mrs Diamond! Mrs Diamond, Sheila say you were coming today.' Greek Paul, who looked larger than life, came walking towards her, his arms open wide. Swallowing her up in them, he almost crushed her. 'Sorry Mrs Diamond, I almost forget myself.'

Patsy smiled at the mountain of a man. He was as wide as he was long, wearing jeans and an open-necked check shirt. Even though it had only been a short while, the French air had done him good. 'So what is happening here, Paul?'

Patsy walked around the chateau and looked at all the alterations. 'When I said sort it out, I didn't expect a complete refurbishment.' Patsy looked at his swarthy face, and he seemed to blush slightly.

'You said to make it look good, Mrs Diamond. That is what I am doing. This kitchen was dated and not fit for a restaurant kitchen; it needed refurbishment. The French trading standards are very high and will only pass if absolutely perfect.'

Patsy relaxed and gave Paul a smile. 'You're doing an excellent job; I just thought I would have a look around and see what was going on. Show me your plans for the kitchen.'

Paul's black eyes, which were hidden behind bushy black eyebrows, sparkled at the mention of the kitchen and he eagerly showed her his pride and joy. 'Here we have meat sink units and vegetable ones. We are waiting for the rest to be fitted. This place look good on the outside, but no one looked after it inside, so we get rid of almost everything.'

Stunned, Patsy asked, 'Do you think it was a bad investment, Paul?'

'Absolutely not! The foundations are solid. It has just been neglected. We want people to come and eat here. We want weddings and for this place to be the talk of France when I have finished,' he boasted, then looked down at the floor before getting carried away, 'but, it is costing money.'

'And you think you can make a success of this?' Doubt ran through Patsy's mind; maybe she had bitten off more than she could chew?

'Yes, Mrs Diamond. We can turn all of this into a successful restaurant and more. This place just needs a little love and organising.'

Grinning, Patsy nodded. 'Then I picked the right man for the job. I have to go now; I have a meeting. But keep up the good work Paul; it's going to look stunning.' Patsy smiled and walked back to the car with Sheila trailing behind her. Paul stood in the doorway and waved as they drove off.

'Well, he's excited, that's for sure. He scares the hell out of me though Patsy. He always reminded me of Frankenstein's monster,' Sheila laughed. 'Christ he's big, and his stomach is like a barrel; I bet he hasn't seen his dick in years.' Sheila turned towards Patsy and together they laughed.

'I didn't realise that the place needed so much money

spending on it. I thought maybe a wall taken out or something...'
Patsy trailed off.

'What did you expect? We both know that Karen woman
didn't have a pot to piss in. She had more front than Selfridges.
That house looked good, but they never spent a penny on it and
her husband gambled everything else away. Let's be honest, no
matter what that costs you in refurbishment, it won't be more
than what you'd get if you sold the place. The land alone is worth
a fortune... Stop worrying, Patsy.'

* * *

Patsy rang the bell on the closed bistro. Puzzled, she looked at
Sheila but then they heard the bolts on the door being slid across.
Patsy's mouth felt dry and she moistened her lips. A man in his
sixties opened the door dressed in brown corduroy trousers and a
white polo shirt. They never saw much of his hair, or even if he
had any, because he wore a flat cap that looked like it was too big
for him.

'Bonjour, Madame Diamond,' he said, holding out his hand to
shake hers. Patsy's hand felt sweaty, and she wanted to wipe it, but
she held it out anyway.

Opening the door wider, he beckoned them inside and
pointed to the hatch in the floor behind the bar. Kneeling down,
he lifted the metal ring on the wooden hatch and opened it. The
smell of cigar smoke was the first thing that greeted them once the
hatch was fully open. Patsy stood back a little and glanced at
Sheila, then, as they had once before, they climbed down the
staircase into the basement of the bistro. Sheila closed her eyes,
but when Patsy nudged her in the ribs with her elbow, Sheila
opened her eyes, surprised. The basement had been freshly
painted with tables and chairs scattered around in bistro style.

The tables had red-and-white checked tablecloths with wine bottles in the middle acting as candle holders, their glow lighting up the dimness of the room. Three men, whom Patsy recognised from last time, were sat at a table. Each one had a glass of red wine to go with their cigars.

'Mrs Diamond, sit down please.' The man Patsy remembered as Jules, stood up and pulled out a chair for herself and Sheila. The others looked Patsy up and down, noting the jeans and T-shirt. This was what she had banked on. Her display of defiance against what they were expecting her to wear had shocked them.

Although she didn't feel strong, Patsy sat easily on the chair and pulled it in towards the table, folding her arms. 'Well gentlemen, I'm here at last.'

'Madame Diamond, take the sullen schoolgirl look off your face. We are people of business.'

'Manne? Is that your name?'

'I'm flattered you remember my name, Madame Diamond.'

'Well, Manne. To start with, business is usually done in an office, not a basement in a bistro down a bloody hatch were I could break my neck. As for the look on my face, how would you know? Can you actually see the look on my face underneath the bruises your driver caused me? Yes, I know I was in a car crash, though somehow you have hidden it well. Everyone thinks I am crazy, and now my fiancé thinks I've dumped him. How the hell do you expect me to feel!'

The three men cast furtive glances at each other and one of them took a drink of his wine. Manne offered Sheila and Patsy a glass, but Patsy refused for both of them. 'You're right, it was a car crash, and we can only apologise for that. The man was one of our drivers and clearly an imbecile. Sadly, the driver of the truck that hit you was killed. You were very lucky, Madame Diamond. On hearing about it, we had everything cleared away. You were taken to hospital and apart from a few minor cuts and bruises, you sound and look on fighting form again.' Manne held his hands up in submission. 'Yes, Madame Diamond, we covered our tracks, so let's not have angry outbursts. Business first always. In fact, to show good faith we have a present for you. We do not suffer fools gladly, and the driver of your vehicle could have caused a lot of trouble for us – so here, I have something for you.'

Sheila and Patsy heard the hatch above them open and a half naked man, wearing only a pair of trousers, was being pushed down the staircase. He looked battered and bruised and the two men behind him pushed and shoved him down the staircase, making him fall to the floor. Patsy heard him whimper, then she noticed the gag around his mouth and winced, tightly grabbing hold of Sheila's hand. Her blood ran cold as the man was picked up and half thrown across the floor. He looked up towards Patsy and as her eyes caught his in the candlelight, she recognised him as the driver of the car. Patsy knew this would only end up one way and she didn't want to bear witness to it. She pitied him. Sheila paled and sat in stunned silence, gripping Patsy's hand under the tablecloth. Her fingernails deeply embedded into her palms of her hands. The damp patch on the front of the man's trousers showed that he had wet himself.

'Stand up!' Manne shouted. 'Stand up like a man!'

The now weeping man tried his best and stood before the three men at the table. He held his hands together, as though in prayer, as tears streamed down his face.

Patsy's blood ran cold and a feeling of nausea washed over her like a wave. She wanted to run out of there, but she couldn't move.

'Take off the gag, he can scream all he likes down here, no one will hear him,' Manne spat out. Then he turned to Patsy, who could almost feel her own tears brimming in her eyes. She was afraid. Wagging a finger in Patsy's face, Manne spoke to her. 'Do not feel sorry for him Madame Diamond. This man could have killed you. Your daughter would be an orphan now, think on that.' Looking back at the driver, Manne said, 'You like to drink, monsieur, well, take a drink.' Manne gently pushed the bottle of red wine towards him. 'Drink it all.'

Puzzled, Patsy cast a sideways glance at Sheila. This was unexpected; Patsy had gritted her teeth and waited for their guillotine to be wheeled out like last time, but no, this was very calm.

Obviously thirsty, the driver picked up the bottle with shaking hands, not knowing what to expect. His eyes darted to each and every one of them then he put the bottle to his mouth and paused.

Manne spied his hesitation and smiled. 'You think it's poisoned? No, we are drinking from it ourselves.' To show good faith, Manne took the bottle from him and poured some into his glass and gulped it down. 'There is no poison in that bottle, monsieur.'

Surprised, the driver of the vehicle picked up the bottle and gulped the remains down, spilling some on his chest in a hurry to quench his thirst. Satisfied, he put the bottle on the table and wiped his mouth with the back of his hand. 'Merci, Manne.'

Jules reached under the table and produced another bottle of wine. Picking up the corkscrew, he opened it and put it on the table before the driver. 'Drink it. All of it.' Patsy and Sheila watched the performance with growing confusion, while the three men at the table remained very calm.

The driver picked up the bottle once more and drank before putting the bottle down on the table.

'I said all of it.'

The driver picked up the bottle and started to drink again, but he couldn't drink it all and took the bottle away from his mouth to take a breath. One of the men that had brought him down the stairs held the bottle to his mouth and pulled his head back, pouring the wine down his throat, making the driver cough and splutter, drenching himself in red wine. In the dimness of the room, Patsy thought it resembled blood running down his body. The driver was choking and tried pushing the bottle away in panic, but the man holding him kept his grip tight and carried on pouring it down his throat until the bottle was empty.

Jules reached down and produced another bottle. 'Drink it,' he ordered.

The driver fell to his knees, crying, 'No messieurs, no more please, I beg of you.'

Patsy felt like she was having an out-of-body experience. She was watching this like some horror movie she couldn't turn off. 'Wait! Don't you think he's had enough?' she shouted.

Raising one eyebrow, Manne smiled at her. 'This man likes to drink, so let him drink, Madame Diamond.' Throwing his hands up in the air, he shrugged. 'Let him drink the cellar dry. Don't you have the stomach to watch your would-be assassin be punished?'

Sitting back again, Patsy felt if that was all they were going to do, she could watch it. They wanted to teach him a lesson.

Shaking his head and trembling, the man had no choice but to do as he was told and picked up the bottle. 'Please, I have had enough; don't make me drink any more.' Then he turned towards Patsy. 'I am sorry, madame, truly I am.' Again, he burst into tears.

Patsy was about to say something, but Manne held his finger to his lips. He turned to the men who'd brought the driver downstairs and pointed to the corner. They each took the driver's arms and pulled him to the far corner of the room. The bottle fell to the ground and smashed, the remains of the wine covering the concrete floor. The man's stomach was extended from all the wine he had drunk, and he swayed slightly. Patsy and Sheila turned in their seats to see what was going to happen next out of curiosity.

They both felt it was a very sadistic situation but couldn't help themselves.

Once Manne nodded, one of the men holding the driver took out a knife and plunged it into the driver's stomach, pulling it upwards and opening him up. Instantly, red wine and blood poured out, splashing onto the floor. Sheila screamed and Patsy jumped up so quickly, her chair fell over as she ran to the other side of the room, trembling. Neither of them had expected that.

Patsy couldn't take her eyes off Manne and his friends as they got up from the table and walked along the wet floor towards the dying man. Manne held his hand out and was given the knife. He stabbed the driver with it. Then, he passed the knife to Jules who did the same. Each in turn the men plunged the knife into the driver, even after the light in his eyes had died and he'd stopped moving.

Sheila and Patsy were crouched on the floor, their heads against each other, shaking and crying with their eyes closed tight. They didn't want to see any more. Patsy felt a light tap on her shoulder and slowly opened her eyes to see Manne standing there holding the bloodied knife out to her. She backed away.

'Don't be foolish; this is your justice day. Everyone knows not to cross the Milieu. This man was paid to deliver you safely but failed, instead putting you in harm's way. We are the Milieu, Madame Diamond. Are you one of us?'

Patsy stared at him. 'You mean you want me to stab that already-dead man with that knife?' she stammered. She couldn't believe what she was hearing; this was unimaginable.

'We have avenged you and now it is your turn... or have we done this for nothing?' Although his voice was calm, it was cold and harsh.

Patsy moved the still quivering Sheila to one side and tried her best to stand up. Her legs felt weak and she felt faint, but as she peered around Manne, she could see the others waiting for her. Her heart was hammering in her chest so loud she thought they could hear it. She wanted to blot out everything she had seen, but afraid of repercussions, Patsy took the knife. If she didn't do as they asked, she knew they would easily kill both her and Sheila.

'You can't be serious, Patsy,' Sheila screamed. 'They are fucking animals! All of you are animals!' Tears fell down her face as she carried on screaming until Manne raised his hand and slapped her.

'Calm down woman. Would you not want revenge if he had killed someone in your family? A truck driver is dead, a man innocently going about his work. His wife and family have lost him because of this fool. People know he worked for us. Are we to be made a laughingstock of? Your friend here could also be dead. Does that mean nothing to you?'

Wide eyed, Sheila stared at him and then back at Patsy while rubbing her face. 'Do as he says, Patsy.'

Patsy's jaw almost dropped, and her hand was visibly shaking as she held the knife smeared with blood. She slowly walked to the dead man's body; her feet were soaked from the puddle of wine and blood on the floor and she couldn't stop the tears from falling. Manne nodded. 'Are you one of us or not? Friend or foe, Madame Diamond; your choice.'

Patsy realised she had no choice if she was to survive. Friend or foe summed it up. Only Maggie knew where they were, but not the address. They were trapped, with no other option than to do as the Milieu requested.

The man's body was full of knife wounds, his stomach cut wide open. Closing her eyes and cringing, Patsy plunged the knife into the dead man's body and pulled it out again. Patsy looked across to Sheila and held out the knife. 'Your turn; we are all in this together remember.'

Sheila shook her head, but looked into Patsy's eyes, which seemed to be pleading with her. Slowly, Sheila stood and walked towards her, grabbing the knife and plunging it into the man, before throwing it on the floor. 'Are you all fucking satisfied now?' Adrenalin and anger took over and she slapped Manne across the face, shocking him and knocking him backwards. 'Don't you ever slap me again you French bastard, or believe me, you will be the next person I use a knife on!'

Rubbing his jaw, Manne nodded at Sheila. 'We will go upstairs now and finish our discussion.'

Wiping away her tears, Patsy looked at him. 'You mean, we're not leaving? What more is there to do here?'

'Business, Madame Diamond. Come on, take off your clothes and put them in these bags. There is more upstairs for you to wear.'

Sheila started stripping off. 'Come on Patsy, he's right; let's get rid of the evidence.'

Everyone stripped to their underwear and went up the staircase and through the open hatch. Wearily, Patsy and Sheila followed, just glad to be out of there. Barefoot and shivering in their underwear, the first man they had met, who had opened the door for them in the corduroy trousers, took them through the back of the bistro where already running showers awaited them. Patsy sat on the floor of the shower tray as the water sprayed her head and body. She watched the blood from her hands wash away down the plug hole. She wanted to scream but didn't. She knew she would never forget this day.

After what seemed forever in the hot shower, Patsy came out. Once dressed, she opened the door to find Sheila, pale faced and still damp, waiting for her. 'Let's not discuss it lassie. Do your business, see what they have to say and let's get out of here alive.'

They both walked into the main bistro. The men were already

waiting for them, drinking and talking normally. It felt like a dream, as though that nightmare had never occurred.

Manne stood up and pulled out two chairs at the table for them. 'I have poured some brandy. I think maybe you will need it. Let's not rake over the past. This is the future, but we still have matters we wanted to discuss with you.'

Knowing her torment wasn't over, Patsy downed her brandy in one, letting the warm liquid soothe her throat. She felt tired, but braver now after her shower. This was the life she had chosen, and she knew it wasn't going to be pretty. She took a deep sigh and rubbed her hand through her hair. Full of despair, she knew this was her own doing. 'So, what was the emergency? Why have you destroyed my holiday, my engagement and my life?'

'Maybe in the future when we ask something of you, you will think twice before snubbing us. We have a partnership, an alliance, and yet, you treat us like we don't exist.' Manne pulled his chair closer to the table and put his elbows on it. The serious look on his face unnerved Patsy. 'Firstly, who is this Greek man that you have sent to the chateau? We know nothing about him. Can he be trusted? Why did you not inform us he was coming. What plans do you have for place? There has been a lot of building work going on, and the builders are not in our circle. We use our own people. Who are you to make these decisions without consulting us? This is our country and our rules, you are the visitor. Respect Madame Diamond, respect!' Manne banged the table with his fist. His face was flushed. 'Do you think you will get the permits you need without us? They will go to the bottom of a very long pile, Madame Diamond, and time is money. This Greek man of yours, does he know you will be laundering money? And this lawyer you're sleeping with, is he in on it too, Madame Diamond? Because they get paid out of your share, not ours.'

Spit dribbled down the side of Manne's mouth as he spoke. He was angry, which made Patsy's blood turn cold. She had no idea what her penance would be for her stupidity.

'That is how we stay out of jail, Madame Diamond; we close ranks and stick together, but you treat us like fools! If you had done as we asked, you would have been on your holiday now and not come to see us looking like you have been hit by a train!'

Patsy winced at his words, but he was right, she reasoned with herself. She would have been on her holiday now if she had just postponed for a day or so and come to France. A couple of excuses to Larry would have been better than having to go home to face his wrath. Patsy realised she had been a fool and impulsive. She had jumped the gun sending Paul and not discussing it with these men. The Milieu didn't like outsiders and she had sent Paul and his brothers here without explanation. It was a stupid oversight, and they were right. It was amateurish.

'Okay, okay, I hear you. I understand. Yes, it was an oversight, and I didn't think. I just wanted to get things sorted out at the chateau. I have all kinds of plans for it and with your approval, hopefully we will build a good smoke screen for our joint venture.' Trying her best to appease the men, Patsy felt it was time to eat humble pie. Better than to be choked by it!

Jules, the younger of the three, spoke up. 'You never informed us of what happened to Karen Duret. Where is she? Don't you think you owe us some kind of explanation as to her where-abouts?' Although his line of questioning was just as direct as Manne's, Jules seemed more relaxed and friendly.

'Karen?' The mention of Karen's name stopped Patsy in her tracks ad she looked around the dimly lit room, her heart thumping in her chest so much she felt they could hear it. 'I am not in contact with Karen. She seems to have disappeared. I'm not sure where to.' Mentally, she reasoned with herself that it wasn't a lie, because she had no idea where her ex-business partner and friend James had buried her after she had met her grizzly end in the cemetery.

'You forget Patsy, Freddie is a good friend of ours. He filled us in on the minor details, but we would like to hear it from yourself. Surely you owe us that much.' Jules spoke without malice. 'We want no repercussions Patsy, and you have not exactly been forthcoming so far...' Raising an eyebrow and cocking his head to one side in a playful fashion, he looked at her questioningly.

'Freddie!' she sighed. Where did she start? To be fair, she had no idea who he really was, nor did anyone else it seemed. She wasn't even sure if that was his real name. He was a known mercenary-cum-bounty hunter, and his job was killing people for money – a lot of money. She'd used his services several times, and he'd always delivered. But his connection with the Milieu was a mystery. They clearly knew him very well, and were possibly the only people that did. When she'd first met the Milieu, Freddie had been with her, and they had spoken to each other like old friends, not business associates. The whole mystery surrounding Freddie and his close gang of associates was intriguing. He was obviously military. Anyone would know that, because he was meticulous in his work and left no stone unturned and no traces of himself near his victims. He appeared like a ghost. No one had contact details for him, but if you spread the word that you needed something doing, he just popped up out of the blue and then disappeared again. He never showed any kind of emotions, that wasn't in his nature, but he had been good to her. She had to admit that. Freddie and his gang had saved her daughter and family, for a price, but it had been worth every penny. He had also tipped her off about James double-crossing her. Patsy admired Freddie. He was a businessman and kept his word. A job was a job to him and he saw it through to the end. But now it seemed like he had reported back to the Milieu regarding her dealings, and she couldn't understand why.

She looked towards Sheila for support; her friend gave her a weak smile. Patsy nodded. 'I don't know where James put Karen, but I do know she is dead and will no longer cause us any trouble, myself in particular. James is also dead. As for Greek Paul, he is to be trusted. He knows all about the money laundering and drug dealing and I have given him a chance as an experienced chef to give him back his life as long as he runs things in...' Patsy was about to say 'my' but stopped herself. 'In *our* favour. My apologies gentlemen, I have made quite a few mistakes, I see that now, but maybe you would consider giving me a second chance.' Patsy felt stupid. She had presented herself as an efficient businesswoman the last time they had met, but had overlooked the most important things. She needed these men on her side. She would get nothing in France without their approval. They had ruined and tortured Karen and Patsy knew they could do the same to herself. It did cross her mind to cry and beg for mercy, but she decided against it. No, she thought to herself, the time called for her to prove herself to be a strong woman. An equal.

'We already know where Karen is buried, we just wondered if you did. By your body language we can see that you do not, but you must appreciate our concerns. Anything that comes back from Karen's demise could also come back to us – do you understand that?'

Confused, Patsy looked at Sheila in surprise and then back at the men. 'You know where Karen is buried? How?'

'Simple enough, by watching you and those you associate with.'

Patsy slammed her glass down on the table. 'You've been spying on me?'

Sheila looked at the men and smiled weakly. She felt Patsy

was being reckless – she was always fiery tempered and some-times that wasn't the best way to solve things. Sheila felt now was the time for her to speak up before Patsy made a bad situation worse.

'Can I speak gentlemen?' Sheila asked politely.

They nodded. 'Feel free.'

Turning towards Patsy, Sheila said, 'Patsy, everything these men have said is right lassie. You haven't told them anything since you left. I thought you were in a partnership. As for spying on you' – Sheila shrugged and made a face – 'we knew that anyway, so what's the problem? You can't exactly say you have anything to hide from these men, they know what we do and who we do it with. They already know we are murderers and drug dealers. What they want is a little curtesy, and I am sure you would feel the same if the boot was on the other foot. The question is, do you want to walk away and not do business with these men or do you want to swallow your pride and talk business? Truly Patsy, have we been through all of this for nothing?'

Defeated, Patsy knew Sheila was right. Sighing, she looked at the men directly and squared her shoulders. 'As Sheila says, we haven't gone through all of this for nothing. What do you want from us?'

Opposite her, the three Frenchmen smiled.

5

THE BEGINNING OF THE END

Once they had all said their piece and their business was finished, they all agreed that the chateau would make a good restaurant, and the rooms upstairs for paying guests would be a good smoke screen for their business dealings.

'Call us anytime if you need anything Madame Diamond. You have our numbers so keep in touch. And you, Madame Sheila.' Manne smiled. 'I like a woman with spirit. The last person that slapped my face had her hand cut off with a machete, but if you ever feel like you want a job away from Madame Diamond, contact me.'

'Me and Patsy are partners...' Sheila said. 'We stick together. You just got what you deserved, but it's all over now... finished.'

Manne nodded. 'I understand.'

They all shook hands and the man in the corduroy trousers walked Sheila and Patsy to the door before locking it firmly behind the two women.

'Did you keep the bags and the knife Francois?' Manne asked.

'Of course. I'm surprised they didn't think about all that evidence. I would have wanted to see my blood-stained clothing burnt before my eyes. It's all stashed away together in airtight bags. Insurance is always for the best in these cases. We don't want them running out of here shouting murder!'

'And who would they shout that to Francois? Your father is the police commissioner.' They all laughed.

Manne smiled. 'Personally, I like them and we owe them. Patsy Diamond could have been killed by that stupid driver. That was our doing. They both have spirit, but they need nurturing. Now they both know the score, I think we will do good business together, but if not, we have insurance. Their hands were the last ones that touched that knife. Their fingerprints are all over it, and we have their clothing. Let's hope they never cross us.' Manne laughed.

* * *

'Get me out of here Sheila. Let's just get as far away as possible. Are you okay to drive?'

'If it means leaving the Godfather and those murdering bastards behind, I can drive.' Sheila started the car and sped off much faster than she realised. 'Sorry, the last thing you need is a panic-stricken overanxious driver. Those men, they are cold and I don't think I will ever sleep again after witnessing what they did. And after doing what they made us do. Monsters, the lot of them!'

Lighting two cigarettes, Patsy passed one to Sheila. They drove along in silence, each with their own thoughts and memories of the day. There was nothing to say and neither of them wanted to bring it to life again by discussing it. After an hour, Patsy took out her mobile. 'I'm going to book us all on the next flight back to Scotland. We need to go home to some sense of normality.'

'I know what you mean. I want to go home. I never thought I'd see Angus and the kids again after today. I miss his egg and chips...' Sheila trailed off. She didn't want to say any more. She knew Patsy felt the same.

As she looked through the list of flights, the countryside passing her by, Patsy looked up. Somewhere in the distance something caught her eye. She thought it was a trick of the light, but opened the window to see better.

'Sheila, stop the car,' she whispered. She didn't dare take her eyes off the figure in the distance. Patsy blinked hard and wondered if it was a figment of her imagination.

Puzzled, Sheila pulled into the side of the road. 'Don't you feel well Patsy? Are you going to be sick?'

Patsy spoke slowly, not daring to move her face from the open window. 'Look in the distance over there. Can you see that figure on horseback? It's a white horse and we're not far from where I had the crash. Come on Sheila, open your eyes!' Excitedly, Patsy moved aside to give Sheila a better view. 'That's the man who pulled me out of the car, I'm sure of it.'

'Patsy, all I see is someone in the distance on a horse... I think. I can't really make it out it's all so far away. Come on, you've had a long day, let's go home.'

'Is there a side road around here? Can we get closer to have a proper look?'

Sheila looked around to see where they could turn off. 'It's just hedgerow Patsy and a straight road. There aren't any turn-offs. Whoever that is, is way over in the distance.'

Deflated, Patsy watched the figure disappear before her eyes. 'I just wanted to thank him Sheila, for saving my life. Well, at least I know I'm not going mad.' Patsy said no more on the subject. It wasn't worth it; no one believed her anyway.

Back at the cottage, Maggie had cooked up one of her favourite Scottish stews. Neither of them felt hungry, they couldn't stomach it, but given the effort Maggie had put in they felt they should at least try.

'Are you two lassies okay?' Maggie didn't want to interfere, but given how they had more or less fallen through the door tired and weary, with pale faces and a change of clothing, she guessed something had gone terribly wrong.

'I've found three flights for us tonight to go back to Scotland, I think we should go home,' Patsy said.

Sheila instantly agreed, but Maggie sipped at her warm broth, frowning. Now she definitely knew something was wrong. 'Are you sure you feel strong enough to face Larry's questioning?'

'I have to face the music sometime with Larry; I might as well get it over with sooner rather than later.'

* * *

The flight back had seemed longer than normal, but stepping out of the airport and seeing Fin there waving to catch their attention made them feel at home.

As she got closer to him, Patsy could tell he had seen her bruises. The expression on his face spoke volumes. Wagging a finger at him as she approached, she got her word in first. 'Not a word; do you hear me Fin.' Patsy raised her eyebrows and looked directly at him.

'I wasn't going to say anything, Patsy; don't know what you mean.' He grinned. 'But now that you mention it, that French make-up isn't up to much if it makes you look like that!' He laughed and picked up Maggie's and Sheila's holdalls. 'The car's straight outside the door; pinched someone's disabled badge on the way here. I thought it would make things easier.'

For the first time in what seemed like an age, they all laughed.

It was good to see him again, even though he was an inconsiderate thief!

When they'd packed up the car and were on their way, Fin said, 'By the way, Patsy, your Larry has been around. Christ, he's like a fucking stalker. Every time I go for a piss, I have to look over my shoulder. I've told him nothing, that's your job Patsy. But everything at home is running smoothly. Oh and Maggie, your parcel came from Amazon. Stupid prats left it outside of your door. Christ, I feel like a bloody call centre.'

'You better not have opened my parcel,' snapped Maggie, pursing her lips in her usual fashion.

'Why not? Have you been ordering those TENA pads again?'

'If you weren't driving laddie, I'd give you a good slap around the back of the head.'

While Maggie and Fin bickered between themselves, Patsy reached across and held Sheila's hand. 'Are you okay Sheila? You seem miles away,' she whispered.

'I was just thinking, would you mind driving me up to Edinburgh first? I want to see Angus and the kiddies... you know what I mean.'

'I understand.' She squeezed her hand again. The last twenty-four hours had been gruesome and made Patsy wish she had an Angus to go home to. 'Fin, can you drop Sheila off in Edinburgh first please.'

Patsy could see his puzzled face in the rear-view mirror as he caught her eye. Normally Sheila would have gone to Glasgow with them for a cuppa and then Angus would have picked her up. But Fin knew better than to ask and came off at the next junction.

Patsy could see the relief wash over Sheila as they drove up to her house and Angus's road recovery truck was parked outside.

'We won't come in if you don't mind. We'll speak later. And thank you for coming to my rescue. Bye love.'

Patsy knew exactly how she felt. They had both been trau-
matised and could only share it with each other. Each time she
had closed her eyes, the image of the driver of her car having
his stomach ripped open and the wine pouring out made her
feel sick and then being forced to stab him made her want to
shower and scrub her hands constantly. Friend or foe, Manne
had said; well, maybe if they hadn't stabbed the man they would
have been classed as foe and wouldn't now be making this
journey home. The very thought of it made her want to telephone Nancy and her parents. In fact, she decided there and
then to go home to London. She was going to take time out
anyway, so she might as well put it to good use, go home and
hug her daughter. Once she had made that decision, she felt
better.

Fin pulled up outside the community centre where Patsy's flat
was situated above. 'There you go Patsy, home sweet home.'

Maggie turned and looked at Patsy in the back seat. 'You're
staying with me. I'll pop back and pick up some of your clothes
later.' Patsy was about to protest, but Maggie gave her a stern look.
'I said you're staying with me Patsy Diamond and that is the end
of it!'

Grateful that she wouldn't be alone, Patsy nodded and smiled.
Fin took out Maggie's bag and walked them to her flat. 'Well
ladies, I'll see you later. You look tired; get some rest, eh?'

Once in Maggie's homely flat, Patsy gave a huge sigh.

'You, young lady, go to bed and get some rest. You're not long
out of hospital. I'll go and put some clean sheets on the bed while
you sort yourself out in the bathroom.'

Smiling at Maggie's motherly bossiness, Patsy did as she was
told. She knew she wouldn't sleep but Maggie was right, her
whole body ached and relaxing in the safety of Maggie's flat was
just what she needed. Coming out of the bathroom, she walked

into Maggie's spare bedroom. The bed was freshly made and on top of the duvet was a floral winceyette nightgown.

'Get changed into that; it's not much, but it's comfy and warm. I've put a hot toddy on the bedside table. Drink it, it will help you get some rest. Shout if you need me.' Once Maggie had left the room, Patsy got undressed, put on the nightgown and got into bed. The steaming whisky and hot water was cool enough to drink. Sipping at it, she could feel it soothing her throat and she drank until she finished it. Her mind roamed over the last few days, but her lids felt heavy and she closed her eyes and finally slept.

* * *

Opening her eyes and yawning, Patsy felt disorientated by the darkness of the room. Blinking hard, she turned her head and saw the bedside lamp. Switching it on, she yawned again and looked at her watch: 7 p.m. Sitting up with a start, she looked around the immaculately clean bedroom. For a moment she couldn't recollect where she was and then suddenly she remembered she was at Maggie's. She could hear the television coming from the lounge and the smell of food cooking wafted to her nostrils, making her feel hungry. Pulling back the duvet, she looked down at the winceyette nightgown and smiled. It was a far cry from her own silky negligees she normally wore, but to be honest, it was warm and comfortable. She opened the bedroom door and crept down the corridor of the flat towards the lounge. It felt warm and welcoming as she popped her head around the door and saw Maggie watching the news from her armchair.

'Hi Maggie,' she yawned, 'I can't believe I've slept for so long. Sorry.'

'Patsy lassie, come and sit down, and why are you apologising? You must have needed it. You haven't been well. Now stop standing in the doorway and sit down. I'll go and make you a coffee.' Fussing and busying herself, Maggie stood up and steered Patsy to the sofa. 'That nightgown suits you lassie; don't worry, I won't tell anyone.' She winked.

'Have you had any sleep, Maggie? You've had a tiring few days, too.'

'I had a quick nap in my chair, while watching the antiques roadshow. Come on, sit down.' Maggie patted the sofa and smiled.

Slightly embarrassed and feeling quite vulnerable with only a nightgown on and no make-up, Patsy sat down. Her hair felt a mess and she needed a hot shower. Not quite the Patsy Maggie was used to seeing. Patsy stared blankly at the television while Maggie disappeared and in no time at all appeared again with a cup of coffee for both of them. 'I can't believe I slept so long,' she repeated. 'I didn't think I would sleep at all, with one thing and another.'

'That will be the hot toddy; I swear by them. Always help me when I have a troubled mind and need some sleep. Now just relax and stop looking like a scared cat. I know you're not your usual polished self, but you will be in no time at all. Now drink up and catch up with what's been going on in the world. That's all there seems to be these days. Bad news! Let's have something to eat and you just relax tonight, then tomorrow you can face the world and do whatever business it is you have to do. But build up your strength tonight and get some colour back in those cheeks.'

Patsy laughed. 'Don't you think I have enough colour in my cheeks? I'm black and blue and some bruises are now going a wonderful shade of yellow.'

'Well, now that you mention it, I could have used a better choice of words. All things considered though, you've been very lucky, my girl. You could have come off a lot worse. Somebody up there likes you.' Maggie raised her eyes and looked at the ceiling.

'I know Maggie. Things could have been so much worse. It almost frightens me to think about it. I've decided to go to London for a while to see Nancy and Victoria; she must be wondering what's happened to me.'

'Sheila called Victoria and told her what was happening and that everything was in hand. But at some point you need to let her know you're safe and sound. I think that nuisance Larry has contacted her, too. I appreciate he's worried and your boyfriend, but he's not your bloody keeper! If you want to be a runaway bride, then so be it,' Maggie snapped. 'I will go and see if those potatoes are ready. A good hot meal inside of you will make you feel better, and then back to bed with you; tomorrow is another day.' Wagging her finger at Patsy, she smiled and left the room.

Feeling like a young girl being lectured by her mother, Patsy found it strangely comforting. Maggie had a heart of gold even though she came across as a bitter, scary woman forever in her black cardigan like the black widow. She could see now why Nick's grandmother, Beryl, had liked and trusted her so much. After a plate of sausage, mash, peas and gravy, Patsy felt stronger already. But the fullness of her stomach and the warmth of the room made her feel tired again, so with Maggie's blessing, she went back to bed and slept soundly.

* * *

The next morning, Patsy woke feeling refreshed. Last night had been the medicine she'd needed. She hoped that Sheila felt better too, now she was back in the safety of Angus's arms.

Walking into the kitchen, Patsy could see that Maggie was already up and about making coffee. She wondered if Maggie ever slept. Maggie busied herself while Patsy made a list of things to do. Her first job was to telephone Victoria and assure her she was okay, then her parents. Saving the best until last, she wrote Larry's name down.

Once showered and dressed, Patsy rang Victoria. 'I'm just letting you know I'm okay and back in Scotland under the careful watch of Maggie. I will come and see you soon, promise.'

Victoria breathed a sigh of relief. 'I've been so worried about you Patsy, but Sheila said not to come.' Assuring her everything was okay, Patsy ended the call, then she called her parents. 'Mum, everything is okay, I'm in Scotland now but I'm coming to London to see you all.' Patsy sent her love to Nancy, who apparently was out. Taking a sip of her coffee, she then dialled Larry's number. Instantly he answered.

'Patsy!' he shouted. 'Where the hell have you been? Why haven't you been in touch? I've been frantic. Where are you now? I'm coming to see you!'

'I'm in Scotland; I am home.'

'I'm on my way, don't move. Don't go anywhere.'

Patsy was about to speak but Larry ended the call and Patsy stared at her mobile blankly. 'I'm going back to my flat Maggie. Larry is on the way.'

Concerned, Maggie looked at her. 'Are you sure you don't want him to come here lassie?'

'No, I will do this alone. He has a lot of questions and it's going to take time to answer them, but thank you.'

Entering her flat, Patsy put the heating on. Even though it wasn't chilly outside, the flat seemed cold. Walking into the kitchen, she started to percolate some coffee. Waiting seemed an eternity, but as she looked out of the window, she saw Larry's car pull up and then heard the buzzer to her flat go. Picking up the intercom telephone, she pressed the button to open the down-stairs' door. She could hear Larry's feet almost running up the stairs and her door flew open. Larry was about to rush towards her when he saw her bruised face. 'What the hell has happened to you? Who did this?' he demanded.

'I was in a car accident Larry, that's why I haven't called you. I've been in hospital in France. I'm okay, just a bit battered and bruised.'

'What about the airport when you were arrested? I went to the police station and they knew nothing about it. What have you got to say about that? Why didn't you come home to me? Why go to France? For fuck's sake Patsy, don't you know how worried I've been about you? All I got was some stupid text from you saying you would be in touch. I've been going out of my mind woman!'

'Stop shouting Larry. My head aches and I'm tired. No wonder I didn't want you to come to the hospital, if this was how you were going to behave. Look at me; don't you think I've been through enough?'

'Are you hurt badly? What happened?' he asked politely but coldly.

'As you can see, cuts and bruises and a sprained wrist. I was very lucky. I was unconscious and in hospital, but they said I was fit to go home so here I am. I've made some coffee; would you like some?' Without waiting for his answer, Patsy walked away. Seeing the anger on Larry's face made her realise this wasn't going to be easy. Laying the cups on the coffee table in front of them, Patsy lit a cigarette.

'What happened after you were arrested, or not as the case may be? It looked real enough to me. I wanted to file you as a missing person, but then I got your text. I tried convincing the police that it could be from kidnappers or something but then Sheila also said she had heard from you. So, who were they? Where did they take you?'

Patsy thought about her words carefully; this was a web of lies that she couldn't untangle easily and Larry's sharp brain would see through them all. 'They dumped me off the motorway at the other side of the airport.' Patsy pondered her next words. 'They were some old enemies of Nick's wanting money and information. How on earth they staged that set-up is beyond me and they had gone to a lot of trouble to frighten me, which they did.' Her heart was thumping hard in her chest and even she felt it sounded hollow and unbelievable.

'So after you were dumped, why didn't you come home? Why didn't you contact me? Why let me worry and panic about you when you were safe? I don't understand Patsy; why didn't you come home!' he shouted. His face was flushed and his eyes were wide in anger.

Trying to remain calm, Patsy's brain darted around in different directions, trying to think of things to appease him, to calm him down.

'I was frightened, Larry. I just wanted to get away. I wasn't thinking straight. Everything was such a shock. I just wanted to run; I didn't think.' Trying to change the subject, she picked up her coffee and looked over the rim of her mug at him. 'What happened to you?'

Larry shook his head and looked up at the ceiling. 'You're never going to believe this, but they dropped me off outside the police station and told me to go in while they parked the car. I wasn't thinking straight either, I was so worried about you. When I asked the desk sergeant about you, he told me you weren't there – you never had been. But he also thought it quite odd that a lawyer like me didn't ask for a warrant card or the name of the arresting officers.'

Hearing his explanation, Patsy felt on firmer ground. Mentally, she thought, she could maybe turn this around on Larry. If he had done his job properly, then none of this would have happened, would it?

Looking at Larry, Patsy couldn't see what she had once seen in him. His lack of concern about her made her realise that. He had gone through the preliminaries of asking how she was, but she could tell it wasn't genuine. All he was doing was shouting, and focusing on how he felt. It was all about him. They say love is blind, and in her case it most definitely was. She had thought she'd been in love, possibly still was, but, she had put off setting a definite date for the wedding. What she had needed most was to be needed, and Larry had been the perfect loving partner and lover. Mentally, she realised how pathetic that sounded. She had been willing to marry Larry, but his attitude of late had made her have second thoughts. He was permanently questioning her movements. Who had she seen, where had she been? The very thought of a lifetime with someone like that made her shudder. Maybe that bang on the head she had received in the car crash had done her good. Considering how swiftly things were moving in her life with the Milieu and her other dealings, she knew she couldn't be the wife Larry wanted. She had to make a choice, and the truth was that however much she loved Larry, she loved herself more.

Wanting to get a little of her own back, she couldn't hold her tongue any more. Looking at him over her mug again, she smiled apprehensively. 'I suppose they had a point; you didn't ask too many questions, did you? All those trumped-up charges they came up with and all you did was shout and protest. I felt it was easier to go with them and get it sorted out as quickly as possible. Everyone in the airport was watching, it was better I just left. You also went with them in the other car. Didn't you ask any questions then?'

'Don't fucking blame me! It's not my fault you're up to your neck in shit! How did those people know we were going away? I hope you're going to report all of this to the police; that is if you haven't already, because I bloody am. You're safe, you're home and now we go to the police.'

Panic rose in Patsy; that was the last thing she wanted. 'No, I'm not up to it.' Shaking her head, Patsy felt it was time to do the womanly thing and squeeze a few tears into her eyes. 'I was upset Larry; I wasn't really looking at them. They warned me about messing around in Nick's business affairs and apparently he owed them money. They wanted money and to frighten me. I'm not going to the police. Sorry.'

Larry's head shot up. 'How much did they want? Did you give it to them? If you sent it via mobile banking then you will have their bank details; we could trace them by that.'

Patsy felt Larry sounded almost excited. It also crossed her mind whether it was really her he was worried about or his own reputation. He desperately wanted to prove himself right to the desk sergeant and police station who thought he was stupid not asking the arresting officers for identification.

'It doesn't matter how much they wanted, I didn't have it. And no, they were not stupid enough to give me their bank details. Let it go Larry; surely if there was anything to find or prove, you would have found it by now. I know they had a police car and everything, but it was a sick joke and I'm just glad to be home.'

'But Nick, he's been dead a year. Who gives a fuck about him now? It doesn't make sense and you know a lot more than you're telling me. Well, that's the last of it; the sooner we're married, the sooner all of this shit stops.'

The mention of marriage brought Patsy up short. 'Why would everything stop if we were married?'

'Because I would stop you hanging around on this estate and the estate trash that go with it. I defend scum like that every day in court, but you choose them as your friends. Well, they are not welcome in my house!'

Patsy couldn't believe her ears. Calm, easy-going Larry was going to stop her seeing her friends and ban her from the estate? For the first time since she'd met him, Larry frightened her. The minute he got the ring on her finger he planned to isolate her from all her friends.

'I choose my friends Larry, not you. I am my own person.' Anger bubbled up inside of her. How dare he dictate to her in this way! Maybe it was just as well everything had happened the way it had and she'd found out sooner rather than later what his plans for her married life were to be like.

'And I am always the last on your list. Well, not any more Patsy. We get married and sort your life out properly. No more of this gallivanting around the country. It's time to rein you in and let Nick Diamond rest in peace. You will have my name and my friends. These people you've been mixing with have caused you nothing but hassle. Let that be the end of it.' His flushed angry face no longer looked handsome; in fact, quite the opposite.

As hard as Patsy tried to compose herself, she couldn't stop herself from feeling angry. Rein her in? Did he really say that? Without a second thought, she blurted out, 'I'm dumping you, Larry! How dare you tell me how to live my life and who I can be friends with. This isn't the Dark Ages. Christ, we're not even married and you're laying down the law; who the hell do you think you are?'

'Dump me? You're choosing this lot over me? Don't make an enemy of me Patsy, it will only end badly for you,' he sneered. 'I'm going to be your husband. We've agreed on that and I'm not letting you treat me like discarded rubbish. Is there someone else? Is that it? Have you been playing me for a mug all this time?'

'No! There isn't anyone else, I barely have time for myself let alone two relationships. It's over Larry. It's been very nice and we've both had some fun, but I can't continue a relationship with someone who wants to rein me in!' she shouted. 'And as for threatening me, Larry; what are you going to do? Complain to the authorities that I've ended our relationship? Grow up; you sound like a teenager!' Patsy half laughed. This was ridiculous.

Very slowly, Larry reached into the breast pocket of his jacket and took out an envelope. Patsy could see that it had been opened and watched as Larry put it on the table. 'I'd almost forgotten about this Patsy,' said Larry calmly. His voice was monotone and coldly threatening. 'It was only when I was frantically looking through my desk drawers that I stumbled across it.'

Patsy stared at the envelope and felt a sense of foreboding. Whatever was in it, Larry felt it held his trump card. 'What is it?' Intrigued and nervous, she looked on as Larry took out a letter from inside the envelope.

'James came to see me on his own a while ago. He rambled on about how you were up to your neck in all kinds of illegal dealings, but he also gave me this letter and asked in the event of his untimely death or should anything happen to him, to read it and give it to the police. He said you were going to have him murdered.'

Patsy paled at his words; she was stunned and didn't know what to say. Moistening her lips to speak, she looked at the letter and then at Larry. 'So what does it say, this dead man's confession?'

'Read it yourself.' Larry handed over the letter. 'But in short, it says that you murdered Karen Duret and he knows where you buried her. He's given the full whereabouts of where she is.' Larry smiled. 'Now, I could burn it and we could say no more about it, or I could do as requested and give it to the police... What do you think? I'm not stupid, I know you have friends in low places, but no one has seen sight nor sound of Karen recently. I know you were angry and upset, and whatever happened could have been an accident. But where have you buried her Patsy?'

'Don't be ridiculous! Have you heard yourself? Twisted, bitter James who tried accusing me of killing his wife and lover, even though he was covered in blood and all the neighbours saw him. You believe his lies against me. For crying out loud Larry, I had no reason to harm Karen. Our partnership was dissolved and Nancy was safe.'

'Well, there is only one way to find out and that is to let the authorities dig up this place he says she's buried, isn't it? I will give you forty-eight hours to think about it Patsy. I love you and I know you love me, and we could be happy away from this place and the people you mix with. But I will not be used and cast aside by you!'

Patsy looked at Larry. This was a very different man to the one she had laughed and shared a bed with. He was evil and manipulating.

'You know Larry, I often wondered why you and your wife split up. You said it was because you worked so hard and were never there when she needed you. But you're always at home, Larry. Maybe your wife didn't like this side of you I'm seeing today. You want to blackmail me into marriage over a pack of lies. Exchange one prison sentence for another. You say I have friends in low places, but they're not as low as you!'

'I'm not blackmailing you Patsy, I love you,' he protested. 'You know that and you are treating me like a fool. All I'm doing is my job as a lawyer. I have been given a letter by a deceased client. It's my duty to pass it on to the police. The fact that it contains incriminating information about my fiancée would possibly make me see things differently. We could burn it together on our wedding day. If you have nothing to hide, it makes no difference, does it? Think on it, Patsy.' Larry had a smirk on his face Patsy wished she could slap off.

The hate that boiled up inside her was indescribable. The bastard. This was his revenge, and he was enjoying it. 'This is more than you doing your duty, Larry. Why didn't you hand it over when you found it? Why wait and tell me now?'

'I thought I would give you a chance to explain first. I'm not as blind as you think Patsy. I know you've been running around like some cheap gangster trying to match Nick. But it hasn't worked, and you're a fool. It's time you grew up and came back into the real world and I am offering you that choice.'

'Get out Larry, just get out!' Patsy screamed at him like a banshee. She couldn't bear to look at him any more.

Shrugging, he took the letter and slowly put it back into the envelope. 'I'd better keep this in a safe place.' He smiled, turned on his heel and left.

Patsy ran to the door and slammed it behind him. Her heart was pounding and she felt pains in her chest. Collapsing to her knees, she burst into tears and sobbed. James had really left his mark on the world. Dead or not, he had been determined to see her go to prison. Breathing in and out slowly, she tried calming herself but her body was wracked with sobs. It was over. One way or another, her life was over. Larry, beloved Larry, would see to that. He was blackmailing her into marriage, just so he could manipulate and control her. Rein her in, even! His harsh, bitter words swam around her head. Forty-eight hours to plan the rest of her life, that was the option he had given her. James had handed him the stick to beat her with. She couldn't believe it. Larry, who she'd thought she loved, had been willing to marry, was turning out to be the worst of all her assailants. For a good business-woman, she was a bad judge of men.

She felt woozy and thought she might pass out, when suddenly she felt Maggie kneel beside her.

'Patsy! Can you hear me lassie? Breathe! Let's breathe together. You're going to be okay, now breathe with me Patsy.'

She followed Maggie's instructions. The pain in her chest subsided a little and she found herself breathing normally again after a while.

'Why are you here Maggie?' she panted.

'Because I saw Larry leave and wondered if you were okay. He left the downstairs door open; good job by all accounts, that was one hell of a panic attack! I thought you were going to pass out. Do you have any whisky or brandy around this place?'

Still on the floor and breathing heavily, Patsy pointed to a cupboard. Her head was spinning.

Maggie got a mug and poured some liquid in. 'Take a sip lassie, this will help. Don't bother trying to say anything, let's just get you right first.'

As Patsy took a couple of sips, Maggie held her arm out to help her off the floor. Slowly but steadily, Patsy managed it and almost slumped onto the sofa. Beads of sweat covered her brow, and she wiped them away with her hands.

Maggie waited then made her take another sip. 'Right, he didn't take the news well then, that you're ending your engagement.'

'He's blackmailing me, Maggie,' Patsy panted. 'James gave him a letter saying I'd murdered and buried Karen. He's told him all kinds of things... I don't know,' Patsy blurted out. 'He won't give the police the letter if I agree to marry him and never come back to this estate and end the friendships I've made here! What can I do Maggie? Who knows what James has put in that letter or how many copies he has. I can't believe it of him, I really can't.' Patsy couldn't stop crying; all her worst fears had come true.

'Patsy, you're not thinking straight. Play him at his own game.

Agree with him. That letter of his has to be somewhere close and we have the perfect burglar to find it – Fin.'

'No Maggie, he isn't going to leave it anywhere for Fin to find. He me trapped into a loveless marriage too much – the bastard!'

Maggie shook her head; she was all out of answers. 'Have a word with Sheila, see what her slant on this is. In the meantime, I'll have a word with Fin anyway.'

'It's the copies that bother me, Maggie. What's the point in me stealing one letter if there are others? He's not stupid.'

'Just agree to his terms for now; we need thinking space. He may be running ahead of you at this moment in time, but we'll beat him eventually. Let's put Sheila in the picture first, then we'll go back to mine. I am not having you here stewing on this all night alone.'

Picking up her mobile, Patsy did as she was told and telephoned Sheila. 'Sheila, I just thought I would let you know that I have spoken to Larry, and well, it's all turned very nasty. Maggie's here with me, she told me to fill you in on the details...' Patsy trailed off.

'What the hell's happened Patsy? Tell me.'

Patsy's choked voice revealed Larry's ultimatum.

'Well, that sleazy bastard has got a real shock coming then, hasn't he? As much as I hate to say it, we need to ring that Manne to confirm something!'

'Why, for God's sake?' Patsy whined.

'Didn't he say that they knew about Karen and where she was buried? I want him to confirm it, then we can let Larry call the police and dig up nothing. He will look like a prize prat! Don't be blackmailed by him, Patsy lassie, and over my dead body are you marrying him! I'm going to call Manne now and I'll call you back.'

Wide eyed, Patsy remembered that conversation – the Milieu knew all about Karen Duret and her body being moved.

Patsy ended the call and looked up at Maggie. 'There might be hope on the horizon Maggie; I do hope Sheila's right.'

Maggie and Patsy waited in silence for Sheila's call and when Patsy's phone suddenly burst into life, Patsy couldn't answer it quickly enough.

'I've told Manne what's happened and he isn't too happy, but then that Manne never is. He's confirmed they can dig where they like but they won't find Karen. I asked him if it was a trick and he was a little angry at my suggestion and called me a few things in French, but he gave me his word. The location on James's letter is not where she is, quite simply because they cremated her and as a sick joke, she is on a mantlepiece at the chateau! I've called Greek Paul and he confirmed there is a valuable urn, just as Manne described, on the mantlepiece. And it's full of ashes, Patsy, hopefully Karen's... What do you think of that!'

'What? They've put her ashes in the chateau? That's sick, really sick.'

'Maybe they felt it was for sentimental value; anyway, who cares? The main thing is that Larry can do what the fuck he likes. Let them get their warrant and dig up this place. They'll find nothing!'

Patsy exhaled deeply. 'Christ, do you think I'm off the hook, Sheila? That fucking James, after everything I did for him! Why are men such bastards? Maggie thinks we should play Larry at his own game...'

'I'd string the prick along for a while, let him have his moment. What we want are those legal papers Karen signed, dissolving the partnership. They have to be in his office, and Larry will want to destroy those papers and make out your partnership was never dissolved and that is why you killed her, or something like that. Christ, I'm not Miss Marple.'

'Yes, you're right. I'll speak to Fin; maybe he could have a look around. Thank you, Sheila. I'd forgotten about that conversation with the Milieu with one thing and another. My head's a bit of a mess.' Suddenly the future looked brighter. Larry had shown his true colours and they were determined to give him his come-uppance.

'You will be fine, Patsy. That bastard Larry calling me estate trash; who the hell does he think he is? Well, according to your French friends, revenge is a dish best served cold. And we are going to freeze that Larry's bollocks off – trust me!'

'Thank you, Sheila. You have been more than a good friend to me. I feel we're more like sisters. I've never had a sister, but if I had, it would have been you.'

'Och, shut up lassie, that bump on the head of yours has turned you soft. Oh, by the way, there is one more thing I didn't mention...' Sheila paused.

'Oh my God what now?' Patsy felt as though she'd been surrounded by more bad news than she could cope with lately.

'No, well, it's not bad, but it's not what you want to hear either. That Manne and his Frenchie mates are having some big dinner dance in a few weeks and are asking that you and me go to it. It's some kind of yearly ball or something. Anyway, it's something to get your glad rags out for.' Sheila laughed.

Relieved, Patsy smiled. 'Actually, that wasn't what I was expecting, and my bruises will have gone by then. As long as it isn't at their favourite bistro!'

'Well, sounds good, eh? He said we can bring plus ones. I know its isn't Angus's thing; he would rather have a doner kebab with the football. But I thought I might invite Maggie or Victoria. What about you?'

'I don't know if Victoria would go; she has her hands full with little Nicky at the moment and she's loving it. What about Fin?'

'I'm sure Fin would love it. He's never been to anything like that – then again Patsy, neither have I,' Sheila laughed. 'Right, lassie. Back to business. Let's get Operation Larry sorted. Speak to Fin first and wait for Larry to contact you. Do not contact him. Let the bastard sweat!'

Patsy sighed. 'What would I do without you? I always seem to bring trouble to your doors and I feel so guilty sometimes...'

'Oh shut up lassie and stop asking for the sympathy vote. That's what friends and families do... we stick together!'

Giving a weak smile, Patsy agreed. She had never had friends like this before. Someone always on hand when she needed them. And what a strange mix they were. They couldn't be more opposite, but there was no question of their loyalty. She had always had to fight her own battles, but now she wasn't alone any more. This was the one good legacy Nick had left behind.

6

A SHOCK IN STORE

When Patsy picked up her mobile and answered it, she saw it was Janine, the manageress of her salons, calling her. She was surprised by the woman's breathless panicking voice on the other end. 'Patsy, it's the salon!' she wailed. 'It's been broken into and they've made a right mess of it. There's graffiti all over the walls, the mirrors are broken and two of the sinks look like they have been hit with a hammer. The floor is covered in water, about an inch deep.' Breaking down in tears, Janine couldn't help herself. 'Oh Patsy, it's all my fault. I should never have questioned those men. I could see they were angry and I know it's them, but I can't prove it.'

'What men? What are you talking about? You're not making sense Janine. Stop crying and tell me properly.' Patsy waited while she could hear Janine sniffing and blowing her nose.

'It's the delivery drivers who bring the money to be laundered. You know who I mean, don't you?'

Stunned, Patsy was trying to make sense of what Janine was saying. 'Of course I do,' Patsy snapped. 'What about them?'

'The last two deliveries have been made by two different

men. The last one was short by £5,000 and this time it was short
by a lot more. When I questioned it after the first time, they just
laughed at me and said you knew all about it. But when it was
short again I said I would call you to confirm this and they got
angry and started shouting. One threatened to rough me up a
bit; he grabbed hold of my blouse and told me to not interfere
in your business. That was two days ago... and now this
morning I've walked into this. Patsy, we've never had anything
like this before. Why would anyone break into a hairdresser's? I
could be wrong, it could just be vandals, but I think it's because
I questioned and upset those men. What are we going to do,
Patsy?'

Patsy agreed that it didn't make sense. Those deliveries of
money had been coming for as long as she could remember and
there had never been any problems, so why now? Angry, but
trying to think on her feet, Patsy almost screamed down the
phone to make Janine hear her above her sobbing.

'Janine, ring as many of the clients you can get hold of, or get
one of the staff to do it. And then call the police. We're going to
need a crime number for the insurance.' Patsy was already
thinking about all the custom she would be turning away, and for
how long, before this was all fixed. 'Offer everyone who is due to
walk through the door this morning half price at one of the other
salons and reimburse them for any further taxi expenses or bus
fares – that might help. I was already planning on coming to
London, but I'm on my way today, now! Don't touch anything
until the police arrive. Oh and Janine, say nothing about the men
– do you hear me? I will sort that when I arrive.' Patsy waited for
Janine's weak reply and ended the call.

'Fuck!' Patsy shouted at the wall. 'If it doesn't rain, it pours!'
Patsy lit a cigarette and stopped to think for a moment. That salon
in particular was her baby. Buying it and renovating it had been

her biggest achievement and it saddened her to think someone had vandalised it.

When she went to tell Maggie she was leaving, Maggie pursed her lips and folded her arms in that matronly way she had about her. 'Aren't you forgetting something in your hurry to get through the door lassie? Like something or someone? With a letter... and I don't mean the postman.'

'Who?' Patsy's mind was already in London and thinking about the million things she would have to sort out once there.

Giving her another meaningful look and tutting, Maggie started again. 'Larry. He's going to think you've done another runner!'

Patsy's shoulders sank and she sat down. 'I'm going to have to tell him, aren't I? Well, Maggie if he doesn't believe me, he can listen to Janine crying down the telephone, that will convince him.' It annoyed her to have to explain herself to Larry, but she also knew she had no option if she wanted to keep him off her back.

Maggie nodded. 'Keep him sweet Patsy and tell him you're distressed by it all. Give him no cause for concern.'

Disheartened, Patsy picked up her mobile and called Larry, who instantly answered.

'Morning darling, how are you today?' he asked, much too chirpily for Patsy's liking. There had been a time when his welcoming dulcet tones had made her smile; now they left a bitter taste in her mouth. Larry was her jailer, and he hid it well, under his loving words. Hypocrite!

'Morning...' she stammered. 'I've just had a call from Janine; you remember, my manageress at the salons?' Patsy waited for a moment; this obviously wasn't the call he had expected.

'Yes, so what of it?' Patsy could already hear the suspicion in his voice.

'One of my salons has been badly vandalised. The police are on their way and Janine's in a terrible state. I have to go to London... today.' Patsy waited again for the penny to drop and put her mobile on loudspeaker so that Maggie could hear him too.

'London!' he shouted down the phone. 'Surely, if she's your manageress, she can sort this problem out. Isn't that what you pay her for?'

Patsy felt disgusted. Larry didn't give a hoot about anyone but himself. He hadn't even asked if Janine had been hurt in the process. This made her blood boil.

'It's my salon, Larry, and Janine's very upset by it all and there are things to sort out, like the staff and the customers for instance?' she prompted him.

Realising his mistake, Larry stopped short. 'Yes, of course, sorry. Was anyone hurt or anything?'

'Not as far as I know, but there is a lot of damage and flooding. I really can't believe you Larry—'

Maggie wagged her finger to stop Patsy's outburst. Reaching over, she picked up Patsy's cigarettes, and lighting one, she handed it over to a grateful Patsy.

'How long do you intend to stay in London for? Have you thought any more about what we discussed?'

'For God's sake Larry, I haven't even got there yet and seen the damage; how do I know!'

Raising one eyebrow, Maggie looked at her and mouthed, 'Nicely,' to Patsy.

'Look, I'm too upset to discuss anything at the moment. I have to go.' As an afterthought, and taking Maggie's lead, she softened her voice. 'Of course, you could always come with me,' she suggested through gritted teeth.

Surprisingly, Larry didn't jump at the chance. Instead, he stammered and coughed, saying, 'I have a big case on today. I have to be in court. There is no way I could drop everything and go with you.'

Not wanting to push her luck, but knowing she had Larry cornered, Patsy said, 'I could do with your support Larry...'

'Can't you go tomorrow? I may be able to come with you then.'

'No, be sensible now,' Patsy reasoned, 'I need to see it for myself and sort this mess out quickly. I've asked you to come with me and help me, but your work clearly comes first and my work means nothing to you. I just presumed as my fiancé you would want to support me.' She grinned up at Maggie, who was too busy stifling her own laughter.

'For God's sake Patsy, it's not all about you. You can't just spring this on me and expect me to drop everything. I have responsibilities too. People are relying on me,' he snapped.

Patsy knew she had won this argument and realised Larry must be cursing himself for not being able to go with her. When she didn't say anything else, he added, 'Anyway, you're right, the sooner you go and get things sorted out, the quicker you will be back. Let me know when you arrive safe and sound, eh, and keep me posted if you need anything.'

Patsy ended the call. Maggie burst out laughing and punched the air. 'Well, that well and truly stuffed him, didn't it? And it's given us more time, although he still wants to keep tabs on you lassie. For goodness' sake, he's worse than a leech. Now, are you getting the train to London? You can't drive with that sprained wrist.'

'Oh shit, yes, I never thought of that. Maybe Fin could drive me?'

Maggie gave a wry grin. 'Fin has other things to do... remember?'

'Indeed, I do. Well, if he gets that sorted quickly, maybe he could meet me there. Janine said something about a problem with some men there. Maybe Fin could shed some light on that too. Right, let's get sorted. I'm going to call a taxi and catch a train. And thanks Maggie; I think I would have bitten his head off if you hadn't been here.'

'I think I would have bitten his head off if he had been here. Selfish little bastard!'

Looking at each other for a moment, they both burst into laughter.

* * *

The train pulled out of the station and the further it got away from Larry and Glasgow, the better Patsy felt. It was like she could breathe again without being suffocated by a blackmailing jealous man. Arriving at the station some hours later, she was pleased to see her dad's face in the crowd.

'Hello Patsy love, it's good to see you. I wish it was in better circumstances. How are you feeling now, after your accident? Your bruises are going yellow, that means they are fading.' He hugged her.

'Actually, I feel okay, just tired. Do I really look that bad?' Don't answer that, I've seen myself in the mirror.'

'Let's put it this way,' he laughed, 'you look much better than that salon of yours.' Picking up her holdall and putting his arm around her shoulders, he walked her to the car.

'You'd better take me there first I suppose... How bad is it, Dad?'

'The police have been. At first, they presumed it was just kids wrecking the place, but the metal shutters had been cut at the bottom and the lock has been broken. The police think it's profes- sional, sorry love. But why would anyone want to break into a hairdresser's? Must've been desperate for a hair dye.' Her dad laughed, trying to make light of it.

Patsy sat quietly, pondering the situation. 'To be honest Dad, it had crossed my mind if Janine had locked up properly, but it sounds like she did. At least I can claim on the insurance. But I agree it doesn't make sense, does it?' Patsy's mind wandered back to the conversation she'd had with Janine. Someone was obviously out to make trouble and rip her off in the process, but who?

Shocked by what she saw as she arrived at the salon, Patsy tiptoed across the wet floor and sat in one of the chairs. Looking around at the devastation, she couldn't believe it. A plumber had been and stopped the water flow and the staff had brushed a lot of the water out the front doors. But all of the mirrors were smashed to pieces, the sink units were broken, and the walls were sprayed with all kinds of different coloured graffiti. Her heart sank.

'Oh God Patsy. I am so glad you've come. The police have checked everything. Their forensic people have brushed and powdered everything for fingerprints. They are making enquiries, but they didn't look too hopeful. Although, if any of those fingerprints match up with anyone they have on record, that's a great lead.' Janine smiled weakly; she was relieved Patsy was there. She knew everything would get sorted now.

A thought crossed Patsy's mind and she pulled Janine aside. 'The money from the delivery, Janine. Where is it?'

Janine blushed and looked down at the floor. 'Well, erm,' she stammered, 'I know you will go bonkers Patsy but...'

'They've taken it, haven't they? That's what they were looking for.'

Janine looked up at Patsy. 'Actually Patsy, the money is in my dad's garage. As I told you earlier, I had a strange feeling about those blokes. I didn't want to leave those boxes of money in the shop and so I told my sister's boyfriend Danny that we were overstocked with shampoos and stuff. He's got a transit van so I asked him if he would drive it to my dad's garage until we could sort it out.'

Patsy's jaw dropped and her eyes widened. 'Oh my God Janine, you're a bloody genius!' Leaning forward, Patsy cupped her face and planted a big kiss on her cheek. 'You clever girl! How long have we got before your dad goes in or looks through those boxes?'

'Forever. I don't think he's cleaned it out since they moved in ten years ago!' she laughed.

Patsy couldn't believe her luck. Fifty thousand pounds hidden away in Janine's dad's garage. Those burglars had caused chaos but got away with nothing. 'It has to be the same men, Janine. They knew what they were looking for. Well, they are fucked well and truly.'

'Well, that's not the end of it. We had a big delivery of hair products in and because I didn't trust those guys and I knew they were skimming money off the boxes, I took the money out and filled the original boxes with conditioners and shampoos. So all they got was six boxes of conditioner, shampoo and perming lotion.' She laughed. 'It was the first thing I checked this morning before the police arrived and true enough those original boxes are the ones that have gone. They are going to be livid when they open them and it's just as well we're closed because we have no shampoo!'

Patsy's mobile burst into life; it was Larry. 'Do me a favour Janine and answer that would you, please. Tell him I'm talking to the police and will call him back.'

Janine did as requested and Patsy could hear Larry interrogating her about the burglary. His suspicions were soon squashed as Janine went into a long story of what had happened. She was boring him to tears and Patsy couldn't help sniggering. The more

Larry tried ending the call, the more Janine babbled on about the plumber and the mess. In the end, Larry gave up and ended the call.

'Sounds like you have man trouble Patsy. Is it the end of the road?' Janine laughed.

'I think so, but he just won't take no for an answer.'

'Well, you know my motto. The best way to get over a man is to get under a new one!'

'Now now, ladies.' Patsy turned to see her dad and behind him was her mum and Nancy, wearing her pink wellies and splashing in the remains of the water.

'Puddles, Mummy!' She laughed and jumped up and down, soaking them all.

'Hey, little girl, where's my hug? Never mind these puddles.' Scooping her up in her arms, Patsy hugged and kissed her daughter.

'Be careful of that wrist, Patsy,' cautioned her father.

'It feels better already now I have my little princess in my arms,' she said, kissing the little girl again.

'Why is your face different colours Mummy?' Nancy asked and they all burst out laughing.

'Because, princess, I had my face painted and it all went wrong. They turned me into Shrek!' Patsy laughed and she realised how much she had missed Nancy and her innocence. Maybe it was time Nancy lived with her properly, although she hated taking her out of school and away from her friends. But kids soon adapt, she reasoned with herself. 'Come on, we'll pop to that pizza shop and get loads for everyone.'

'Can I have a McDonald's instead, Mummy?'

Patsy rolled her eyes.

* * *

Once the locks were secured and the shutters were fixed, they all left for home. Patsy had organised the staff to work at different shops doing the same kind of shifts that suited them, including a bonus to cover any extra travelling costs.

Looking around her family home felt good. It was a relief to be home. Patsy hadn't realised how much she'd missed London and the hustle and bustle of it all. Tentatively, her parents asked about Larry and to stop them digging any further, Patsy gave them a near-to-the-truth version. 'I've had second thoughts about the engagement. I want to end it, but Larry won't take no for an answer.'

After a home-cooked lasagne, Patsy put Nancy to bed and read her a story, but as the little girl fell asleep Patsy felt sad. If Nancy lived with her, she could do this every night, couldn't she? She had hidden Nancy away for long enough and maybe it was time for a fresh start. But she could see how attached her parents were to Nancy and what a wrench it would be for them, so she decided to shelve it for now until she got herself sorted...

Sitting down in the cosiness of the lounge, Patsy picked up the hot chocolate her mum had made with a drop of brandy in. It tasted delicious. Even though it was warm, her dad had still lit the log burner and sitting by it and drinking the hot chocolate, Patsy suddenly realised how tired she was. She hadn't felt this relaxed and safe in a long time. It was true what they said, there was no place like home.

While having a long soak in the bath, her mobile started ringing, and when she saw Larry's name, she let out a deep sigh and shimmied deeper into the warm bubble bath. Wiping her hand, she finally answered. 'Sorry Larry, it's been a hectic day and I've only just got back to my parents' house.'

'That's okay darling. I just wondered how you were, having not heard from you. I'm afraid I won't be able to get to London tomorrow Patsy – this case is running on a bit, I'm afraid. When will you be coming home?'

'I'm not sure. Possibly a few days if I'm lucky.'

'Oh, I see. We do have things to discuss, and I did say something about forty-eight hours Patsy. Does that mean nothing to you? By my counting it's already been over twenty-four hours. So, I'm asking again, when are you coming home?'

Patsy couldn't believe what she was hearing. Even though she was in distress, he didn't care. All he cared about was his ultimatum. 'Larry, I am trying to control my voice here. Not only for the sake of my parents, but for my own sanity. I'm afraid my business is my first priority. Do what you will. Personally, after the day I've had, I really don't care about your ultimatum.'

'I know it's your business Patsy, but you're my business. I love you and miss you. And just for once I would like to be first on your list for a change. I'm not blackmailing you. How could I be, if you're innocent?' His smug voice annoyed Patsy and the sarcasm that was dripping from his mouth made her blood boil.

'If you want to believe a criminal above our relationship, do it Larry. Do what you will; as I say, I'm too tired to care.'

'I know you have a business to run; is that the point you're making? That I'm just one of the minions, unlike the great Nick Diamond who was a partner in his law firm. Good old Nick, womaniser, adulterer, drug dealer and not to mention the despised and feared Undertaker!'

'My God, is that your problem? You're jealous of Nick?'

'Nick Diamond was born with a silver spoon in his mouth! He never worked hard at anything!' Larry shouted down the phone. It was then Patsy realised that Larry had been drinking. His words seemed slurred.

'Is Nick your Achilles' heel, Larry? Do you want everything he had, including his wife?'

Suddenly everything made sense to Patsy. Larry was jealous of Nick.

'Oh, for God's sake Patsy. Isn't it time you let your torch for him die out? He dumped you for another woman, but I love you.'

'What is love, Larry? I've been in love and like you say, I was dumped for another woman, and now I'm being blackmailed by another man who claims to love me. So tell me Larry, what is love?'

'You will find out Patsy fucking Diamond! If I can't have you, no one will.' He abruptly ended the call. Patsy stared at the phone, and then called Sheila and told her what had happened.

'Mmm, well at least you know the truth now. Odds are he's going to inform the police about that letter. The bitter twisted bastard. He's jealous of a dead man, how sad is that. Have you heard from Fin? I know he's on his way to London.'

'Already? No, I haven't heard anything. Any good news Sheila? God knows I could do with some.'

'Yes, he's been to Larry's house and that letter is nowhere to be found. He has the papers Karen signed – all of them – and there was also a file about Karen he had from the beginning when you wanted to find out who she really was. Fin has taken that as well. As far as I'm aware, anything that links you and Karen Duret in Larry's office is safely in Fin's notorious thieving fingers. Our thoughts are that Larry has that letter with him. Anyway, Fin is on his way. All we can do is wait Patsy and see what Larry's next move is.'

Fin had worked fast and Patsy found it comforting to know that he was on his way. As she got out of her now cold bath, she thought about the conversation with Larry. She had been a fool falling for Larry's boyish charm. She had once thought he had no devious sides to him, but she'd been wrong. She was thankful she had snubbed the Milieu when they'd called, because without all of that fuss, she could easily have married Larry and not found out what he was like until after it was too late. Talk about a close shave.

After saying goodnight to her parents, she walked to Nancy's bedroom. Watching her sleeping soundly made Patsy's heart ache. Pulling back the duvet, Patsy crept into the single bed and slipped her arm under Nancy's head, holding her tight. A tear escaped her eye and ran down the side of her face. Kissing the top of Nancy's head, Patsy was soothed by her daughter's breathing and closed her eyes, quickly falling into a deep sleep.

7

DAYLIGHT

Patsy was woken by knocking at the door.

'Who the hell is that at this time of the morning?' she heard her father muttering as he crossed the landing.

Looking at the clock, she saw that it was 4.45 a.m. No wonder her father was annoyed. Hearing voices at the door, Patsy got out of bed and looked over the banister at the top of the landing. Instantly, Larry crossed her mind.

'Is everything okay Dad?' she called down to him.

'It's for you Patsy!' her dad shouted back.

'Morning, morning, Patsy.'

'Fin!' Relief washed over her when she realised it was him. Tying her bathrobe around her, she ran down the stairs and hugged him, almost squeezing the life out of him.

Exasperated, her father looked at his watch. 'I guess I'll put the kettle on.'

'Sheila said you left yesterday; where have you been?' Patsy asked, while steering a very cold Fin towards the kitchen.

'Stuck on the motorway, that's where.' Fin rubbed his hands together and blew on them to warm them. 'That sat nav of yours is rubbish, led me straight down a blocked road which meant I had to turn around and go miles up the motorway where I'd just come from.' Fin looked very sheepish as he watched Patsy's dad opening cupboards and taking out mugs.

Patsy laughed to herself. If Fin had got here earlier and without a hitch, she would have been very surprised. Patsy's mum came down the stairs, yawning. 'George? Who is it?' Walking into the kitchen, she stopped when she saw Fin and Patsy. 'Well, I didn't know we had company.' Embarrassed, she started stroking her dishevelled hair down into place.

'Sorry it's early.' Fin blushed. 'I should have waited, but I was so cold and dying to use the toilet.'

'Off you go, top of the landing.' Patsy's mum smiled. 'What did you say your name was again? You can call me Emma.'

'Fin; that's what everyone calls me, missus.' Not able to hold his bladder any longer, Fin bolted up the stairs.

George put the coffee mugs on the table. 'Who the hell wakes someone up at this time of the morning? It's either police or fire brigade. Not some Scottish half-wit who takes a wrong turn off the motorway.'

'Oh shut up grumpy George.' Emma laughed.

Fin came running down the stairs. 'Phew, that's better. Did I miss anything?'

'Only the bloody motorway signs,' George muttered.

'Dad, behave, Fin's driven a long way to come and help me. Stop moaning.'

'Let's not have an argument you lot. I think we could all do with another hour; you must be shattered Fin. There's a spare room upstairs. Why don't you go and have a nap? I'll get you some bedding.'

'Oh, that's all right Mrs Patsy, just the duvet will do me. Thanks.'

'It's Emma, Fin, and come on, I'll show you your room and get you some bedding!'

Patsy followed her mum and Fin upstairs, while George secured the locks on the front door. Patsy walked back into Nancy's room and checked she hadn't woken. It seemed none of the noise had bothered her.

After her mother left Fin's room, Patsy heard a low whisper. 'Psst, Patsy.'

Opening the bedroom door, she saw Fin standing there. Putting his fingers to his lips and pointing at her parents' bedroom door so that she didn't make any noise, he started unzipping his bomber jacket. Curiously, Patsy watched him, wondering what on earth he was doing. She was about to speak when Fin stopped her again. 'Shush, can I come in?' he whispered.

Nodding, Patsy opened the door wider. 'What's wrong?'

'Nothing but put this somewhere safe.' Fin took out an A4 brown envelope that was close to his chest and handed it to her. Nodding, Patsy watched him turn to leave. Opening the envelope, she saw all the paperwork that linked her with Karen Duret, including the private detective's reports when he had tried tracing the mysterious woman for Larry. The most damning evidence was the dates on the paperwork that had been signed by Karen that day in his office. Karen hadn't been seen since that date and that was the date that James had put in his letter accusing Patsy of murdering her. The paperwork was better out of Larry's clutches – who knew what he would do with them.

* * *

'Phew that's a real stink Patsy,' Fin moaned while holding his nose as Patsy raised the shutters of the salon and opened the doors. She too took in the stale stench of damp.

'This is what I wanted to talk to you about Fin. Find a seat and sit down.' He swivelled in one of the hairdresser chairs. Patsy stopped him. 'Will you behave and listen for a minute.' Patsy filled him in on what Janine had told her. Once she'd finished, she threw her hands up in the air and walked around the damp devastation she had once called a salon. 'Look at the bloody walls Fin, they are covered in all kinds of coloured graffiti. They've ruined this place.'

Fin sat silently, while Patsy surveyed the damage.

'That seems like a shitty message to me.' He pointed at some graffiti on the wall.

Patsy looked, frowning. 'So what of it, Fin? All the fucking walls are written on. It's not exactly Banksy, is it?'

'Look at the letters, Patsy, there's a message. The capital letters are in black. I can't believe the police didn't see that.'

Puzzled, Patsy looked at again. She couldn't see anything but a load of illegible writing sprayed across the wall. It meant nothing to her.

'Those three words underneath each other don't make sense, but if you look at the beginning of the words, it spells out RIP. Randy ice prick? What the fuck does that mean? Rest in peace; that's what it says, I'm sure of it.' Once Fin had pointed it out, Patsy saw it. It was as plain as the nose on your face.

'But who is out to get me here Fin? I thought all of my enemies were in Scotland...' Frowning, she looked at the wall again. Her blood ran cold.

'Some London mob maybe? Who delivers your money Patsy? They are the only ones that knew the money was here.'

It always surprised Patsy how Fin could change so suddenly. One minute he was acting the clown and the next his business head was firmly screwed on. He had spotted that message left for her the moment he got in, yet no one else had.

'The same people that delivered it for Nick. There was no need to change things, everything has run smoothly up until now.'

'Yeah, but Nick has been dead over a year. Don't you think it's time you changed your contacts? You don't really know these people, do you? This agreement has just carried on. Someone has been taking the money from the drugs and bringing it here to launder through your salons. I presumed you knew who did it.'

'Well, after Nick, James was sorting that out. He said he had done it for Nick and so I carried on...' Patsy trailed off.

'James! So James organised the deliveries for Nick so that Nick didn't get his hands dirty and convinced you to carry on and do the same – is that right?' Fin asked.

Blushing, Patsy sat down and looked at the floor. 'Yes. How fucking stupid is that? We launder plenty through the pizza shops, but the overflow is far too much and so it goes through the salon. It has for years and there has never been a problem. Let's make no more drops at the appointed places Fin. With no more drops there will be no more deliveries, will there?'

'No, but you're going to get some angry men who want you to rest in peace Patsy. James had a flat here or something didn't he? I remember him mentioning it once.'

Patsy pondered what Fin was saying. 'Yes, I do recall him saying that Fin, but I don't know where. But you're right, he definitely had connections here in London. You know, he actually sent me some money here once.' Patsy thought back and remembered when Noel, an Albanian gangster, and his men had sent threatening messages in a box, but then James had sent her some of the drug money she was owed. Her mind spun so much she felt dizzy.

'Whoever these people are Patsy, they now know James is dead and not in charge of things any more. They are taking their commission plus extras. It's a free-for-all with your money and they intend taking over the lot. Christ, how could you not see this coming!'

Patsy stood there, stunned. Fin was right. She hadn't seen this coming. 'We need to find out who they are Fin. Let the money go to the usual drop off and see if they deliver it; that way we'll find out who they are.'

'No, we won't. They will be sending some leg breakers to deliver it, oafs who probably do money collecting. We need muscle on this and fast. I remember James talking about a pub in south London in Boxall or something,' Fin mused.

'Vauxhall! That would be Vauxhall because there isn't a Boxall. So that is where they all drank and met, but which one?' Patsy asked and let out a huge sigh. 'There is a load of pubs around that area.'

'I'll go and find out. I'll say I'm just out of prison and looking for James. I will let it be known he promised me a job or something when I got out.'

'That sounds like hard work and dangerous stuff Fin, anything could happen to you.' Patsy's concern was genuine. These people weren't playing games and Fin was right, she had overlooked all of this; if anything happened to Fin it would be her fault.

'What other plans do you have Patsy, because I can't see you coming up with any ideas. We have no choice; this is only going from bad to worse. These people mean business.'

Patsy listened to what Fin was saying. She knew he made sense, but she didn't know what to do about it. 'I don't like it Fin, but it seems we have no choice. If you can find anything out, then do so, but don't put yourself in harm's way.'

'I'll stay in a local youth hostel around here or Vauxhall. If I do get a lead on the guys that did this, I can't be connected with you. I can't be seen coming out of your parents' house. I'm just out of prison, remember?' Fin winked at her.

Interrupting their conversation, Janine suddenly burst through the doors. 'Phew, it's cold out there. I went and picked up some coffee and saw your car.' Suddenly she stopped short and looked at Patsy, then Fin. 'Am I interrupting anything?'

'No, not at all. Janine, this is Fin, a good friend of mine from Scotland. Fin, this is Janine, my manageress and saviour.'

'Is your hair always pink?' asked Fin, holding out his hand to shake Janine's.

Smiling and chuckling to herself, Janine shook Fin's hand. 'No, it's what we do, experiment with hair and colours and when the customers see it, hopefully they will want theirs done the same way.'

Patsy glared at Fin and frowned; a beautiful young woman like Janine and all he could think of to say to her was about the colour of her hair. Although, the way they had shaken hands and still hadn't let go surprised Patsy.

'I like your hair, it gives you a pink glow,' gushed Fin.

'I like it too.' Janine blushed.

Pondering the sight before her, Patsy looked on as Janine and Fin tried hard to think of something to say to each other. Oh my God, she mused to herself, is Fin blushing? Has he met a woman who actually makes him blush?

Coughing to interrupt the happy scene before her, Patsy spoke. 'Well, now that we're all introduced, maybe we could get on. Janine, I called the insurance company and they say we can't get a builder in until one of their surveyors come and have a look around, but we can continue cleaning this place up and check the rest of the stock. I've also called an electrician to make sure the electrics are okay. I want the rest of the customers in the diary contacting. They need to know the situation, that is if they haven't heard about it already.'

'Is that your car outside?' Fin asked, looking out of the window. He whistled.

Parked outside of the shop was a union jack Mini. To Patsy, it lacked taste, but Fin found it fascinating, which surprised her.

'It is, I love it. Everyone knows my car. Maybe you could get one with the Scottish flag,' laughed Janine.

Feeling like a gooseberry, Patsy stood and watched them both laughing at Janine's joke. Patsy turned her back on both of them and smiled to herself; Fin was smitten and it seemed so was Janine. What an odd couple!

Janine popped out to her car to get some supplies and Fin watched her out of the window.

'Has she got a boyfriend Patsy?' he asked seriously.

'Not that I am aware of. I think she's in between boyfriends at the moment,' Patsy answered offhandedly. 'Anyway, back to what we were saying before Janine came in. Do you think you can put your ear to the ground and see who has caused all of this devastation Fin?'

'One condition Patsy. I will put my life in danger,' he laughed, 'if you get me a date with that Janine bird.'

Patsy laughed. 'No, I won't blackmail Janine into having a date with you. If she wants to go out with you, let it be her own choice. If it's meant to be Fin, it's meant to be. Ask her yourself; she didn't exactly find you repulsive from where I was standing.' Patsy gave him a knowing look and winked at him.

He straightened himself up and brushed his hair back. His stubborn stance only made Patsy laugh more, 'Right, I will then, and I will take her somewhere posh!'

Patsy clapped her hands together. 'Bravo Fin. You go for it. And just for the record Fin, don't go dressed like a street urchin or a pimp, and treat her like a lady. And don't try and get into her knickers without asking nicely.'

Fin was blushing to his roots as Patsy scolded him. 'I wouldn't do that Patsy. And I will dress properly, if she agrees to come out with me. You will help, won't you?'

Patsy looked at his hang dog eyes. 'Of course I will you lovesick muppet. Never let it be said that I'll stand in the way of true love.'

8

UNSETTLING TIMES

The peeling paint on the outside of the first pub Fin tried reminded him of home. Considering this was London and the capital, he had expected better. The pub was fairly busy so walking up to the bar, he made his Scottish accent even stronger and ordered a drink. Looking around him with expert eyes, he saw a fat, balding man in his sixties behind the bar. That was definitely the landlord, Fin thought to himself. After taking a sip of his drink, Fin smiled at the landlord. 'Do you own this place?'

'What of it? You're a long way from home,' was the snub he received.

'I'm looking for James McNally. He said he could be found around here in the pubs.'

There seemed to be a hushed silence at the end of the bar and the landlord shook his head. 'Can't say I do.'

As he walked away, Fin felt he had touched a nerve. Taking his time with his drink, Fin looked around a little more. It was obviously some kind of thieves' den, especially the way the landlord was so quick to deny he knew James. He knew him, Fin was sure of it. Drinking up, he walked out. There was another pub, just across the road; maybe he would have better luck there.

As he was leaving, he felt a hand on his shoulder. 'I hear you're looking for James McNally. Who is he to you?'

He turned to face the man. 'He's a friend who offered me some work,' Fin lied. 'Just thought I'd look him up while I'm here.'

'You don't live around here then?' the man asked suspiciously.

'No, I'm going back to Glasgow. Just got out of prison. James told me to look him up in these parts if I ever needed a job.' Fin grinned.

'You're way behind the times mate. James is dead. Hanged himself in his cell, didn't you know?'

Feigning surprise, Fin shook his head. 'No I didn't. When did that happen? We were on remand together and then we got split up.'

'Not too long ago. You didn't keep in touch then?' Eyeing Fin suspiciously, the man fired question after question, until eventually, he invited Fin over to meet his friends and have a drink.

'So how do you know James then?' another man asked.

'We're both from Scotland, although James did say he had connections here and a flat.' He felt sticking as near to the truth as he could, would be much more convincing than trying to lie his head off. 'We both used to work for the same man in Scotland until someone decided to take a shot at him. Anyway, thanks fellas, I had better be on my way.' Fin felt he had dropped more than enough bait for them to pick up.

'Do you mean that Nick Diamond bloke, the dealer?' one asked. 'I've heard about him.'

'Yes, but we didn't find out his name until after his death. He was known as the Undertaker, for whatever reason.' Shrugging, Fin smiled.

'So what was you inside for?' they all seemed to ask in unison.

They had each in turn told him they had been in prison, and they all seemed to have that brutish manner of bravado most ex-cons had when they came out.

'Bit of this, bit of that. I'm sure you have an idea if you knew James. Anyway, it seems I have come to a dead end so to speak. I was hoping to get some work and make some cash before moving on, and it would have been nice to have a catch up with him. It's been nice meeting you.' Fin held his hand out to shake theirs.

'Why don't you pop in tomorrow before you go back to Glasgow? Have a drink before you leave.'

Grinning like the idiot they thought he was, Fin agreed. He knew that would give them enough time to check his story out and follow him to his hostel. He had scored a home run here.

* * *

Fin felt uneasy walking in the darkness to the overground train station. He could hear footsteps behind him, but furtively glancing back, could see no one. His bravery seemed to be leaving him a little. Especially once he realised he was in the middle of nowhere, in a city he wasn't familiar with. He had hidden his mobile phone on the inside of his trouser leg and switched it off. It was an expensive one and one the local men in the pub knew he wouldn't have now that he had just come out of prison.

Fin took a sigh of relief when he reached the station and got on his train. Hopefully this would be the end of the line for whoever was following him, but when he got off the train at his stop, his natural instincts kicked in. He knew he wasn't out of the woods yet. The platform was empty, and suddenly he was jumped from behind. A hood of some kind, which felt like rough sacking, was thrown over his head and pulled tight around the neck. He tried to struggle but felt a hard punch to his face. His body was tossed to the ground and kicked. Pain ripped through him and he could feel the warmth of blood dripping from his nose, almost into his mouth. Although struggling to breathe, he tried screaming out. Then he could hear laughter as he felt hands roaming through his jeans pockets. He felt them take his wallet out of his jacket and for a moment the abuse stopped.

'Shut up and walk,' he was instructed as they dragged him up by his arms to his feet. Fin was barely able to stand on up his legs he felt so weak. He could feel himself trembling, not knowing if these would be his last moments alive. 'If you don't walk Scottie, I will throw you under the next train.' He could hear laughter and knew by the feel of the arms dragging him around there was more than two men. He felt very afraid, and prayed silently to God that he didn't wet himself. That would be the ultimate humiliation in his eyes.

Swallowing hard, he followed the instructions to walk. His knees felt sore and scraped and his body ached. Consumed with fear, he tried breathing hard to get some air into his lungs. The hood seemed thick and all he could feel was his own hot breath and the sweat on his brow falling down his face.

After what seemed like hours, but was probably only minutes, he was pushed so hard, he banged his head on something metal and was consumed by total darkness. He heard the slam of a door and then an engine of a car start up. That was when he realised he was in the boot of a car. It seemed to speed along, but thankfully, they hadn't tied his hands and so reaching up, he pulled up as much of the hood as he could to try and get some air into his lungs. He could hardly see in the darkness, but at least they hadn't tied the hood around his neck. His face was almost wet with sweat and his hair clung to his face.

He could barely move. His knees were cramped and almost up to his chest. It was a very small car indeed, he realised. Tears began streaming down his face. He didn't know what to do, then suddenly, he remembered his smartwatch Patsy had bought him had a tracking device on. He hadn't liked the idea in the beginning but now he breathed a sigh of relief. There was no way he could have reached his mobile, but through the smartwatch he could make calls, depending on the signal. Trying to move around, he could see the internet bars were low, but this was his one and only hope. He managed to press Sheila's name. She answered, but it kept cutting out. 'Sheila, I've been kidnapped, I'm in the boot of a car, in London. I don't know if this gang is going to kill me. Can you hear me?'

'I'm on my fucking way to London. Hide your phone up your arse if you have to, but keep it on, I might be able to track you. Turn the sound off. Hide the bastard Fin, we're coming to get you, dead or alive.'

The very idea that Sheila had said 'dead or alive' made his blood run cold. Before he had time to dwell on it, the car came to a halt. Pulling the hood down again, he felt the boot of the car open. Roughly, they pulled the sack off his head, letting him gulp air into his lungs. Raising his hand and blinking hard to see, he saw that it was two of the men he had met in the pub stood before him. Dragging him by the arms, they let him fall out of the boot onto the floor. Excruciating pain overwhelmed him as he banged his head on the ground, dazing him and almost knocking him out. He was panting for air and could taste the blood from his nose and face in his mouth. His only salvation was that Sheila knew what was happening to him. He wasn't alone.

'Come on Scottie, we have someone who wants to meet you,' they laughed. They grabbed his arms and dragged him along on his knees.

Able to see more clearly, Fin looked around. He was at an old scrap yard. Huge iron gates were before him, locked with a large chain. Behind them he could see numerous old cars on top of each other, some burnt out, others with doors and other things missing. It seemed to be in the middle of nowhere.

Someone was waiting for them on the other side.

'Is that James McNally's bitch?' the man said, unlocking the gate.

In his misery and torment, Fin realised this had more to do with James than it did with Patsy.

* * *

Frantic, Sheila called Patsy and told her what had happened. 'Get him on that tracker thing now. Christ I am so glad you made us all download it!' When Patsy had suggested it to keep them all safe, Sheila hadn't liked the idea and had said it felt like Big Brother, until Patsy had explained that one day it might come in handy. Never a truer word had been spoken.

'I can see where he is,' Patsy said. 'I'm going there now.'

'You can't Patsy, you're going to be no better off than him if you walk in there alone. Is there anyone there that you can get to cover your back until I get there? Shit!' Sheila exclaimed. 'It's going to take me hours to get there!'

'Fly Sheila, that's the quickest way, and see if you can rally anyone in Scotland to come to Fin's rescue. God knows we have enough people on the payroll!'

'Fly?' Sheila hadn't thought of that. 'How long will that take?'

'You will be about an hour and then an hour from the airport to Fin. In fact, get them all to fucking fly!' Patsy shouted.

Turning around, Sheila saw Angus behind her, and her heart sank. This was truth time. She needed Angus's help.

'What's going on Sheila?' He sensed trouble and seeing Sheila's panic-stricken face frightened him.

'We need to talk and you're not going to like what I have to tell you. What you decide about our relationship is your business and I will accept it, but for now I need you. Just this once Angus and I swear to God I will never ask again.'

'That bad eh lassie? Get the girls and your coat. Tell me what you can in the truck.'

With a heavy heart, she got the girls together quickly. She knew she would have to tell him the truth and he would feel betrayed. Trying to push that to the back of her mind, she walked out of the house to where Angus was waiting in the truck with the engine running.

'Explain on the way. In short sentences,' he warned, casting a furtive glance towards the girls in the back of the truck. 'I take it Maggie's babysitting?'

'Yes.' Sheila's voice was barely above a whisper. She felt embarrassed and ashamed at having to confess her drug dealing ways to Angus. She knew what he would think of her. He would loathe and despise her considering the amount of lies she had told him in the past.

As they drove along, Sheila explained that Fin was in trouble, that he could even be dead by now for all she knew. She explained about the smartwatch tracking him. She needed to gather an army to go to London, she told him, and even threw in that it might include firearms. A possible shoot out. Slowly but surely, Sheila told Angus what had been going on, while casting sideways glances at the girls who seemed oblivious to their conversation. Angus sat there stoney faced while he drove; he never said a word, which frightened her more than if he had screamed and shouted at her.

Lighting a cigarette and opening the window of the truck to blow the smoke out, she waited, but still Angus said nothing. Once they arrived at Maggie's in record time, she gathered the girls together and walked to her flat. Even though Maggie was in her nightgown, she was still wearing her black cardigan and wrapped it around her herself tightly. 'What the bloody hell is going on Sheila?'

'Will you take the girls? Fin is in real trouble, and I have to go to London. In fact, I have to get anyone that will go with me to London.' Sheila's face paled and she almost burst into tears. Maggie looked out of the doorway and saw Angus's truck. The rescue service light was flashing on the top of it, although she couldn't understand why. Raising one eyebrow, Maggie ushered the girls into her flat. 'I'd come with you, but my hands are full. What does that poor bastard know?'

'Enough to put me behind bars. I presume we're finished. It was too good to last Maggie.' Putting on a brave face, Sheila fought the tears back and looked towards Angus in the truck and back at Maggie. 'Fin once told me that you had a spare key to his flat just in case. Is that true?'

Maggie folded her arms. 'Why do you want to know Sheila?'

'Because I'm going to see if Angus will drive some of the things Fin has in his flat to London. I think we might need them.' Sheila looked down at the floor. She knew Maggie knew she meant weapons.

'That's going to take hours Sheila. And that is, if he agrees,' Maggie scoffed. 'He's straight, your Angus; he won't want to get involved in all of this.'

'He might as a favour. One last favour. I know it will take hours, but I'm going to fly to London and I won't be able to get that kind of stuff through customs will I?'

Exhaling deeply, Maggie walked down her hallway and took a key off the keyholder. 'This is the only one I have; I don't know if he's changed the locks since he gave it to me. I'm going to see the girls into bed. You'd better speak to Angus...'

Sheila nodded and walked back to the truck. 'Angus, I know you don't like me very much at the moment, and what I am about to ask you is illegal and unfair, but I need you on my side.'

Angus was still stoney faced as he looked towards her. 'Spit it out Sheila. You're not one to usually mince your words.'

'I need you to drive some guns to London for me. These men mean business and when they have killed Fin it won't end. They will kill Patsy and myself probably. Will you do it?' Clenching her fists at her side, Sheila could feel her nails digging into her palms. Her stomach churned and she felt sick.

'They are going to kill you?' Frowning, Angus was finding this situation hard to comprehend.

'Possibly, but definitely Patsy. She is my friend Angus. The closest thing I have to a sister. She picked me up when I was down. I can't desert her now.'

Angus rubbed his face with his hands. He was trying to take in what Sheila was telling him, but it all seemed so far-fetched, he couldn't believe it. 'You really are up to your neck in it, aren't you lassie? Okay, I'll do my best... but I'll need to use someone from the estate's car to put on the back of the truck.'

Relief washed over her. 'Come with me.' Angus got out of the truck and walked with her to Fin's flat. She put it in the lock of the door. Once the key turned, she looked up at the sky. 'Thank you God,' she breathed.

Sheila led Angus into Fin's bedroom.

'Help me move the bed,' she said. Once they had pushed the huge double bed aside, Sheila dropped to her knees and indicated Angus do the same. 'The floorboards will come up; under there he has some of his stash.'

Sheila looked down at the floorboards. On one floorboard was a hole, and Sheila put her finger inside it. Pulling at the floorboard, it came up, and then she started removing two others around it. Angus looked down the hole.

'What's down there?' he asked meeting Sheila's eyes and then looking at the black hole again. Angus felt confused, but curious.

'Hopefully, everything we need. Fin used to sell weapons now and again and he always knew a man who knew another man, if you know what I mean.'

Angus started heaving up the holdalls and bags from inside the hole. Quickly, Sheila unzipped one of the bags and sat back on her haunches and breathed a sigh of relief. Just as she thought, the bag was full of all kinds of guns, knives and hand grenades.

'What the fuck!' exclaimed Angus, pulling back from the sight before him. He had never seen anything like it, apart from in movies. 'He sleeps with all that in the house? Is he fucking crazy!'

'Please Angus,' Sheila pleaded, 'you said you would help. Are you a man of your word? I promise when all this is over, I will tell you the full sordid story. And believe me, it is sordid.' Blushing to the roots, she stared at him. Her face burned with shame.

'Am I allowed to be a little shocked, Sheila?' Angus snapped. 'I'm a man of my word, you know that. But I am also human and shit like this frightens me. This is not my world Sheila.'

'Let's not talk about it now. I promise when all this is over, I will confess everything.' Sheila half smiled, though mentally, she was already weighing up the bits she would tell him. She would skip the parts about murdering people!

When it seemed they'd removed everything from underneath the floorboards, Angus reached down and felt around. He could feel something, but it was heavy. Angus adjusted his position on the floor, and using both hands, he pulled with all his might to lift whatever it was he had grasped. Sheila's eyes widened. She hadn't expected this. Angus jumped back in shock. 'For fuck's sake

Sheila, that's a machine gun. Where the hell did he get that from? Jesus! What have I got myself into?'

Ignoring him, Sheila looked down the hole. 'These things have magazines, don't they? Are there any down there?' Half bending into the hole, she felt around. 'Hold my waist Angus, I need to get closer, I can feel a bag.'

Totally disbelieving at her calmness, Angus did as she asked as she pulled up a bag. Unzipping it, she saw boxes and boxes of magazines. 'This will definitely do the trick. I didn't think Fin would have a weapon like this without the ammunition.'

Angus's mouth felt dry and he swallowed hard. 'You want me to drive a machine gun to London. Is that what you're saying?'

Sheila looked up at him, her eyes pleading with him. 'Yes, and the rest of this stuff.'

'You're asking a lot, Sheila. Most women want a new cooker, but you're asking me to put myself in danger. Not only that, but I am looking at years in prison if I'm stopped on the motorway. Don't you understand?'

'Why should you be stopped? Do rescue vehicles usually get stopped?'

Angus sighed. 'No, they don't,' he said, resigned to the fact that he was about to do this. 'Where am I taking it all to Sheila? I need a bloody address at least.'

'I will give you an address. That is where you say you're going if you're stopped,' Sheila snapped. She didn't have time for this. She had what she wanted and now she needed to get to London and rescue Fin. Sheila looked at her watch. Time was passing and she wasn't at the airport yet. Frantic, Sheila ran and banged on the door of Beryl Diamond's old flat, which Patsy had rented out to local prostitutes. Bernie, a lesbian who had been in and out of prison and was a known distributor of drugs, was the girls' minder. She was scary looking, with her head shaved, tattoos from head to toe, and weighing about twenty stone.

Opening the door, Bernie stood there in a white vest top, holding a baseball bat, ready for action. She was clearly shocked to see Sheila. 'What the fuck do you want at this time of night Sheila? We're busy; it's rush hour.' Bernie was about to close the door in Sheila's face, but Sheila put her foot in the door and stopped her.

'Help, that's what I want. Fin's in trouble, in London. Someone is going to kill him, Bernie. Can you rally any of the lads around to come and help?'

Frowning, Bernie pulled her inside. 'Do you realise it's going to take six hours to get to London? He could already be dead by then,' Bernie whispered.

'Patsy says we can all fly if you're willing to help me. Do you have a passport?'

'I don't live in the Dark Ages Sheila. It's the only identification people take nowadays, that and driving licences. Of course I do, and yes, of course I'll come. Who have you contacted so far?'

Sheila shook her head; she had been too busy to contact anyone else.

Bernie took out her mobile phone and dialled. 'Coke head Steve, is that you? Well, sober up, you're coming to London, Fin's in trouble. Get as many as you can with a passport and meet me at Glasgow airport. Now, you little fucker or else!' she shouted down the phone.

Sheila didn't need to ask who it was, the clue was in the name, but she was relieved that Bernie was now in charge of that side of things.

Bernie's dark eyes glared at Sheila. 'Do we have any tools?' Bernie asked next. 'I'm not going to war empty handed.'

'Yes, I've been to Fin's flat and he has quite a collection. Angus is driving them down there.'

'I'm coming to the airport with you now. Just give me a minute.'

Running from the flat, Sheila walked back towards Angus. True to his word, he had strapped a car to the back of his truck and was securing it.

'Don't worry Sheila, all your ill-gotten gains are inside it.'

Sheila thought he almost smiled, but she couldn't be sure. Maybe it was just a trick of the light, or just wishful thinking. Maggie came down to meet them.

'Did you get everything you needed?' she asked, holding her hand out for the key.

Handing it back, Sheila nodded. 'Yes, thanks Maggie. I'll be in touch.' Without thinking, Sheila leaned forward and kissed her on the cheek, making Maggie blush.

'Away with you, lassie.' She waved her hand in the air. 'And bring that useless idiot Fin back home.'

Bernie appeared and opened the door of the truck. 'Move up, Sheila; surely your skinny arse can get further up than that.' Sheila moved closer to Angus as Bernie shifted her huge bulk inside the truck. Angus cast a glance at Sheila, shook his head and drove them to the airport.

9

TURF WARS

'Victoria, do you still belong to that club?' Patsy asked tentatively.

'Which club is that darling, the WI? And why do you sound so flustered? What's happened?'

'That club you had those special cabinets for? Fin is in London and he's in trouble, a lot of trouble.' She hoped Victoria would understand what she meant. It had occurred to Patsy in her panicked state that Victoria belonged to a shooting club. Clay pigeon and all those kinds of country things. She was a crack shot and had won lots of cups and stuff for her shooting. She also had, Patsy seemed to remember, a gun cabinet. Her guns were obviously registered, but as far as Patsy was concerned, a gun was a gun, and that was exactly what she needed.

Realising what she meant, Victoria took a sharp intake of breath. 'Those cabinet trophies are traceable and licensed Patsy, but I still have them. What about Fin, you sound worried.'

'Life or death. He's been kidnapped and seems to be in an old scrap yard near Battersea.'

'I'm coming to help you. Don't do anything until I get there. If you go there alone, you're going to be no better off than him. You too will end up in that scrap yard, possibly dead, so what good is that going to do?'

'And what about Fin?' Patsy shouted down the phone. 'It's my fault he's there in the first place.'

'We cannot go in there blind. I'm on my way and... I may just look in my cabinets...' Victoria trailed off and ended the call.

At least that was hope, Patsy mused to herself, but she felt helpless. Everyone seemed to be on their way, but it was going to be hours before they all arrived. She couldn't just sit there and twiddle her thumbs. Staring at her phone numbly, she could see exactly where Fin was; she only wished she knew what was happening to him...

* * *

Angus dropped Sheila off at the airport. Thankfully Bernie had taken the hint and already got out to let them say their goodbyes. 'Thanks Angus, see you in London.' Reaching forward, she went to kiss him on the cheek but Angus pulled away.

'Be careful Sheila; we'll talk if you get through this.'

Sniffing back a tear, Sheila nodded. She understood his reservations, but even if he didn't want to kiss her, he was still helping her and that mattered more than anything.

As Sheila got out of the van, Bernie pulled her aside. 'Actually, Sheila, I am going with Angus. He has the tools in there, right?' Sheila nodded. 'There are enough of the laddies inside waiting for you to buy them a ticket. I will go with Angus and keep an eye on him and the stuff just in case he gets cold feet, eh?'

'Well maybe I should travel with him and you should go,' Sheila said.

Bernie turned and looked at Angus in the truck with the

engine running. 'Gonna be a long drive with you two not talking. Patsy needs you, so go. Go on, fuck off!'

Reluctantly, Sheila walked into the airport and looked around, not knowing who she was looking for.

'Sheila! Sheila!' Hearing her name, she looked and saw a group of men and women. Some she knew vaguely, but the others she had no idea who they were. 'Sheila, where have you been? Come on, there is a flight in half an hour.'

Flustered and upset, Sheila nodded. 'Did Bernie give you an idea of what she wanted and what is happening?'

'We know why we're here. Now, are you going to buy these tickets or not?'

Walking up to the desk Sheila bought twelve tickets to London on her credit card. No sooner were they bought than they were flying off to London. Sheila was surprised they had all passed security. They all looked like a bunch of druggies, but nothing was found on any of them and even better, they were all sober!

* * *

The inside of the scrap yard was littered with all kinds of broken cars and looked a mess. Looking up, Fin could see the huge car crusher and cringed. Was that his fate? In the darkness of the night, he could see scattered tyres and nearly stumbled over one on his way to a building on the premises. Inside, the room was littered with paperwork, and chairs that didn't match and had seen better days were scattered around. The floor was plain cement, making the room cold and uninviting. Two bare light bulbs hung from the ceiling.

Not including Fin, there were four men. Fin could feel himself trembling.

'Shall we make the bastard dance,' one laughed. 'Maybe he

could do the highland fling.' Jeering and laughing at him, one got off his chair and kicked him hard in the balls, making Fin cry out in pain and collapse to his knees, holding his crotch.

'That, you bastard, is for my mate. He went to that salon the other day and all he came back with was a box of shampoo. You helped them hide it, didn't you? Where is the money!' Fin felt a blow to his face as the man kicked him. The searing pain almost made his head burst.

'I know nothing about shampoo!' Fin shouted and rolled on the floor, groaning, spitting the blood out of his mouth. Fin heard the footsteps of one of the other men and felt his face become wet. As he looked up, he saw the man holding his penis and urinating on him. All the others laughed and egged the man on. Fin raised his arms and tried to shield himself. Tears ran down his face, and his body was wracked with pain. His heart was hammering in his chest and he knew this was the end of the line. They didn't care what they did, they were going to kill him, but they were going to torture him first. Through the slits of his swollen eyes, he glanced at his watch. It was his only salvation, but no one had come. It seemed like hours since he had been taken and no one had turned up to save him. Spitting blood out of his mouth, he felt one of his bottom teeth come loose and spat it out. Blood and urine ran down his chin.

'We're going to ask you one last time. Where is the money? That slut of an assistant of hers called us thieves. Fucking bitch! When we went back to the salon the money was gone and replaced with bottles of shit. My mate took a real kicking for that and then you walked straight into our pub boasting you knew that grass James McNally. Everyone knows he worked for that Diamond woman who thinks she is some kind of gangland queen. She's a fucking hairdresser!'

Fin groaned. He felt miserable and in pain. Spit dribbled and foamed at his mouth.

'You wait till the boss comes, he will slice your nuts off and use them as earrings!'

'I was on remand with James for a month,' Fin muttered. 'He said when I got out, he would find me a job.' Weeping, Fin lay on the cement floor. His clothing was wet, and he could feel his own urine running down his leg. 'My dad knew him.' It was the first time Fin had ever mentioned his own father, the notorious Billy Burke, but he thought the connection might help.

'Who is your father then? Who is this big man that worked with that scum bag James?'

'Billy Burke,' Fin muttered. His voice was a low whisper and could hardly be heard.

One man crouched down to get closer. 'Who?' he asked. Fin spoke again, and the man laughed. 'Billy Burke fathered a wimp like you! Don't make me laugh. Anyway, what does it matter, he's dead too. And for your information, James and that Albanian pal of his had your dad murdered in prison. The very man you became mates with murdered your own dad. He would have been real proud of you wouldn't he?'

For a moment, the pain stopped and Fin listened to what he was saying. He knew the Albanian boss Noel had organised his father's death, but he didn't know James had also been behind it.

Fin felt a searing pain and cowering into a ball on the floor, screamed out. Through the slits of his eyes, he saw one of the men had a whip and was well practiced at using it. Fin watched him coil it around his hand and then with one stroke of his wrist he let it fly out towards. The searing pain was too much for Fin to bear and he slipped into unconsciousness.

'Charlie, bring that bucket of water,' one of the men shouted.

Picking it up, the man called Charlie walked over to Fin and poured it over him to wake him up.

'This is no fun if you can't feel it sonny,' he snarled. Fin coughed and spluttered. Somewhere in the dark recesses of his mind, he could hear footsteps. They were new ones, from well-heeled shoes.

'Boss,' Charlie shouted. 'This one says he's Billy Burke's son. You remember that Glaswegian bully?'

'I do.' The crisp well-spoken voice wafted into Fin's ears and while face down on the floor, he managed to raise his head to look up. The man they called boss looked around fifty, maybe older. He was wearing a tuxedo, which Fin thought was odd. His grey hair was slicked back from his face. As Fin looked up, their eyes met. The man was wearing horn-rimmed glasses, but Fin could see his eyes boring into him.

One of the men pulled up one of the wooden dining chairs and placed it before the boss. 'Here you go Mr Duke,' he said.

Sitting down, the man took out a cigarette and waited for one of the others to light it for him.

'I know that Diamond woman is in Glasgow running a shit operation, with shit people like you. But I own London, sonny. People do what I tell them to do. This is my turf and yet she is laundering good money through her hairdressing shops and has no respect for me. She has never offered me a commission on any of it and now 50,000 pounds is missing. That's a lot of money. What do you think lads?' Each in turn, the men in the room agreed with Mr Duke.

Fin felt the blood from the whip which had torn his clothes and bit into his flesh, running down his back. Doing his best to look at the duke, sat on the chair, Fin spoke. 'I don't know anything about any money,' he muttered.

'You work for the Diamond woman; I know you haven't

recently been released from prison. I have friends in high places. So I can only presume you are working for her and taking me for a fool. I own the fucking streets and I don't have time for this. I am supposed to be at a dinner with my wife. If you know nothing, then we have no need of you. Your Mrs Diamond will be dead soon, too.' Mr Duke blew his smoke into the air and looked down at Fin again. 'Pieces of shit like you are two a penny.'

Fin saw Charlie raise his leg and tensed himself for the kick to come. Screaming out in pain, he begged for mercy. 'Please, I know nothing. Let me leave; I won't say anything to anyone.'

Looking down at the cement floor, Fin saw another pair of boots approach him. Tensing himself, he waited for the kick to come, but nothing happened. Tentatively, he looked up, stunned to see the man standing before him, peering at him closely. Fin couldn't believe it. Now he knew he was going to die.

Fin watched as the boots walked away from him, and stood beside the duke. Fin knew this new man and his reputation made his blood run cold. 'Just get it over with,' Fin shouted in despair. 'If you're going to kill me, get on with it.' Fin had lost all hope, he didn't care any more.

'Freddie, you have your money, finish him off and get rid of him, then kill that Diamond woman. I want no trace of her or her friends, but I want the money. I'm sure you can persuade her to part with it. Come on lads, leave it to the professionals.' Fin listened to the cold, harsh demands of the boss. They made him feel sick.

'If that's what you want Mr Duke; it's your money.' Freddie's calm voice filled the room. Just as Fin remembered him, he showed no emotion. Fin knew him as the mercenary that had worked for Patsy and done her bidding, for a price.

Freddie took out his gun. 'Well, it's not going to take a lot to finish him off.' Freddie pointed his gun at Fin.

Fin closed his eyes, praying for release from the pain he was feeling.

Freddie turned towards Mr Duke and smiled. 'Of course, Patsy Diamond has bigger and better friends than you have.' Freddie fired his gun directly into Mr Duke's head.

Fin opened his eyes and saw Mr Duke lying on the floor in a pool of blood. Freddie's colleagues and friends seemed to come out of nowhere, firing shots at the other men in the room, leaving a massacre in their wake. As bullets flew around the room, Fin cowered and put his arms over his head to block out the noise, knowing the next bullet was his, but in an instant, the gunfire stopped. As Fin looked up, he saw Freddie approaching him. 'I'd say you're one lucky bastard! For a cat with nine lives, I'd say you just lost eight of them. Can you stand?'

Fin did his best to crawl onto his knees but couldn't stand. He could see and feel that his leg was broken. 'You know,' said Freddie, 'I've worked for Mr Duke on a few occasions, but Lady Diamond works with the Milieu, which just happens to work in her and especially your favour tonight. Even I wouldn't cross them. Live to fight another day, eh? Two of you,' he said to a colleague, 'help him up and dump him at a hospital nearby. The rest of us will finish off here and meet at the usual place.'

Freddie waited while two of his men did their best to pick Fin up and carry him to a car outside. Once gone, Freddie and his men rolled and pushed two metal barrels full of petrol into the middle of the floor and kicked them over, letting the petrol pour out. Then Freddie took a huge drag on his cigarette and threw it onto the fuel. Instantly, it burst into flames as Freddie and his men ran to their own van and got in. Each one of them looked back at the inferno behind them. Glass shattered and then an explosion erupted, blowing the building up.

'That will do boys, let's go,' Freddie ordered.

* * *

Patsy texted Victoria that she was going to the airport. She couldn't sit twiddling her thumbs any longer. Looking at her phone, she saw that Fin was on the move again. Suddenly the tracker showed that he was at St George's hospital near Battersea. Perplexed, she looked at her mobile. Why would they be going to the hospital? Her head swam with all kinds of thoughts about Fin's fate.

Sitting in the busy airport, she looked up at the board of arrivals. She wanted to smoke but couldn't; her nerves were in tatters and she felt helpless. With each flight that landed, her heart sank. She didn't see Sheila's flight anywhere. Where the hell could she be?

'Patsy!' Suddenly, she heard her name and that familiar Scottish accent. Relief washed over her, and she almost ran to greet her friend.

'The tracker shows Fin at a hospital in Battersea!' Patsy blurted out.

'Take a breath Patsy for Christ's sake. Look, the cavalry is here.' Sheila looked behind her and then back at Patsy. 'I appreciate they don't look much but apparently they are up to the job.' Sheila's weak smile spoke volumes.

Patsy looked at the crowd of people as they approached her. They were a mixed bunch, she had to admit, but for the moment they were all she had.

Hearing her name again, she looked around, puzzled. Victoria came running towards her. 'Thank God I've found you, I thought I might have missed you.'

Letting out a deep sigh, Patsy felt she could half smile again. It had been a long few hours not knowing when someone was going to turn up, but she was more than pleased to see them all.

Victoria looked at the group of people behind Sheila, frowning. 'Who are they?'

'They, Victoria lassie, are the cavalry. Allies of the Diamond family who have come to help us out.'

Victoria felt humbled. All of these people had turned up to help when the chips were down. Victoria stood in front of them all as their chatter stopped. 'Thank you everyone.' She felt it was the least she could say in the circumstances.

'We'll take the tube back to London from here; God knows how many taxis or how long it would take otherwise. Once we get there, I want a couple of you to go and find Fin,' said Patsy.

'Isn't that why we're here, Mrs Diamond?' a woman asked up, puzzled by Patsy's remark.

'Yes, sorry, what's your name?' asked Patsy. The woman looked strangely familiar, but she couldn't remember from where.

'Sylvia, Mrs Diamond. I work in one of your pizza shops.' The look of disgust she flashed Patsy said it all. She worked for Patsy and Patsy didn't even know her!

Trying to cover her tracks the best she could, Patsy smiled. 'Sorry love, of course it is. My mind is just all over the place at the moment. No,' Patsy carried on, 'I have been tracking Fin and for some reason he is now at St George's hospital. I need someone to go there and find out about him. Whether he is dead or alive...' Patsy trailed off. The very thought of it made her blood run cold. She had been so busy trying to organise things, the very truth about what could have happened to Fin hadn't sunk in.

Sylvia nodded. 'Me and Aitch will go. What's his full name? We can't go into a hospital and just ask for Fin, can we?'

Patsy looked at Victoria, stunned. As stupid as it sounded, Fin had always been just Fin. She had never asked him his surname and he had never volunteered one. It sounded crazy, but's that how it had been. She felt stupid in front of this crew of people.

'William Finnigan,' Sheila piped up. 'Or rather, that is how he was known at school. If he's changed it since, we're fucked!'

With that sorted, Patsy walked ahead to the tube station and got the Gatwick express back to London. Everyone seemed in awe of the place, which puzzled Patsy.

'Don't forget,' Sheila whispered in her ear as they sat side by side on the train. 'This may not be a day trip to you, but it is to them. Some of them have never been out of Glasgow. Now, Bernie and Angus are on their way with the weapons.'

Nodding, Patsy smiled and looked at the crowd as they laughed and chatted. Sylvia caught Patsy's eye. She was one of the thinnest women Patsy had ever seen and the tallest. She had to be mid-thirties, but she was definitely a size zero and her chest was as flat as an ironing board. Her bleach blonde hair showed the dark roots growing through, which as a hairdresser, Patsy couldn't fail to notice. 'Sylvia,' Patsy interrupted, 'who is Aitch?'

Sylvia looked across and pointed to the woman next to her. 'Harriet,' she replied. 'We call her Aitch cos she hates Harriet, don't you lassie.' Sylvia smiled, showing a perfect set of teeth apart from a huge gap in the middle of the top set.

'Fucking Harriet! I don't know what my mother was thinking of,' laughed Aitch. In comparison, Aitch was overly plump with a very bad black hair dye on her short bob. Her eyebrows were thick, like two leaches walking across her forehead.

At last, after what seemed forever, the train stopped and excitement grew amongst the crowd, which annoyed Patsy somewhat. She wanted them to understand this wasn't a day trip. 'Sheila, are they going to take any of this seriously? All they seem to do is laugh and chatter on. This is serious stuff and I want no fuck ups.'

'For God's sake Patsy, give it a rest. I know your blood's boiling, and you're anxious about Fin, but these laddies and lassies know the score. They are here for a turf war. Your turf war. Let them have their fun before a stray bullet kills them, eh?'

'Sorry, you're right.' Patsy exhaled. Once on the station platform and walking towards the exit, Patsy turned and looked around for Sylvia. Opening her purse, she took out forty pounds. 'Take this and go to the hospital. Give me your mobile number to keep in touch. Find out what you can about Fin. According to my tracker he is there, or rather, I hope it's him and someone hasn't pinched his watch.'

'I will be in touch if I have news. Hopefully,' Sylvia said, 'it's good news.'

Thanking Sylvia, Patsy turned to Sheila. 'Let's get this lot off the street. It looks like a bad stag and hen night. Then we need to get to the pub that Fin visited. He walked in there like a lamb to the slaughter all because of me and I am damned sure I will pay those bastards back.'

'Calm down Patsy, we will sort this out, and Fin will be okay. He's a survivor,' Sheila replied.

Turning to the crowd behind her, Patsy clapped her hands to gain everyone's attention. 'Right, you've had your catch up, now were going to get a couple of black cabs to take us where we need to be.'

'What happened, Mrs Diamond? No one has really said anything apart from the fact that Fin is in deep shit!' a voice bellowed from the back.

Patsy looked towards where the voice was coming from. Patsy's eyes widened – he was a huge brute of a man. 'What's your name?' Patsy queried, feeling that this was becoming a habit.

'Tiny, Mrs Diamond. Everyone calls me Tiny. I work for you as a collector for your loan shark business and I always get paid.' Tiny winked.

Turning towards Sheila, Patsy had to stifle the laughter

bubbling up inside of her. Patsy beckoned them all towards her in some kind of semi-circle. She ignored the onlookers walking past, curious as to what they were all doing.

Patsy didn't really know where to start and she wanted to make a long story very short because she was freezing as the cold air bit into her. She explained in short that Fin had gone to find out who was threatening not only her life, but her business and possibly the lives of the people she was associated with, including the ones stood before her.

Letting out a deep sigh, Patsy looked at them all. Patsy felt ashamed that she didn't really know the people that worked for her and yet they were willing to put their lives on the line for her, or rather Fin. 'Look, if none are you are up for this, just say so and get the next flight back, okay?' This was their opt-out card. If they wanted to leave, they could.

Tiny spoke up for the rest of the crowd. 'Well, I'm in.'

Patsy smiled. 'Let's get out of here before everyone thinks we're street walkers!'

Patsy marched across to the taxi rank and stuck her head through the window of a cab. 'Take five of these to this pub in Vauxhall, will you?' She handed the driver the address.

'I ain't going anywhere near Duke's pub. And I want my money up front.' The cabbie tapped in thirty pounds on his meter.

Patsy was just about to give him a nasty retort when suddenly she stopped. 'Duke? Who is Duke?'

'Lady, if you don't know who he is than you are a tourist. He owns Vauxhall and the surrounding territories south of the river. That pub is his turf. Are you sure you want to go there?' he questioned.

Patsy ran her contactless card across his machine, ignoring him.

'Is that with or without a tip, missus?'

'You will get your tip if you shut your mouth and take us where we want to go – got it?' Patsy could feel the anger bubbling up inside of her.

'Rather you than me love; get in, but don't say I didn't warn you. Mr Duke owns that place, well not officially but that is his meeting place.' Laughing, he held his hands up in submission. 'But I never told you that missus; even the police don't go in there.'

'Listen to me,' Patsy warned, 'Mr Duke is a big fish in a small pond and an arsehole. I am Patsy Diamond. Remember the name, sonny. I am going to bring him down and teach him to learn some respect,' she snapped.

The cab driver raised his eyebrows and gave a low whistle before starting the engine.

* * *

It looked like a busy night at the hospital when Sylvia and Aitch walked in. The accident and emergency department was packed to the hilt with people as they tried pushing their way forward to the reception area.

'We're looking for a William Finnigan. We've been told he's been brought in here,' Sylvia asked.

A nurse came forward. 'Excuse me, did you say Finnigan?'

'Aye lassie, what big ears you have,' Sylvia quipped and then winced when Aitch elbowed her in the ribs. 'Yes, we were told he's been brought in here,' she said again.

'He has indeed; he's in acute assessment. Who are you please?' The young nurse had probably said more than she should have without asking who they were first, but at least they had their information. Suddenly, Aitch felt a tap on the shoulder. Turning around, she saw a police officer standing there.

'Excuse me miss, did I hear you ask about Mr Finnigan?'

Swallowing hard, Sylvia looked up at him. 'Yes that's right offi-cer. My brother. I've just had an anonymous call saying he was here...' In time-old fashion, Sylvia used the only weapon she had and burst into tears. 'What's happened to him officer?' she asked politely between sniffs; she could see that the policeman felt embarrassed and reached into his pocket for a packet of paper tissues.

'He was found in the car park a while back. He's in a pretty bad way. He only had his driving licence on him.' He asked them to follow him to a side room. Stunned, Sylvia and Aitch looked at a very battered Fin in a hospital bed surrounded by machines. His swollen eyes were already turning black. His leg dangled in the air in a plaster cast. This time Sylvia's tears were for real.

'Oh my God, Fin, who did this to you?' said Sylvia while holding his hand. Aitch went and stood around the other side of the bed and looked at all of the machines surrounding him. Bleeps and lights flashed everywhere.

Sylvia looked up at the policeman. 'Is he going to live? I mean, is he okay?' she stammered.

'He's going to be fine,' the nurse chirped up, 'but he's taken one hell of a beating. Looks like a mugging to me; not sure how he got to the car park though. He either stumbled here and passed out or someone has dumped him anonymously. Possibly the same person that took his mobile phone after they called you.'

Sylvia smiled at Aitch; without knowing, the nurse had just filled in all of the gaps for the policeman.

'He been very lucky.' The nurse smiled. 'That face looks bad, but all the scans and X-rays don't show anything else major. He's sleeping now, probably from the beating and the morphine we have given him for the pain. All this' – the nurse waved at the machines – 'is just precautionary in case of internal bleeding.

We're just monitoring him, love.' Shaking her head, the nurse walked up to Sylvia and put her hand on her arm. 'I will go and get you both a nice cup of coffee.' As she walked out, the nurse gave the policeman a meaningful stare. 'If any of your lot had been walking the streets you might have found him sooner,' she quipped.

Ignoring the nurse, the policeman looked at Sylvia and Aitch standing beside Fin's bed. 'I will be wanting to speak to you two later...'

Sharply, Sylvia looked up. 'Speak to us about what? You know more than we do,' she snapped. 'Bloody coppers,' she muttered under her breath as he left the room.

* * *

Patsy's mobile burst into life; seeing Sylvia's name, she answered it quickly. 'Sylvia, what's happened? Have you found him?'

'Too right lassie, we're sat by his hospital bed now. He looks like he's been hit by a bus and has a broken leg. He's drugged up to the eyeballs, which he will enjoy,' she laughed. 'But according to this lot he's going to be okay. The police are here, because he was found in the hospital car park. Strange though. Apparently his driving licence was left in his pockets for the police to find, but everything else had been taken.'

Relief washed over Patsy. 'Stay with him Sylvia and let me know if he comes around. Keep me posted.' Ending the call, Patsy let out a huge sigh and relayed the conversation to Sheila. She sat back in her seat while mentally thanking God for Fin's survival, although she couldn't imagine what he had been through.

As the cab pulled up, Patsy looked around but couldn't see a pub. The cabbie turned to face her.

'This is as far as I go missus.' The cabbie pointed around the corner of the street. 'The pub's just there, love.'

Disgruntled, Patsy and the rest of them got out. 'Fucking coward,' she snapped as a final retort.

Sheila ran ahead to the corner of the street and true enough, the pub was there. It seemed desolate and had no other houses around it. There might have been at some time but, on the corner of two streets the pub now stood alone. As far as Sheila could see it was bouncing with life and she could hear loud music playing.

A car's headlights flashed at Patsy and looking up, she saw that it was Victoria's car and quickened her pace. Victoria opened the window and Sheila and Patsy stuck their heads through it. 'Christ, you got here quick. Are you okay?'

'I'm fine, but this is a God-awful place. There are some pubs further down at the other side, but this stands alone, like a cactus in the desert.'

'We've just heard Fin is alive, battered and a few broken bones, but okay,' Patsy blurted out.

'That's good. So what is your plan Patsy? You have found the pub, but now what?'

'Did you bring anything from that cabinet of yours, Victoria?' Patsy bit her bottom lip, waiting for an answer.

Victoria opened her glove compartment, and took out a handgun. 'This is loaded, the safety catch is on and its only to be used if necessary. God, I feel like some villain in a detective drama. All this cloak-and-dagger stuff Patsy. If any of this goes wrong and they want to check my cabinets, they have to be in order... Do you understand?' Victoria warned. She felt uneasy about all of this, knowing how impulsive Patsy could be. But this was her life on the line, too.

'Victoria, you don't have to stay. Thanks for this, but, really, you can go if you want. I don't know what is going to happen when I enter those doors and I am going to be too busy watching my own back, never mind yours.'

'Don't worry about me love. I'm the one with the guns.'

'Right, next I need a lift up the road to the petrol station. Can you take me there?' Patsy opened the door and got in.

Confused, Sheila looked at Victoria. 'Why do you need a garage lassie?'

'I've just had an idea Sheila, and I am going to give that pub and the bastards in it a drink on me!'

10

DIAMOND ARMY

'Well, let's get on with it, Mrs Diamond. We have been travelling for hours. Can we do what we have to and then go and get something to drink?'

'Tiny, I am ready when you are.' Patsy was now prepared for whatever came their way.

Tiny nodded. 'You two,' he shouted across at a man and a woman. 'You go in as a couple. We're going to drip feed this. No one goes in mob handed until we have sussed the place out.'

The man and woman nodded and opened the pub door and walked in. The music blared out and it seemed full of people.

'Typical dealer den Patsy; it's Friday night and everyone has come for their "hit" now they have a bit of cash,' Sheila said.

One by one, Tiny instructed them to go in and mingle. People were already falling out of the doors drunk and some men even came out to urinate against the brick wall. 'This is a good atmosphere, Mrs Diamond. It will take a while for them to notice us. They are so pissed and wrapped up in themselves, we're irrelevant.'

Patsy nodded. All seemed good so far, and the mixture of men and women was working in her favour. It didn't look too suspicious.

'Ring Angus, Sheila, I know he's driving but Bernie will answer for him if necessary. Find out where they are.' Sheila did as she was told, but she didn't really want to speak to Angus and have to answer any difficult questions. Once Angus had answered on his hands-free, Sheila had seemed satisfied and ended the call.

'Christ, that was short and sweet Sheila. Normally we can't get you off the phone,' Patsy remarked.

'We're not on the best of terms at the moment. This is his first and last favour, so let's make good use of it. He says he's about an hour and a half away. He knows London so he knows exactly where he is heading for.' Sheila's curt answer stopped Patsy asking any more questions. She felt quite guilty that whatever the problem was, it definitely had something to do with her. Musing to herself, she realised Sheila was right, this ambush had to count. And she would make damn sure it would!

'Tiny! I don't want you to go in, I'd rather you stayed out here. You're a great guy, don't get me wrong, but you're noticeable, and I would like someone on the outside just in case.' She gave him a knowing look. They both knew what she meant.

'Fair dos Mrs Diamond. I'm on watch. You take care now, but if you think I'm noticeable, you're going to stick out like a sore thumb in there with those clothes on,' he remarked.

Swallowing hard, with her heart in her mouth, Patsy took hold of the handle on the pub door and opened it. She hadn't realised how dark it was inside, considering from the outside it looked well-lit with all its disco lights. People were drinking, laughing and dancing around. Ignoring them, she walked straight up to the bar and pushed her way through. It was heaving and the bar staff seemed run off their feet. The bar was soaking wet with spilt beer and people stood with their hands in the air holding their money, hoping to catch the eye of one of the bar staff.

Patsy noticed a man at the end of the bar where the hatch was. He was stood holding court with a few friends and was obviously the landlord, Patsy thought to herself. Especially when she saw him turn to the optics where the whisky was and fill his glass and the glasses of his friends without paying. Squinting, she looked around to see if she could see any of her allies. She spotted one or two, but not the others. Wherever they were mingling, it seemed to be working.

Patsy slowly walked to the end of the bar where the landlord stood laughing and joking with his friends. Instantly, their laughter stopped. 'If you're waiting to be served love, wait your turn; the staff are doing their best,' he remarked, and paused, waiting for her to leave their gathering.

'It's you I want to talk to. I am looking for Mr Duke, I have a meeting with him,' she lied.

A grin appeared on the landlord's face.

Raising one eyebrow, she gave him a disgruntled look. 'Maybe I can have a private word with you. I have something for him.'

The men seemed to feel this was a private joke, and looking her up and down, they grinned. 'He's not come in yet... are you his latest flame?'

'The name is Patsy Diamond and I want him. But as you're his monkey I will talk to you.' Patsy's comment stopped the laughing instantly and the stunned landlord looked at her angrily.

'Fuck off, I am no one's monkey, you bitch and let's see what Dukey says about his latest screw's manners. If you're hoping for a free drink while you're waiting, there are none. Now either buy one or go and wait on the streets where a slut like you belongs.'

'Actually, I have a drink for you, smart arse. Now is he here or not? Remember my name, because I intend it to be embedded into your brain for a long time.'

Suddenly the mood changed and the landlord stopped leaning on the bar and stood up straight. 'What's your gripe missus?' he asked more soberly.

'A friend of mine came in here. A Scottish guy, and now he's in hospital. I feel you and Mr Duke could tell me what happened to him.' As an afterthought, Patsy remembered James. 'He was looking for a friend of his, James McNally, I believe.' Patsy watched and even in the dark lighting, she could see him pale. She had been right; he knew exactly what had happened to Fin.

The landlord adjusted his glasses as he took in the way she was dressed. He recognised real designer clothes and peering at her more closely, he took in her stance and her authoritative air. She seemed to mean business.

'So I am right then? You do remember my friend.' Patsy raised one eyebrow and glared at him, a wry grin on her face. 'Was it you who tipped Mr Duke off, whoever he is?' Patsy laughed mockingly. 'Well, I am Patsy Diamond and that snivelling rat has trashed one of my hair salons. If he wants trouble, he has come to the right place. Trouble is my middle name.' Patsy smiled. Putting her hand in her pocket, she pulled out a bottle of water and put it on the bar. Unscrewing the top slowly, she gently pushed it with her finger and let it fall over, letting the liquid pour out. The petrol fumes from the bottle made the landlord and his friends stand back.

'What the fuck are you doing, lady?'

Patsy took out her lighter. 'Turn the lights up; I want to let everyone see you fry.' Patsy laughed as the petrol ignited. There wasn't a lot in the bottle, and even she was surprised by how quickly the fire spread. The landlord threw wet bar towels at it to stamp it out, which only seemed to ignite it more.

'You crazy woman! Clear the bar; everyone move!' the land-lord shouted.

Everyone nearby screamed and threw their drinks over the flames to put them out, but Patsy just stood there watching, smiling, hoping it would spread further and show these bastards who was boss. They'd frightened Janine, trashed her shop and Fin was in hospital; enough was enough. Suddenly the lights turned up and she walked into the middle of the floor, clapping her hands together to attract everyone's attention.

'My name is Patsy Diamond. A friend of mine came in and has been half beaten to death because of it.'

The landlord and his friends were still dowsing the flames in a state of panic and cursing her. That part of the bar had completely cleared.

'You'll get yours when Duke comes in!' someone shouted.

Taking out the gun from her pocket, Patsy pointed it towards the voice. 'And you will get yours if you don't shut your mouth. Go on, all of you. Go and find this Duke you're all so afraid of, because I am afraid of no one. Where is he to protect you when he is needed? What exactly do you pay him for?' she scoffed. The room silenced, even the music had been turned off. What she was saying was slowly sinking into their drunken brains. One man threw a glass towards her but she ducked, avoiding it, and fired a shot in the air, causing some of the plaster from the ceiling to fall like snow above her. People put their arms over their heads to protect themselves, some even ducked under a nearby table.

'I remember the guy you're talking about, skinny little runt from Glasgow. Said he just got out, fucking loser. Yes, Mr Duke was called to sort things out. Money was owed and your guy knew where it was. He didn't mention that he hung onto a woman's skirts,' the man laughed, almost spilling the pint of beer in his hand on the floor.

'Ring your boss, big man. I take it you have a phone number. Then call it,' Patsy commanded. Patsy was angry and she wanted justice, not only for herself but for Fin. She was sick of being treated as a silly woman to be blackmailed and scoffed at, by the likes of Larry, Nick and this mob. This time she meant business. She had no idea how this night was going to end, but she was determined to see it through – no matter what.

Patsy looked around for the landlord and noticed his absence. He was doing just as she wanted. This turf war needed sorting one way or another and now Fin seemed to be out of the woods and alive, there was no better time.

Unexpectedly, the landlord reappeared with two other men she hadn't noticed earlier. Each of them were holding shotguns. 'There!' the landlord spat out. 'Do you really think you were the only person in this pub with a gun? I was one of the men that went to your salon, when that stupid assistant of yours dared to question how much there was. She's a loser and so are you. You women are only good for one thing!' With his jeering insults, the crowd laughed and mocked Patsy.

Standing there stoney faced, she didn't care; she had her own plans. She wanted to meet this Mr Duke face on. If there was a turf war, she intended to win it. Although, at the moment, even she knew she was outnumbered and mentally wondered if she had started her war too early. She had no guns and no idea when Angus was going to turn up. She knew she stood there with a target on her back, but she didn't care. Tonight, she would face this London gangster they were so afraid of and show him who was boss.

Tiny stood in the shadows at the corner of the pub; he was just about to light his cigarette when he saw car headlights coming towards him. Stepping backwards into the shadows, he saw the cars screeching to a halt. Knowing it was trouble, he texted Sheila quickly.

Enemy outside

Tiny rushed to the pub door in front of the four men who had got out of the two cars and stopped them. 'You seem in a bit of a hurry laddies. Anything special going on?'

The four men tried shoving past him and he could see they all had guns, ready for action. 'Fuck off you fool,' one of them said. But Tiny wasn't about to be moved.

'I suggest you go home laddies, there is nothing in there for you.' Tiny threw a punch; he knew there wasn't much he could do but he was trying to buy time. He had no idea if the others needed to escape, or what had happened inside. He wasn't 100 per cent sure Sheila had even got his message.

Impatiently, one of the men took his gun out of the inside of his jacket, pointed it at him, then as an afterthought, struck him on the side of the head with it, almost knocking Tiny off balance. Dazed, he held on to the wall to balance himself. Putting his hand up to his head, he looked at his fingertips, and saw they were crimson from the blood trickling down his temple. With one last attempt, Tiny threw another punch, and was hit again by the butt end of the gun. He staggered and swayed, and this time he slumped to his knees. The four men looked at him in disgust and pulled the pub door open. With their guns in their hands, they ran in. 'Right, who's looking for trouble?'

Patsy looked around. Her allies were waiting for her signal, but even she knew there wasn't a lot they could do against four guns pointing at her. Swallowing hard and keeping her nerve, she gave them an icy stare. 'So I take it none of you are Mr Duke.' Her heart was pounding; any moment now, any one of those guns could fire at her and it would definitely all be over.

'One last chance lady, fuck off and we'll forget all about your little tantrum. Mr Duke is on his way, so I wouldn't hang around. You've had your fun, and we're paid to protect this place. Now just leave.' They shouted and patronised her like some young child. This made her angrier than ever.

Patsy threw her hands up in the air, the odds firmly against her. 'Okay, guys, do whatever you can,' she shouted.

This was the signal the others had waited for. Suddenly punches flew in the direction of the crowd from her own allies. This disturbance took the heat off her for a moment as Mr Duke's foot soldiers were confused by the people in the crowd starting a fight at a time like this.

'Call the governor,' one of the armed men shouted. 'She's buried half of her army in here and you didn't even notice. You fucking idiot!' the men with the shotguns shouted at the landlord.

Shocked and in panic, the landlord reached into his pocket for his mobile and started shouting down the phone. The pub was now becoming one big brawl.

'You have one smart mouth missus, and the next word is going to be your last.'

Patsy looked down the barrel of a gun. Everyone else seemed oblivious to the fact that she was going to die and lashing out towards the man threatening her, she slapped him. Adrenalin and anger made her braver than she felt. 'Don't threaten me, you puppet,' she snarled.

He grabbed her by the hair. Patsy struggled, kicking and spitting at the man who held her, but he was much stronger than she was. Forcing her mouth open, he put the barrel of his gun inside and turned to the crowd.

'This is your fucking Patsy Diamond, who turns up ready for

war with nothing but a few punches. Stop fighting! Others are on their way, and you lot are going to be tortured, believe me,' he laughed with his friends. Patsy glared at him; strangely enough she wasn't frightened, she was just furious.

'Duck!' a woman shouted out and two gunshots rang out in the silence. Patsy fell to her knees and instinctively covered her head with her arms. The man holding Patsy fell to the floor in front of her. Looking up, she saw crack-shot Victoria holding up her rifle, which she'd hidden in her long coat. Coolly and calmly, she had shot the man holding Patsy in the head. Screams rang out from some of the people in the crowd, and they scrambled towards the door.

Shaken, Patsy stood up again. Her mobile phone buzzed, indicating a message.

This one is on the house Lady Diamond. Duke already paid me.

Lady Diamond?
The only person that had ever called her that had been that mercenary Freddie.

* * *

Outside was mayhem too. 'For crying out loud Angus, who are all of those people going into the pub?' As Bernie and Angus got closer to the pub, cars were suddenly overtaking their rescue truck.

'Shit Angus, that was gunfire, and those bastards are mob handed.' Bernie opened the door of the truck and was about to climb out.

'Where are you going?' Angus asked as he took in the carnage around them.

'I'm getting in the back of this trailer and you're going to save your girlfriend. Sheila is in there and someone is firing guns, and you can bet it's not our lot because we have them, remember? Into the pub Angus, reverse up and drive straight in, this is not the time for pleasantries!' Bernie shouted.

Angus could see through the frosted windows that there was a brawl going on and people were staggering out of the pub, smeared with blood.

He couldn't see Bernie, nor did he know what she was going to do, but she was right. Sheila was in the thick of whatever was going on in there. Reversing up, he revved up the engine and slammed his foot down hard on the accelerator. The long heavy tow truck crashed through the wall of the pub and Angus shielded his face with one arm as he carried on steering forward. The jolt as it hit the walls almost knocked him backwards. Bricks and dust crashed around him as the windscreen cracked and shattered, spraying remnants of glass everywhere. As he slowly opened his eyes, coughing from the dust, he realised he was inside the pub, truck and all.

Angus covered his ears as loud gunshots rang out; he couldn't see where they were coming from, and rubbing the dust from his sore eyes, he looked around aimlessly. Turning, he saw Bernie on the back of his truck. She had set the machine gun up and was firing into the crowd. Round after round, she fired into the walls, the lights and the bar itself.

People were shouting and screaming and the pub was now in total mayhem. Men who had been stood beside the landlord with their shotguns were now firing aimlessly at the truck. Thankfully and much to Angus's relief, it was so big and high up, he could kneel down under the steering wheel without getting caught in the crossfire. Frantically, he peered up amongst the broken windscreen, searching for some sight of Sheila.

In the hysteria, Patsy pushed her way through to the bar, picked up her gun and aimed it at the landlord whose eyes widened with fear. Patsy fired. 'That's for Fin, you bastard.' She shouted as he fell face down onto the wooden bar.

People were heading for the door as they picked up tables and chairs to shield themselves from whatever stray bullet was heading their way. It had now become a free-for-all. While kneeling down and firing the machine gun, Bernie had reached into one of the holdalls and was throwing out guns to the rest of her friends. Now, all of them were armed and safe.

The duke's men were shooting aimlessly and most of the time were firing at their own accomplices and customers.

'I want that bitch!' one of Duke's soldiers shouted out, running towards Patsy. Sheila fired her own gun into the man's direction, but Victoria, who was much further away, held up her rifle and shot him.

'This is better than clay pigeon shooting,' she shouted and laughed maniacally.

Sheila made her way to Angus and the truck. Seeing her, he kicked the dented door open. 'That was a brilliant idea Angus... thanks,' she panted.

Sliding onto the seat, Angus watched as Sheila leaned forward in the truck to where the windscreen had once been and started shooting. 'It's like the wild west Angus, but those foot soldiers of this Duke fella mean business. There are dead bodies everywhere and they have killed most of them.' Adrenalin spurred her on; she was hot, sweaty and had blood smeared across her top.

'Have you been hit?' said Angus, hoping to be heard above the riot.

'No, one of their lot fell on me. I'm okay though; it's just as well they're all crap shots. Angus, will this thing still drive?'

Angus nodded. 'Yes, of course it will, the engine is still running.'

'Good. Then I am going to shout for all of our lot to try and get in or on the back of it and you're going to put your foot down and get us out of here. Sooner or later, someone will call the cops. I'm surprised no one has already.'

Slightly shocked and stunned by Sheila's nonchalance, Angus put the truck in reverse.

'Patsy! You lot, get the fuck on here. We're leaving!' Sheila shouted. She couldn't see Patsy, but she was determined not to hang around. This whole place with its blood-smeared walls, and dead bodies scattered around the floor was one big crime scene. Suddenly, Patsy put her head through the truck window. She was covered in plaster dust and balancing on one of the steps outside of the truck while holding on to the open window. Her hands were bleeding from the broken glass of the shattered windows.

'Drive!' she shouted.

Angus put his foot down and drove off. He could see people balancing on one leg while holding onto the truck. He wasn't sure how many there were. He had never seen anything like it. It was like something out of the movies and seeing this side of Sheila and Patsy terrified him. As though on autopilot, he drove until Sheila gave the command to stop down a side street. Sheila, who had been hanging on to Patsy's arms to make sure she didn't fall off the side of the truck, opened the door. Patsy almost fell to the ground in exhaustion.

Sheila got out of the truck, and steadied Patsy. 'How many of the others are here? Where's Victoria?' Sheila asked. It was dark, and the only lights they had were the headlights from the truck.

'I'm here.' Victoria slowly held up her head from the back of the truck. Her clothes were torn, and she too was smeared with blood. 'I'm okay,' she croaked, panting.

'I got her lassies; she was going to fight to the last man standing, that is until she ran out of bullets,' laughed Bernie. 'Donny has got a bullet in the shoulder. He's bleeding bad; we need to drop him off at a hospital or something... I have tried tightening his belt around his arm to stop the blood flow. There's a few of us missing, Patsy. I don't know if they're alive or dead.'

For a moment, Patsy looked at Sheila and wiped her face, then swept her hair back. It was caked in plaster and God knows what. They both knew they had been lucky.

'Angus, this is the address to my parents' house. Drive us there if you can. Everyone!' Patsy shouted. 'If possible, get into the truck or into the car. We have to get to safety and assess the damage.' It was the only place Patsy could think of and hopefully they would get there without being stopped by the police. The truck had bullet holes in it and no windscreen. Her only hope was to get the rest of them to safety.

* * *

Patsy hammered on her parents' front door. Once she saw the hall light turned on, she breathed a sigh of relief.

'What the hell?' Her father stopped short when he saw her. Looking past her, he saw the rescue truck and injured, bleeding people limping and walking up his drive. Some were holding each other up with their arms around each other's shoulders. For a moment, he stood there disbelievingly watching them.

'We need to come in Dad... all of us,' Patsy panted.

George woke from his stunned state and immediately opened the front door wider. Wrapping his dressing gown around him tighter, he stepped forward to help the others inside.

'George!' shouted Patsy's mother as she ran down the stairs. 'What the bloody hell is going on? Who are all these people?'

George glanced at her and gave her a look. 'I'll put the kettle on. Get everyone into the kitchen.'

Understanding now wasn't the time for questions, Patsy's mother led everyone into the kitchen and busied herself getting out mugs.

'Emma, get the whisky out of the cabinet. This lot look like they have been in a war, and I have a strong feeling who's behind it,' George snapped and glared at Patsy.

Doing as she was told, Emma disappeared into the other room. Angus eventually walked in, his large bulk tired and weary. He found a seat and sat down, wiping his brow.

'You need to get rid of that truck, son. Is it yours from work?' George asked, taking charge of the situation.

'It is Mr...' Angus was about to call him Mr Diamond when it occurred to him that wasn't his name – that was Patsy's married name.

'George will do just fine. What the hell you are going to say happened to that truck is beyond me, it's full of bullet holes and one of the tyres is flat. How the hell did you drive that here?'

'I don't know George, I just did. But you're right, my work are going to go bonkers.' Angus seemed to pale under his dirty face. He knew he was for the high jump. There was no explaining this.

'Just tell them it's been stolen. You were in Glasgow, weren't you? And it's arrived in London. Shit like that happens, son.' George sat beside him and put his arm around his shoulder. 'There isn't a lot we can do with it, it's too big to hide. Drive the truck a couple of miles from here and I will follow you and bring you back home. We need to dump it and you need to get home to report it missing to your bosses.'

Angus wearily nodded his head and stood up. He knew George was right, but his legs felt like lead and he was exhausted, but he had to get the truck as far away as possible.

'Anyone who can walk,' George shouted, 'there are two showers, one en suite in our bedroom and a bath. Go and use them and
get cleaned up, and don't wake Nancy.'

Emma poured out whisky for each of them and watched them
gulp it back to clear their dusty throats.

'We need a doctor, Mum,' Patsy wearily whispered. Now the
adrenalin had left her, she was exhausted.

'It's a bullet wound, missus,' said Bernie. 'We can't just call a
doctor.'

'Aunt Mabel is a sister at the hospital. I will call her; she will
do what she can, but he may have to go to the hospital. He's half
unconscious.' Emma had walked over to Donny and pulled his
hair back to see his face.

'He's lost a lot of blood missus, but I stopped the bleeding with
that belt.'

'Well, thank goodness I am not squeamish. I will make the
call,' Emma said and left the room.

For a moment they all sat in silence, thinking about the
evening. The air was sombre. Patsy looked around towards Sheila
and Victoria. 'You two go and get a shower first; there are loads of
towels in the ottoman in the bathroom.'

Remembering Nancy, Patsy more or less hobbled up the stairs
and quietly walked into her bedroom. It was dim with only the
night light on. Looking down at the little girl sleeping while
holding her favourite doll, realisation hit Patsy, almost an after-
shock of the evening.

She could have been killed tonight, she realised that now.
What the hell was she doing playing gangsters when she had
Nancy to think about? It all seemed ridiculous. Tears streamed
down her cheeks, making pathways in her dusty face. The past
couple of years had gone so fast, and her life had been turned

upside down. But that was no excuse for that fact that she had neglected her daughter.

Leaving the bedroom so as not to disturb her, she sat on the top of the stairs and cried. Tonight Nancy could have become an orphan. It had been an awful ordeal and she had gone in there without a thought for anyone else. How selfish was that? Some of the people who had come to her aid were obviously dead. The head count alone proved that. Tiny wasn't amongst the people sat in her parents' kitchen and she wondered what had happened to him. If Tiny and some of the others were dead, she thought to herself, it was all her fault. These good people had come to the aid of a friend and she had led them into battle, risking their lives on a whim of her vanity. Her heart was in her mouth, and she felt sick.

Stifling her sobs so no one could hear her, she brushed away the tears and went to the bathroom. Turning on the taps, she rinsed her face to hide the tear stains. It was the first time she had caught sight of herself in the mirror. She looked shocking. She had blood smeared on her and her clothes were torn from the brawl. Her fists were swollen where she had thrown punches, but tonight she knew she was nothing but a cold-blooded murderer. She had been determined to kill that landlord of the pub herself and once given the opportunity, she had shot him. Looking at herself in the mirror, she faced the truth. She was glad she had killed that landlord and worse still, she had enjoyed it. Watching the shocked expression on his face and seeing him slump before her with a bullet in him had given her sheer satisfaction.

Composing herself, she walked downstairs. Her parents seemed to be in control of the situation, and she was sorry, almost ashamed, that they had been dragged into her lifestyle again. What they must think of her was anyone's guess, she thought sadly to herself.

11

TAKE OVER

Mabel had worked her magic, while saying nothing, and had patched everyone up and managed to remove the bullet from Donny. Once everyone was showered and bandaged, it looked like a hospital ward, but everyone looked and felt better, although saddened that their numbers had dwindled.

If any of the others had survived, they hadn't made contact, so they could only presume they were dead. The others knew who they were, and Patsy vowed she would try and make good with any family members and see they were financially secure. It was the least she could do for them and for herself, she mused. Her act of charity made her feel better. It was a small offering for a loved one, but it eased her guilt.

Angus had said his reluctant farewells to Sheila and followed George's advice and caught the milk train back to Scotland after they had disposed of his truck. This way he could call his office and report the missing truck, letting them believe he had been in Scotland the whole time. That was also his alibi. Sheila knew they had a lot to talk about, but now wasn't the time. Angus had been there for her when she needed him, and she had betrayed his trust. He was a good man, but it took more than a good man to forgive this. Mentally, she accepted that their life together was over. This wasn't what Angus had signed up for and her lifestyle wasn't the one he would want. It saddened her, and she felt her heart was breaking as he left, but there was nothing she could say or do about it at this moment in time.

Emma had arranged makeshift beds for everyone once they were all cleaned up and they were so exhausted they had all fallen asleep.

Once Angus had left, Patsy had showed Sheila her mobile. 'I got this message during that massacre. I think it's from Freddie; he is the only person I know that called me Lady Diamond, but what does he mean about this Duke guy?'

Puzzled, Sheila read the message. 'Does that mean while we were going through that slaughter, the boss behind it all was already dead?'

'I don't know.' Yawning, Patsy rolled her eyes to the ceiling. She didn't know anything any more. 'I need to go and see how Fin's doing. You stay here and get some rest.'

'I think we should both get some sleep. Anyway, I think your dad wants a proper talk with you. He's been really kind about everything, but he wants answers. What are you going to tell him? We need to sing from the same hymn sheet if he asks me,' explained Sheila.

'I know. I think he deserves some of the truth. He knows about the salon, but he doesn't know about Fin and what happened to him. The guns and the gang coming to the rescue, well, seeing the bullet holes in the truck and the state of everyone, he isn't stupid. Maybe I should just come clean,' Patsy sighed. Sitting at the dining table with Sheila, everything seemed so clear, but even she knew not everything was as black and white as she hoped.

Confused, Sheila took a sip of her very strong coffee and

narrowed her eyes. 'What did Freddie have to do with all of this? Was this Duke guy was paying Freddie to kill you? So why didn't he do it? He doesn't care about anyone. The man is a mercenary, that is his job.'

'I don't know, I really don't.' Looking up at Sheila, Patsy grinned for what seemed like the first time in ages. 'Maybe he has a soft spot for me,' she giggled.

'Aye lassie, or a hard-on!' laughed Sheila and chinked her mug against Patsy's. 'Well, whatever it is, thank your lucky stars.'

When Patsy thought of the near miss she had had, her blood ran cold. Today, she realised, she could have been a corpse. Only time would tell what Freddie's involvement was in all of this. Or she might never find out. Whatever, she was alive and that was all that mattered.

'You two look mischievous with your heads together like that.' Victoria yawned and walked over to the kettle, shaking it to see if it had any water inside it then switching it on. 'Your mum's up and about Patsy; she is trying to cope with the situation, but I can see she is finding it hard. She has just asked me what they would all like for breakfast... Be kind, Patsy.' Picking up their mugs, Victoria smiled and went to fill them up again with coffee.

'I will Victoria, and thank you. You saved my life last night with your sharp shooting.'

'Well, I didn't win those trophies for nothing, but let's not talk about that now.' Victoria put her finger to her lips and rolled her eyes towards the staircase and the sound of Patsy's mum coming down them.

'Morning, I have just made some coffee Emma, would you like some?' asked Victoria and took a mug off the hook.

Feeling that she had walked into a private conversation, Emma smiled and looked around the room. 'That would be nice Victoria – thank you. What do Scottish people eat for breakfast?'

They all burst into laughter, especially Sheila. 'Well lassie, I presume we eat the same as anyone else. It's not all porridge and haggis.' She winked.

'Sorry Sheila, no offence.' Emma blushed slightly and turned her back on them, emptying the contents of her fridge onto the counter. 'I'd better get started; there will be a lot of hungry mouths coming down soon and we need to get some food into that poor lad Mabel sorted out.'

Victoria spied Patsy and gave her a knowing look. Taking her lead, Patsy got up and walked up to her mum who still had her back to her and put her arms around her waist. 'Thank you, Mum; you and Dad have been great.'

Turning around, Emma hugged her tightly. 'My Patsy, you're safe and sound.' Choked up with tears brimming on her lashes, she almost squeezed the life out of Patsy. 'Whatever it is you're up to, be careful.'

'I will Mum; I am so sorry you and Dad got dragged into this, I couldn't think of anywhere else we could go.'

'Where else would you go but your family? That is what families do – we stick together no matter what,' she scoffed and turned again to the work top to sort out the breakfast.

Victoria gave Patsy a smile and a nod, which Patsy took to be her approval of her appreciation for her parents' help. They had a lot to think about, and last night would haunt them for a long time to come.

* * *

Arriving at the hospital, Patsy and Sheila went into the side room Fin had been put in. Patsy was shocked at the state he was in; his swollen eyes were barely open. Sylvia and Aitch had stayed with him all night and looked up wearily when they walked into the room.

'How is he?' Patsy asked, knowing that was a stupid question.

'He's half awake, although you wouldn't know it. He has mumbled to us a couple of times, but he's so drugged up we can't understand him. It's the first time Fin's been off his head on drugs that he hasn't had to pay for,' Aitch joked.

'Here is the address of my parents' house. Most of the others are there. Go and get some rest; you have been good friends staying with him all night.' Patsy opened her purse and handed them a wad of money and a piece of paper with her parents' address on. 'That will pay for the taxi and then some.'

'My arse is numb Sylvia. Come on, let's get some proper breakfast instead of that weak water they call coffee. Incidentally Patsy, there is a copper sniffing around at the moment – okay?' Standing up, they both rubbed their backs and stretched, while Patsy waited until they had left the room.

Leaning closer to Fin's ear so he could hear her, Patsy whispered his name. 'Fin. Fin love, it's Patsy. Can you hear me?'

Slowly he reached out his swollen hand and squeezed it. Patsy looked up at Sheila and they both gave a sigh of relief.

'Can you speak?' Patsy looked at his swollen lips.

'Christ, Fin, you look like you have had an overdose of Botox. Come on, spill the beans,' Sheila urged. Her jokey manner made her seem braver than she felt, but she tried raising the morale of all of them. They had been in a warzone last night, but Fin looked worse than all of them put together. 'I suppose you're going to milk these aches and pains and get everyone to sign your plaster cast. Well, don't waste your time because most of your friends can't even spell.' She smiled and squeezed his hand. The nurse walked in, and Sheila stopped talking.

'It's time for his medication, and I need to change the drip. Is that okay ladies or do you want to leave the room?' she asked chirpily.

Patsy gave her a weak smile. 'What's the damage nurse? Is he going to be okay?'

'He's going to be fine, although he has taken quite a beating. No real damage done, although he won't be winning any beauty contests for a while.' She smiled and carried on regardless. 'Are you family? Where are the other two?' she enquired.

'He's my brother-in-law on my husband's side. I've just found out and come as quickly as possible.'

'Well, he's not short of visitors, I'll give him that. He'll be okay in a few days; he's already starting to rouse, but we want to keep him stable and take away the pain.'

Patsy and Sheila both nodded, as relief washed over them. Fin was going to be okay, and that was all that mattered. That was why his friends had come, to help him. It was little consolation, but at least their loyalty had not been wasted.

Leaning in even closer once the nurse had left, Patsy pushed a little more. 'Fin, can you tell me anything, can you remember anything? Just one thing, squeeze my hand. Was Freddie there?'

Fin squeezed Patsy's hand and mumbled, confused. She cast a glance at Sheila, and almost laid her head on his lips to hear what he had to say.

'He saved me,' Fin mumbled. 'Shot the boss, before they shot me.' Exhausted, Fin went limp again.

Sheila pursed her lips. She was puzzled by all of this. 'Your mobile message was right. Freddie was there, but why he saved Fin, killed... well, I presume that Duke bloke and not you... puzzles me.'

'We'll find out more when Fin wakes up properly, that's for sure. At least we have the information we need.'

'So we went through all of that last night, for nothing,' snapped Sheila.

'No, those bastards in the pub set Fin up good and proper. They were all in on it. and I'm glad we avenged Fin. But I'm not sure what Freddie wants for his trouble.'

'Money! That's all he does favours for; maybe he thinks you pay more than the others. I'm sure we will soon find out. You do have another problem to deal with though, unless it's slipped your mind.'

Letting out a huge sigh, Patsy sat on one of the nearby chairs. 'I know, I have a million texts from Larry, he's driving me crazy. Christ, I hate that bastard. I curse the day I listened to all of that shit. I'm giving up on men, especially relationships. I'm no good at them.' Patsy pushed her hands through her hair, which hurt the bumps on her head and made her wince.

'Have you thought any more about what you're going to do?'

'No. I suppose I could marry him, but that's swapping one prison sentence for another. Fin has got me my paperwork, but not the letter. I honestly don't know what I am going to do Sheila. At the moment I can't think straight.'

'Well, Patsy lass, you could always call his bluff and let him go to the police. When they find nothing, he will look like a real prat, won't he?'

'Yeah, but I have a bad feeling he'll find something else to tie me down with. He's become bitter and twisted. I could agree to marry him and make his life hell. Every day he will wish he had never gone through with it.'

'Or every day of his life he will have that smug satisfaction that he has the sword hanging over you. It will do his ego the world of good, sad bastard. Is that the only way he can keep a woman, by blackmail? Hey, don't forget, those Frenchie's are having that ball and expecting us to go. Let's not decline again; the last time wasn't pretty.' Sheila grinned.

Patsy rolled her eyes to the ceiling. 'Christ! I'd forgotten all about that.'

'Well, you had better get your skates on and buy a posh frock lassie. Got to look your best, before they have you arrested again and driven to them by a madman.' Sheila couldn't help laughing at her own joke, but seeing Patsy's serious face, she stopped. 'Sorry Patsy, I think a touch of insanity has crept in after last night. I don't mean to mock your accident.'

Patsy's mind wandered back to that day when the French driver had crashed, and she had been saved. A flashback to the man on a white horse holding her and taking her out of the car came floating back to her. She had thought about it often, but it annoyed her that she couldn't remember what her saviour looked like.

'That gives me an idea Sheila. I think I will agree to marry Larry and get him off my back as we agreed, but we have to go to Paris to choose my wedding gown. That way we can see what Paul and the Frenchies are getting up to and it gets me out of Larry's clutches for a little longer. After all, he can't come with me to choose my bridal gown; it's not traditional.' Patsy grinned.

'Patsy Diamond' – Sheila shook her head – 'what a little minx you are!' Sheila laughed. They both grinned at each other. 'In the meantime, lassie, we have to go and get our friends back home so they are not missed. You have to face your father's wrath and I am prepared for Angus to dump me.' She shrugged. 'Who is going to stay with Fin now? We can't ask Sylvia and Aitch to come back, they are shattered.'

A fleeting thought passed through Patsy's mind, and she nodded. 'I have just the right person to lift Fin's spirits, and she has time on her hands. Janine, my manageress. They liked each other before all this, and somehow, I don't think she will mind.'

'She's a bit upper class for Fin isn't she…? I mean, she knows how to use a knife and fork!'

'Behave Sheila, he may be full of pain killers, but he can hear you I'm sure of it. Anyway, I think Janine might be just the tonic to make our Fin feel better. I'll make the call; she can only say no, but I doubt she will.' Patsy took out her mobile and started calling Janine. 'You never know Sheila, she might teach him to use a knife and fork!' They both burst out laughing.

Once Janine had jumped at the chance to play nurse maid, Sheila and Patsy left, feeling satisfied that Fin would be in very good hands.

Back at her parents' house, Patsy was surprised at how everyone seemed to have fitted in. Bernie was teaching Nancy Scottish songs and laughing with her, the others were resting and helping with dinner preparations. And as much as he wouldn't admit it, George was quite enjoying the male company. Mabel had visited in Patsy's absence and checked on Donny who was in a lot of pain, but doing well, so after changing the dressing and giving him some more painkillers she had left.

Entering the lounge, Patsy turned to everyone and said, 'Can we all have a meeting around the kitchen table please? We need to sort things out.'

'Not much to sort, Mrs Diamond,' said one of the men. 'The news is full of a massacre in Vauxhall. The police are swarming all over the place. We should have torched it. By the way, my name is Josh. I'm Tiny's mate. He is okay, took a bashing, but has already got the train back to Glasgow.'

Patsy nodded. 'That's good to know.' She stopped short as Nancy ran in from the garden.

'Mummy, I'm going to a birthday party and I need a new dress.

Tessa's got a new dress and she's telling everyone she looks like a princess!'

Beaming, Patsy hugged her. After the last few days, listening to this trivial information that was so important to Nancy made her smile. 'There is only one princess around here, and that's you. We're going to find you a dress full of sequins so you can look like a posh lady. Grandma will put some nail varnish on you as well.' Her heart swelled when she saw the smile on Nancy's face. 'Now' – Patsy winked – 'which grandma is going to paint those nails of yours?' She looked up at her mother and Victoria.

'We both will, and I think we should shop for this amazing dress. Mothers are always serious about these things, but grand-mothers understand what princesses need, including a little tiara,' said Victoria.

'A tiara!' shouted Nancy. 'I really will look like a princess then.' Everyone laughed. It was good to hear some innocent laughter again, and Nancy's excitement was infectious. It seemed in no time, both grandmothers were collecting their coats and bags.

Patsy waited until Victoria and Emma left with Nancy before continuing. 'Back to business now they have gone. All of you need to leave. Preferably not together. Each of you choose your times and your ways of getting home. I think Donny should be driven home and if there is no one else, Maggie will look after him... I'm sure of it. You will all be compensated for your time, with cash.'

Patsy could almost hear a collective sigh of relief. 'I might need one more favour off you all first though.' Patsy paused. Seeing their faces, she wanted to bite her tongue. She could see they had all had enough of her already.

'They say the boss of that area we were in is dead....' She paused again, waiting for it to sink in. 'That means his area is up for grabs and that is where we come in. If anyone is going to sell anything around these parts, it's us. This will now become our turf and I am sure last night will put a lot of people off presuming they can take it over. They know someone is behind it and that someone is going to be me. The only problem is, there will need to be deliveries made to my salons as normal, by my own people. The point is, I need someone to be here to keep an eye on things. I can't be in three places at once. I have Scotland, Paris and London to deal with. Any of you prepared to move to London?'

'I will. Me and my other half,' interrupted Bernie. 'I could do with a change of scenery and no bastard Sassenach will cross me, that's for sure.'

Patsy almost smiled. 'What about your brothels Bernie? Have you got tired of those already?'

'Nah Mrs Diamond, but they are doing fine, and there are others I can put in my place. That Leandra has things under control, and she knows you're there to protect her.'

Patsy nodded. 'That's agreed then. I will find you somewhere to live and you can spread the word that you're in charge, under the Diamond reign of course. We need to find out who owed money to Mr Duke, because they now owe us money. Were his only soldiers those lot who turned up the other night? I doubt it. So we need to fish them out and find out what we can. Can I leave that with you Bernie?'

'Can I choose my own gang Mrs Diamond?' asked Bernie pensively.

'Whatever you like as long as all of my affairs are in order and you are responsible for all laundering, collecting and deliveries – you and you alone are responsible.'

'Suits me, I can do that. You just find me somewhere to stay Mrs D and I will do the rest. Better than relying on some bloke. They are all distracted by a pair of tits.'

'Aren't you, Bernie? Seems to me that's the pot calling the kettle black,' laughed one of the others.

Bernie picked up a cushion and threw it at him, laughing. 'I'm not dazzled by them laddie; if there's a drought I can feel my own! We need to go door knocking in that area to see who owed money to that sleazy bastard. He must have some mates hanging around somewhere; they will be keeping their heads down if the police are sniffing around. We'll sniff them out and more to the point sort them out. I'll make you proud and you will make me rich! Anyways' – Bernie pursed her lips, deep in thought for a moment – 'Victoria is what? Only a couple of hours away from here. She can be my first point of contact if you're busy; God knows her shootouts are going to be legendary, and I like the way she talks.' Bernie blushed.

Patsy cast a sideways glance at Sheila. It seemed Victoria had found herself an admirer. Patsy shook Bernie's meat hook of a hand. 'It's a deal Bernie, and the start of a great business relationship.'

Sheila listened and nodded; she felt Bernie was a good choice and no one would mess around with her. She also liked the idea that the Diamond reign was all women, strong women. 'Me and Fin can always look after things in Scotland Patsy, you know that.' Holding up her hand to stop Patsy's interruptions, she carried on. 'I know you like to keep your finger on the pulse, but that gives you time to concentrate on bigger fish.' Sheila raised her eyebrows and gave Patsy a knowing look.

Patsy knew she meant Larry. She was right of course, that was one problem that wasn't going away soon. Her hands were tied, and she knew it. The whole thing sickened her and she wanted to run out into the street and scream loudly and let all of the stress and hate inside of her pour out. She looked at her mobile and saw the numerous messages Larry had left for her. It was time she called him back to keep him sweet. That was next on her agenda.

'Patsy, while the men are watching the football, I think now is the time for us to have a talk.' Patsy recognised her father's authoritative voice. It reminded her of being a teenager again when she had come home late at night.

Gritting her teeth and looking at Sheila before she left the room with her father, Patsy waited. She knew this scolding was inevitable and given his good mood, she thought she could avoid it, but this was one bullet she couldn't dodge.

As Patsy sat down in the lounge away from everyone with the door shut, her heart was pounding. Her palms felt sweaty, and she rubbed them together. The silence was deafening. Looking up, she saw the smile drop from her father's face.

'What on earth do you think you are playing at dragging innocent people all the way here to face death! You turn up here in the dead of night after some shootout. Who the hell do you think you are? The Godfather! For fuck's sake Patsy, you have gone too far this time.'

'I'm sorry Dad,' Patsy began, her mouth dry; she could feel herself burning with shame. 'I didn't know where else to go. They had kidnapped Fin and...' Painfully, Patsy explained what had happened and why it had come to a head like it had.

George sat and listened stoney faced. He wasn't surprised at her impulsive actions; she had always been the same. He could even understand her reasoning, but to put hers and others' lives in danger like she had, he couldn't understand.

Patsy looked at her father from under her lashes; her chin was almost resting on her chest. 'I'm sorry Dad,' was all she could think of to say. She was lost for words and all the apologies in the world wouldn't help. 'Everyone will be leaving soon, me included. Thanks for everything you have done. I promise you, whatever happens, I won't bring trouble to your door again. In fact, I've been thinking about Nancy. It's time she lived with me; I am her mother after all, and it's time to move on.'

George paled. 'You're taking Nancy away from us? With your lifestyle, do you think that's wise?' His voice was choked with emotion. 'What about her stability and school and the friends she has? Are you going to take her away from all of that?' he argued.

'Dad, this was never meant to be permanent, you know that, but it's time, don't you agree? Children adapt, she will make other friends in another school. It's not as though she is studying for her exams, is it?'

'And what part of the country is Nancy to be brought up in? You have no roots, Patsy.'

'Does it matter where, as long as it's with her mother?' Patsy argued.

'Yes, it bloody well does, and don't use Nancy as a weapon against us just because you're up to your neck in it. This was about you causing havoc, leaving a trail of disaster all over the news and dead men in your wake, not Nancy!' he barked. 'I think you need to sort your life out first, get a home and settle properly and stop playing cops and robbers before you even consider moving Nancy. That is my word on it, Patsy, and don't even think of crossing me, or your night of terror in Vauxhall will feel like a fucking tea party when I've finished with you!'

Standing up, George opened the door and slammed it behind him. His angry footsteps up the stairs made Patsy's stomach churn. She hadn't meant it to sound as though she was using Nancy as a weapon. Full of despair, she stared at the blank television for what seemed like forever. She could hear everyone down the hallway and in the kitchen, talking and moving around. Obviously, they would have heard her argument with her father, or rather him shouting at her and putting her firmly in her place.

12

A LEARNING CURVE

A few days later, almost everyone had returned to Glasgow, and Patsy knew she had to face the music again too.

'I'm coming home today, Larry; there is nothing else I can do here until the decorators and workmen go into the salon.' Patsy's voice sounded like treacle pouring down the phone, but it seemed to satisfy his vanity, even though he complained that she never answered his texts. Each complaint set her teeth on edge, but she sweetly appeased him, all the while cursing him under her breath.

Sheila and Victoria sat opposite her, listening, and they were there not only for moral support, but to prompt her to be nice if her temper got the better of her. Ending the call, Patsy sighed. 'Jeez, that was hard work. What am I going to do when I face him?'

'You will think of something Patsy, you always do,' Victoria chimed in. 'Just step back and take a breath before you do anything else.'

Emma joined them for their morning coffee. 'Just dump him Patsy and to hell with the consequences. He's a rattle snake; no one blackmails someone into marrying them. I haven't told your father the full story because he will wage war, but I know the truth... Victoria told me,' she confessed.

Seeing that Patsy wanted to change the subject, Sheila let out a huge sigh. 'I've heard from Angus; it seems his work has believed his story. After all, he has worked for them for years and nothing has ever gone missing before; he's a trusted employee.'

'Is that all he said?' asked Patsy. 'Did he say anything about the two of you and your future together?'

'Well, he has gone back to the house and collected the girls from Maggie, so I suppose that sounds promising, although I do feel I'm going to have one of those heart to hearts you had with your father Patsy. I'll cross that bridge when I come to it. Anyway, I don't know what you think about this, so don't fly off the handle, but why don't you try and contact Freddie? You want to know what happened and Fin still isn't up to it yet, so why not get the truth from the horse's mouth? Surely it's worth a try?'

'No, I'm going to wait for Fin first. Freddie can only tell me half a story and I want Fin's version, too. I am popping to see him before I leave. Where's your car Victoria? Have you managed to find it yet?'

'Yes, your fantastic dad has sorted it. Drove me up there, even though it was on bricks. Someone had pinched all the tyres. So we called the rescue service which seems a little ironic, given the circumstances, and they have towed it home to Dorset. I will catch the train home. It's not a problem. The news reports are still digging into that pub business.' Victoria didn't want to call it a massacre or shootout, even though that was what it was. 'I'm surprised no one has mentioned your name, Patsy. To be honest, I thought they might have done.'

Sheila scoffed and took a sip of her coffee. 'The last thing they want to do is point the finger at someone who shot the pub up. I see they've also reported Mr Duke and some others as missing. The police know exactly what's happened, and they also know no one will speak up for fear of repercussions.'

Frowning, Emma asked, 'What, you mean like honour amongst thieves?'

'No lassie, more like I'm saving my own fucking skin in case that mad bitch comes back with a rescue truck and finishes the job!' Sheila laughed. 'My guess is that they will lay all of this on that Duke guy, especially if he's gone missing. It's him they are looking for – not us.'

They all agreed that what Sheila said made a lot of sense.

'My other guess, Patsy, is that when some of those lowlifes are feeling better, they might contact you or Bernie to see if there is any work going. Their drug selling or whatever they did will have dried up by now and they will be skint. Some will try and go it alone, they always do and they will come a real cropper once Bernie is on the case, so be prepared for that. There is no loyalty in crime; they will want to jump ship, believe me.'

Nodding, Patsy agreed. 'Well, as you say Sheila, we'll cross that bridge when we come to it. In the meantime, does anyone want to come and see Fin? Janine has given me hourly reports, and according to her he is mumbling more coherently. I knew she would cheer him up.' Patsy winked.

Sheila couldn't help laughing. 'Well, if she fancies him the way he looks now, she will think he's God's gift when the bruises are gone. He's onto a winner there and she obviously likes a bit of rough.' They all started to laugh, but for Patsy it was hollow. She knew she had to go back to Glasgow to face Larry, and no matter how many times she had gone over it in her head, she knew she had no option but to see it through, that or put a bullet in his head!

Victoria could sense Patsy's apprehension and she wished she could do more. 'We'll all come. God knows, if he's awake he will want to hold court.'

'Sounds like a good idea to me,' said Patsy. 'Come on then, let's go. Are you coming, Mum?'

Emma smiled, grateful to be included in the girl gang. 'I'd like that. Nancy is at school and I will be back before then.' Emma paused and let out a little sigh. 'Your dad says you might be taking Nancy away with you, is that right?'

Everyone could see and hear the sadness in her face and voice. Victoria flashed a look of disapproval at Patsy.

'Not this minute Mum, but eventually I have to, don't I? I think you and Dad have done more than your fair share, don't you?'

The smile appeared back on Emma's face. 'So it's not imminent then, just when you get sorted? Because your dad and I were going to go back to the villa in Greece for a few days and were planning to take Nancy with us; she likes it there.'

'Greece, eh?' Victoria smiled. 'That sounds like a lovely idea Emma, and I don't think there are any plans to take Nancy anywhere yet. After all, there is this Larry business to sort out first. Things need to be organised before you bring a child onto the scene, isn't that right Patsy?' Victoria cast Patsy a knowing look, which prompted her answer.

'Oh yes Mum, I didn't mean today,' she stammered, 'just at some point. As Victoria says, there is a lot to sort out. I need to buy a house to start with and that isn't done in a day, is it?'

As much as Patsy's heart ached for both her parents, it ached for herself as well. She wanted to build a life with her daughter, and deep down she knew it was time.

To lighten the mood, Victoria said, 'And after Greece, you're all coming to Dorset. Maybe for a long weekend; how does that sound?'

They all agreed. When Emma picked up her car keys and

headed for the door, Sheila behind her, Victoria pulled Patsy aside. 'Don't push it, Patsy. They have looked after Nancy for years, there's no rush. Don't be a heartless bitch.'

Surprised at Victoria's outburst, Patsy stood there stunned for a moment, lost for words. Victoria rarely said anything bad to anyone, and so even Patsy realised she had pressed the wrong button for her to speak to her like that.

* * *

When they all walked in to see Fin, they could see the immediate change in him. Janine was sat there reading to him from the newspaper, and although groggy, he was awake. His hair had been combed, and his face had been washed. There was even a smell of aftershave or perfume in the air.

As they stood there in the doorway, they cast sideways glances at each other and grinned. Seeing his overflowing fruit bowl, Sheila hid her hastily bought grapes back into her bag.

'Och lassie,' Sheila said to Janine, 'if you keep looking after him this well, he will never want to go home. Come on Fin, stop milking it,' joked Sheila.

He tried to smile, but his lips were so cut and swollen she could see it hurt and watched him wince in pain, which made Janine instantly stand up and dab his mouth with a tissue. Fin had a definite admirer, and he liked it.

Patsy pulled up a chair beside him. Looking up at the others apologetically, she couldn't help herself. 'Fin, do you remember what happened? Why was Freddie there? Who got you here?' She fired question after question. All these things had been going through her mind since he had turned up in the hospital.

Fin turned his head towards Patsy. She looked at the slits of his eyes and leaned closer. 'Freddie, he got me here,' he panted, trying to make himself understood under his mumbling. 'He was there.' Fin's answers were in short bursts, but he was telling her what she needed to know. 'Freddie shot Duke; he was supposed to shoot me, then you.' All talked out, Fin lay back on his pillow and breathless, closed his eyes.

Patsy looked up. The others hadn't heard Fin's mumblings; they were barely above a whisper. 'Well, Janine,' she said softly, 'are you sure you want to hang around here much longer? I can get someone to sit with him if you're tired. I have to go to Glasgow this afternoon – we all do I'm afraid, so it will just be you and Fin until he can fend for himself in a couple of days, if that's okay?' Although Patsy already knew what Janine's answer would be, she felt it only polite to ask.

'I don't mind Patsy. I like looking after him. I even got him some new pyjamas, but he can't get the bottoms over his leg, being in plaster, but he can wear the top.' Proudly, Janine pulled back the covers. 'Me and the nurse helped wash and change him.' They all stared down at Fin with his *Star Wars* pyjama top.

Stifling a giggle, Sheila couldn't help herself. 'Does he have matching boxer shorts too Janine?'

Innocently and proud of herself, Janine smiled. 'He does actually.'

Not being able to resist herself, Sheila spoke again. 'And I suppose you helped him into those with the nurse as well?'

Blushing, Janine made her excuses, and said something about getting a sandwich and left. Sheila looked around at the others and burst out laughing. 'My God lassies, she has certainly checked him out good and proper.' Tears ran down her face and she couldn't stop laughing. They all laughed. Fin was in good hands; Patsy was sure of it.

'Let's leave Darth Vader and Princess Leia to it.' As they were leaving they passed Janine in the corridor near the vending machine. Patsy stood by her. 'Thank you Janine; if you need anything, give me a call and keep me informed how he is please.' Patsy kissed her on the cheek.

After saying goodbye to Nancy and giving her a hug that almost squeezed the life out of her, Patsy climbed into the rental car with Sheila and dropped Victoria off at the train station. With a heavy heart she drove back to Glasgow.

Lighting two cigarettes, Sheila opened the window and blew smoke into the air. 'By the way, Bernie texted me saying she already has a black book about the people who owed Duke money. She started at a block of flats around the corner and Bingo! God knows how she's managing it, but her finger is well and truly on the pulse.'

Patsy was in a world of her own as Sheila rambled on. So many things were going through her mind, she didn't know where to start first.

'Are you listening Patsy, or are you in Larry land?' Sheila snapped.

'I'm fine, and I'm glad Bernie is sorting things out; she doesn't hang around, does she?'

The rest of the journey was spent more or less in silence, and after dropping Sheila home, Patsy went directly to Larry's house. The quicker she saw him and got it over with, the less painful it would be.

13

WEDDING PLANS

'I expected you back hours ago; where have you been?'

Looking up at Larry's angry face made Patsy's heart sink. Was this the start of the rest of her life? The great Patsy Diamond, being ruled by another solicitor. His attitude made her feel sick.

'Well, hello to you too Larry. I'm tired, I need a bath and I've had a long journey and all you can do is snap at me. Welcome home, Patsy,' she snapped and pushed past him. She didn't care what he said or did any more. She knew now she had two options. One was to see this farce through until she could come up with something better, or as suggested, she could let him go to the police and look a prat.

Realising his mistake, Larry said, 'I'm sorry Patsy, I was just worried about you. It's been hours since you said you were coming home.' Walking up to her, he attempted to put his arms around her, but she yawned, and walked towards the stairs.

'I'm going to take a bath.'

'Do you need someone to scrub your back?' Larry shouted after her.

Patsy's bored expressionless voice floated back down the stairs to him. 'No, I'm tired and I need a nap, so that will give you time to cook something, won't it?' Once in the bathroom, she slammed the door and slid the small lock across it. Turning on the taps, she gave a huge sigh, but at least he hadn't mentioned her fresh bruises.

No sooner had she slipped into the warm soapy water than there was a knock at the door. 'I've brought some wine up for you Patsy; I can't seem to get in though because the door's locked.'

Getting out, she unlocked the door, stuck her head around the corner and took the glass of white wine from him. 'Thank you,' she said and promptly shut and locked the door again. She needed the drink and the smug satisfaction she got from seeing his face drop when she shut the door in his face made her feel better.

Staying in the bath for as long as possible, to the point she was almost a prune, she knew she had to make an appearance sometime. The smells of cooking from the kitchen floated up the stairs. She didn't realise how hungry she was until she smelt the food, the aromas were almost making her salivate. Still in her thick towelling bathrobe, she went downstairs to the kitchen.

'You look better; did you have a nap?' Larry asked, while stirring something in his pots and pans.

'What's for dinner?' Patsy asked, ignoring his questions and sitting at the table while helping herself to another glass of wine.

'Goulash, in red wine. You said you liked it before, so I thought I would do it again. So how are things at the salon? Have you sorted out the insurance and stuff yet?'

'Yes, it's all in hand. It's just a case of getting the workmen together. Janine and the others can handle that. It's been a nightmare.'

As she looked at the man before her, she realised Larry's handsome face repulsed her. She could hardly believe what she had once seen in him. Placing the cutlery and plates before her, he jabbered on about all kinds of immaterial nonsense. It was all superficial and Patsy waited impatiently for him to get to the point...

'Have you thought any more about us Patsy?' he asked eventually.

'About us? Well, I thought that was all sorted. After all, I'm here, aren't I?' Patsy smiled, before picking up her fork and taking a bite of the goulash. 'This is delicious Larry.'

'I see that, but have you thought about setting a date for our wedding yet?'

'Blimey Larry, people are going to think I'm pregnant if we rush it. Anyway, if I am going to do this, I want to do it properly.'

For the first time Larry laughed. 'Pregnant? Well that's a thought; maybe a bit further down the line eh?' Then his brows furrowed. 'What do you mean "properly"?'

'Well, I need a dress, a wedding planner, a venue. You have to get a suit...' Patsy laid it on thick. She could see Larry beaming at the thought of a society wedding.

'That all sounds expensive, very nice but expensive. Any idea of a venue? And please don't say the community centre,' he joked and poured another glass of wine.

'I haven't looked around yet to see what's available. Some places are booked months in advance.' Patsy paused before she dropped her bombshell. Larry seemed all softened up by her proposals and she felt now was the right time. 'Of course, I would want my dress handmade. Nothing off the peg. I was thinking about that beautiful wedding house in Paris. I think I would like it made there.' She paused.

'Paris! Why do you need to go to Paris for a wedding dress? For Christ's sake Patsy, can't you do something simple for a change? There are loads of wedding shops here; surely you can go to one of those,' he snapped.

'No! If I am to get married, it's in a dress I choose. I want a Parisian handmade dress, is that so bad? It's my wedding and I want it to be right for me! It's okay for you blokes, all you need is a suit, but everyone wants to see the bridal dress.' She pouted. She knew she was making her point, but Larry didn't like the idea of her going to Paris.

'We could go together Patsy. Spend a weekend in Paris. It might be good for us?'

This was what Patsy had anticipated him saying. 'What? You want to see my wedding dress before we're married? Are you joking?'

Her indignant manner shocked Larry and he put his fork down and sat back. 'No, no, Patsy, calm down. I never said that. I just can't see why you need to go to Paris when there are a million shops here and online that you can get one from.'

'For fuck's sake Larry, you will have me going to the local charity shop soon to see if there's a bargain. You've blackmailed me into getting married, so at least let me have the wedding I want. Give me something to look forward to,' she snapped. She couldn't help herself any more. She needed to get it off her chest.

Angry and red faced, Larry picked up his plate and threw it at the wall. 'So you don't love me then? You don't want to marry me really. If it wasn't for that letter, you would walk away and I would be a distant memory, is that right? All I can say Patsy, is that you must be shitting yourself with guilt. You're up to your neck in it. Fine, go to fucking Paris and spend a fortune; it makes no difference to me just as long as you're there on the day, or I guarantee the police will be knocking at your door, you murdering bitch!'

Although shocked at his harsh words, Patsy was glad that at last the gloves were off. Larry had made it perfectly clear what he thought of her. Murdering bitch? Now that was an idea...

Composing herself, she picked up her glass of wine. 'I'm innocent Larry. I have murdered no one, and if that is the case, why do you want to marry me? What do you hope to achieve? Don't tell me... I'm the golden goose and you want your own practice. But you will never be Nick; it takes more than money and stature. It takes class and style and you have neither!' Picking up her glass, Patsy threw the contents at him.

Coughing and spluttering, Larry rubbed his face with his shirt. 'If you're so innocent, why are you going through with it?'

'Because I don't know what trumped-up prosecution you have made against me. I'm no prize Larry and I am not flattered. If it's a cash settlement you want, why don't you just ask?'

'I love you Patsy, and you said you loved me. Two people who love each other usually do get married, don't they? Why are you being so unreasonable?' He really didn't understand why she didn't want to be with him. He was deluded. Patsy's blood ran cold. He was crazy, because he felt justified in what he was doing. The very thought of staying with him made her skin crawl. Larry was manipulative and downright evil. Why had she not seen past this façade earlier?

Calmly, she smiled. 'I will book to go to Paris next week.' Suddenly she didn't feel safe around him.

'Let's have an early night Patsy, start again. We always seem to be arguing these days. I love you, I've missed you. Hopefully once we're married you will stop all of this running around you've been doing lately. Delegation is the key, and then we can spend more time together.' With each word he spoke, Patsy cringed. Talk about having your wings clipped.

Suddenly, there was a bang at the door and the sound of footsteps coming down the hallway. Patsy looked up at the ceiling and thanked God. She knew instantly who it was.

'Dad, are you in the kitchen?' Larry's son Paul shouted.

Flustered and taken unawares, Larry jumped out of his seat to meet Paul at the kitchen door. 'Mum's going out tonight, so I've been told to come around here. Is that all right?'

Larry's weak smile betrayed his feelings. Gone was his night of passion with Patsy that he had planned.

Patsy stood up, beaming, her mood changed. 'Actually boys, if you're having a boys' night, I might just slip off home. You two enjoy your evening, and we'll speak tomorrow.' Within an instant, Patsy ran upstairs and changed into her clothes. She couldn't believe her luck and vowed to put something on the church dona-tion plate the next time she passed one. Almost skipping down the driveway, Patsy waved her goodbyes and got into her car.

* * *

'Where do we stand Angus? I need to know.' Her heart in her mouth, Sheila had taken two mugs of tea into the lounge and put one in front of Angus and sat down.

All afternoon he had been polite and acted normally in front of the girls, but now they were alone and he still wasn't angry. She had expected him to hit the roof, but his silence was somehow even worse.

'I'm not angry Sheila, I'm disappointed. Disappointed that you don't trust me. I always had some kind of idea that you worked for Patsy in some form or other and that possibly it wasn't always legal. What I didn't realise is that she is the king pin around these parts, isn't she? This is not a world I'm used to Sheila. I know I'm not a handsome man, I know I'm not everyone's cup of tea, so I was flattered and happy with you and our little family, but you have lied to me all this time, which makes me wonder if you have lied about your feelings about me?' For a huge man, his voice was soft and gentle, which made Sheila feel worse.

'I love you, Angus. I never lied about that. You're the only man that has ever looked after me. As for Patsy, she gave me the opportunity to get out of the slums and make a life for myself and the girls. She is like my sister Angus and yes, she has fallen into this Godfather role, but not of her own doing, it just sort of happened and then spiralled out of control. You were there the other night when I needed you, and there is no one else I could trust the way I trust you. If you want to end our relationship I fully understand and I appreciate you not grassing me up. After all, you could go to the police and tell them all that happened that night. It's your call, Angus.' Sheila couldn't stop the tears from falling. For the first time since she had met Angus, she realised just how much she loved him. Now she was on the verge of losing him, her heart was breaking. Snot ran down her nose and she rubbed it with her sleeve.

Angus pulled off a piece of kitchen roll and handed it to her. 'I'm here, aren't I? But I really don't know what to do. I feel numb. My Sheila and the mafia boss. Seeing you hold that gun, I realised it wasn't the first time you had used one. You knew exactly what you were doing. Although, I must say, a part of me is impressed. And I am very impressed by your loyal friends. Your old estate may be the dregs of society, but I see now it's full of good people who look out for each other and make a living any way they can. You're lucky. I have never had anyone like that... until now.'

'So, are you staying Angus? Staying with me and the girls? They love you, you know.' Sheila felt nauseous. She didn't know what to do to make this right.

Angus took a sip of his tea. His face was grim and he searched his short vocabulary for the words he needed. He was tired of loneliness and seeing and hearing all of his colleagues going home to their families. Over the last few months, he'd been able to talk about his family and what they were doing. For once he had felt like the 'in crowd'.

'Tell me what I can do to fix it, Angus. I will do whatever you want, cross my heart.' Sheila genuinely and desperately wanted Angus to stay, but it had to be his choice.

Angus scanned the room for ideas. 'What I want Sheila is for us to start again. I should have realised the first time we met, and you wanted that car crushed, that something wasn't right, but I'm a giant oaf with no brains, aren't I?'

'Yes and no,' Sheila confessed. 'You are a giant with a big bushy beard. And you're innocent to my lifestyle because you had proper parents and a good childhood. Mine was shit. You're my gentle giant, without a bad bone in your body. Tell me what I can do to make things right!' Sheila cried. Her body was wracked with sobs and she sat beside him on the floor and laid her head on his knee.

'You can do two things for me Sheila if you want to make things right between us. Firstly, I want the truth. The whole truth. I know your husband was shot, but I get the feeling that has something to do with your relationship with Patsy. So I want the whole truth.'

Sheila nodded and sniffed. Blowing her nose on the now-wet kitchen roll, she agreed. 'Fair enough, you're not going to like it, but I might as well. What's the second thing?'

'If you're truthful, you have to agree to marry me and if you go away again, I need to know where you are. No more lies. I have no rights if you are killed and those innocent wee lassies in bed are orphaned. We marry and I adopt them properly. I have a good wage coming in, and we don't need any dodgy money coming in to pay the bills. I'm not going to put my foot down Sheila and tell a grown woman how to live her life. I love you, but I worry about what you're getting yourself in to.'

Sheila could hardly believe what she was hearing; somewhere in the dark recesses of her brain she could hardly comprehend that Angus was proposing. 'Are you asking me to marry you, Angus? Is that because you love me or because you want to protect the girls?'

'Both, for my sins. I don't want to lose you, but I know you would choose Patsy above me. You're good friends, as you say, sisters, and I like her a lot. So I suppose I am asking you to marry me, but those are my conditions.'

'And very reasonable they are too Angus. Well, if you're asking me to marry you, you ask me properly on one knee and everything. I've never had that before, I've only ever seen it in movies. I'm going to make us another cuppa and then as requested I am going to tell you the whole sordid truth about me and Patsy.'

Sheila almost skipped to the kitchen. She couldn't believe what Angus was saying. He was staying and he wanted to marry her; more to the point, he wanted to adopt the girls. This was the only man in her life who hadn't served a prison sentence, was off his head on drugs or turned up after being held in custody all night. She had never known this happy-family status. Angus made her feel different, like an important woman in his life. Not some prostitute that sold her blow jobs in graveyards to make ends meet. That had been another woman completely. She had almost forgotten about her. These days, she didn't have bleached blonde hair with black roots. It was dark and shiny, hanging around her shoulders. Her skirts weren't up to her arse any more to get custom.

While waiting for the kettle to boil, more tears ran down her face, only these were happy ones. She couldn't believe how lucky she was. She was the luckiest girl alive. Walking back into the lounge, she saw Angus on one knee holding out a box. Stunned, she put down the mugs. She didn't dare look at the box and couldn't take her eyes off him. Rubbing her red, tear-stained eyes again, she smiled. 'Well ask me, you big bear.'

'Marry me, Sheila. Marry me and let me adopt our girls.'

'I love you and I will most definitely marry you.' Sheila fell to her knees opposite him and looked at the shiny diamond in the box. She held out her hand and Angus slipped it on her finger.

'I measured it by my little finger,' he said, grinning.

'You're mine Angus, and you're stuck with all three of us forever.' Sheila threw her arms about him, but Angus pushed her away.

'The truth now Sheila, let's clear the air.'

Sheila nodded and moved to sit in the armchair. Angus did the same. They picked up their mugs and Sheila confessed her dealings with Patsy and Fin. She hadn't been sure where to start but, once she had it in her mind, she felt the Diamond reign started with the death of Nick Diamond and the shooting of Steve by Natasha's young son. After Nick's death Patsy had wanted to know what Natasha knew about Nick's secret life. Once or twice she saw Angus's eyes widen with horror, but he said nothing.

'Patsy wants me to go to Paris with her next week to help her choose her wedding dress if that's okay, although, while I am there I might choose something for myself.' She grinned.

'I don't want one of those showcase weddings Sheila, I'd be embarrassed.'

'It doesn't matter where it is, but for once, I am wearing a wedding dress and not my jeans with a borrowed ring from one of Steve's mates in a registry office. We're getting married!' Sheila flung her arms around his neck and kissed him. Strangely enough, she felt better for sharing some of her troubles with him.

She knew Angus wouldn't say anything. He was the strong and silent type.

They made love many times that night, and each time Angus was on top of her, Sheila looked over his shoulder and held up her hand to look at her ring. Her beautiful engagement ring.

14

A BREATH OF FRESH AIR

Sheila made no bones about announcing her engagement. It surprised Patsy that it wasn't on the six o' clock news. Whatever the conversation, it always turned around to her engagement. Patsy and Victoria were pleased for her. If anyone deserved this, Sheila did. Her life had been pretty hard going but she had soldiered on and now it seemed it was her time for happiness.

Sheila turned up at Patsy's flat at the community centre. 'I wanted to speak to you in private. Angus wanted to know the truth about our dealings together.' Sheepishly, she looked up at Patsy. 'I've told him most of it, Patsy. Let's be honest, after what he saw there was no point in being coy, and that was his condition for staying with me – no lies. But I feel bad because I have still lied, haven't I?'

'Not really Sheila. You've told him what he needed to know. I suppose he wants you to stay away from me now? Does he think I'm a bad influence?' Patsy was prepared for the worst. She suspected Sheila had come to tell her that she would no longer be working with her. She steeled herself, while digging her nails into the palms of her hands. She didn't want to lose Sheila's friendship, but she understood her motives. She loved Angus, and she had to make a choice.

Sensing her apprehension and nervousness, Sheila sat down. 'Angus isn't Larry, Patsy. He doesn't want me to stop seeing my friends. He just wants me to be honest and if I have to go away, he wants to know where I am and get no surprises from the police telling him that I'm dead. Nothing's changed, only the lack of cloak and dagger.'

Puzzled, Patsy looked up. It was the first time she'd smiled all day. 'Are you telling me that Angus isn't going to stop you working with me, or us being friends?'

'Well, he'd rather I stocked tins at the local supermarket, but he's accepting me warts and all, and he knows how close we are and to part us would make me unhappy and he doesn't want that. There is a lot I haven't told him Patsy. I couldn't do that. But everything we have done, I told him was in self-defence, and to be fair Patsy it was, well in the beginning...' Sheila trailed off. 'Anyway, how are things with you and Larry? Any change?'

Patsy slammed her fist on the table. 'I can't stand it Sheila; I wish he would actually go to the police. I think it would be a better option than having him puffing and panting on top of me...'

'We're going away tomorrow, Patsy. That will give you time to get yourself together. Breathe some clean air and get away from him. Have a rethink if you want, but don't do anything impulsive. He's the sad bastard...'

Patsy smiled. She would have missed Sheila's company. Even in the worst of times, she made things look brighter.

'Come on Patsy, let's kick our heels in sunny Paris. It's summer, Greek Paul will be in his element. The truffles are growing and the dogs are sniffing them out. The chateau is looking great and we're going on a wee hen weekend. Cheer up, you miserable cow; it could be worse, you could be staying here having to fuck old misery guts!' They both burst out laughing and Patsy felt she could fight the world with Sheila on her side.

'Indeed Sheila. I was thinking of asking Victoria to come with us. Maybe Maggie would be up for it, too? God knows she deserves a break. She drops everything to help us out. Let's make this holiday count.'

'Have you heard about Fin? They are ready to discharge him so he'll be coming home soon Patsy. Maybe then you will get all the answers you wanted about what happened between him and Freddie?' said Sheila.

'Ah.' Patsy drummed her fingers on her chin, a mischievous look in her eyes. 'For the moment, I am leaving Fin in the capable hands of Janine. Let's leave them to it.' Patsy giggled. 'You never know, Sheila, she could make a silk purse out of a sow's ear.'

'I doubt that Patsy; Christ, she has her work cut out for her. The lads in Glasgow won't believe Fin has a girlfriend he doesn't have to blow up first,' she laughed. 'But Fin's a good man. I know he has more front than Selfridges, but underneath he has a good heart and he's much smarter than people think.'

'Right, Sheila.' Standing up, Patsy walked towards her. 'If you can bear to prise yourself away from amorous Angus, get your bags packed, we're going to Paris, and who knows what will happen!'

Sheila jumped with excitement and clapped her hands together. 'I can't wait to show off my ring to all those Frenchies.'

Patsy rolled her eyes at the ceiling, almost feeling sorry for anyone they bumped into. They were going to see nothing of Sheila but her hand, and of course how Angus went down on one knee, but Patsy was happy that Sheila had found not only happiness but peace. If anyone deserved a bit of normality in their life, it was Sheila.

* * *

Everyone was in high spirits as they boarded the aeroplane for Paris. It felt like a work's outing. Sheila sat beside Patsy. 'Well did you have to appease Larry last night with a parting gift?'

'Sheila,' Victoria snapped, embarrassed, 'people are listening.'

'This is business class Victoria, we're not all squashed together in economy.' Feeling light-hearted and laughing, Sheila stood up and addressed the other passengers. 'Who wants to listen to stories about my friend Patsy's sex life, or rather the lack of it?' she shouted.

The other passengers laughed. Some shouted out, 'I do,' and others just smiled at Sheila's brashness.

'Sit down, Sheila, you've had too much champagne,' Patsy whispered.

'There is no such thing as too much champagne Patsy, and we're on holiday. Chill out a little bit, let's have some fun.' As the hostess walked by with a tray of champagne, Sheila held out her hand and took another one off her tray. 'Here's to fun!' she toasted. Getting herself comfortable, she nudged Patsy with her elbow. 'Well, was it okay then?'

'I told him I was on my period so he settled for a blow job; at least I didn't have to look at him.' Patsy grinned.

Sheila laughed and held up her hand for the hostess. Picking up another glass of champagne, she handed it to Patsy. 'Here, lassie, it will take the taste out of your mouth.' She laughed. Victoria and Maggie looked at each other and shook their heads, but they also started to laugh.

* * *

The long drive to the chateau was pleasant as the sun shone. Patsy had asked Sheila to organise a rental car and she had, but it wasn't what any of them expected. She had ordered a black sports car with pink leather interior. The roof was down, and the breeze ran through their hair. For once Patsy felt free. Free of all responsibility. This was her holiday and what other way to spend it but with good friends. She also felt Sheila was using it as her hen weekend before she married Angus, which was absolutely fine by all of them.

As Patsy drove along the long, winding country roads, with their green fields on either side of them and the long hedgerows before them, she felt the sun was playing tricks on her. Lifting her sunglasses slightly, she looked across into the distance. What she saw stunned her. 'Look Sheila look!' she shouted.

'At what?' she asked. Patsy pointed into some fields as they sped past them. 'What am I supposed to be looking at, Patsy? I can only see green fields.'

'There was a man on a horse; well, I think it was a man, but it was so far away, I can't be sure,' Patsy stammered, feeling stupid at the way she had shouted out. Many times, she had thought back to that fateful day when she had been in the car crash and she'd been rescued by the man on the white horse.

Patsy looked in the rear-view mirror behind her. All she could see was empty fields and her heart sank. She didn't know why, but something was niggling at the back of her mind.

They had decided to stay at the cottage near the chateau like the last time and had telephoned ahead to Paul to let them know they were coming. He was there to greet them. Instantly, Patsy could see the change in him. He'd caught the sun, which made him look swarthier, but he looked happy and content. The worry lines seemed to have left his face.

He couldn't stop talking and as they walked in; they could see he had prepared a ham salad buffet with crusty bread. He told them all about the building works and how they should come and see the chateau as soon as possible. He then went on to tell them about the truffles. They all sat down at the wooden kitchen table, while Maggie, in time-old fashion, put the kettle on.

'And what about your restaurant Paul; is that nearly ready yet?' Seeing Paul nod, Patsy smiled. 'Good, well, if people are crazy for our truffles, they will enjoy you cooking them even more, won't they?'

Paul nodded his appreciation and stood in the doorway of the cottage, his huge bulk almost blocking the sunlight. He liked the way Mrs Diamond spoke to him; she made him feel like a human being.

'We're a little tired at the moment Paul, and want to freshen up. Would it be okay if we came and looked at your handywork tomorrow? I don't mean to put you off, but it's been a long dusty drive and I want to give all of your hard work my full attention.'

Paul beamed a happy smile. 'No problem, Mrs Diamond, no problem at all,' he gushed, 'everything will be ready for inspection as soon as you're ready.'

As Maggie poured the tea, she smiled. 'Well, France certainly agrees with him. I never knew he could smile.'

'So, what are our plans while we're here – any agenda?' Victoria asked as she sipped her tea.

Sheila couldn't hold back her excitement. 'Well Vicky lassie, we need to pop into Paris, the big city of romance, and buy a couple of posh frocks. That Milieu lot are having a ball and we're invited. And supposedly, Patsy is looking at wedding dresses, but we'll say no more about that. We don't want to spoil our holiday.'

'I take it myself and Maggie aren't invited to this ball, then? When is it?' asked Victoria.

Patsy shook her head. 'Come if you want Victoria; that lot know you are my family and friend.' Patsy looked up at Maggie. 'Do you fancy it, Maggie? What's a couple of extra people at a ball?'

'It's not really my thing,' Maggie replied, 'but while we're here, there are a couple of things I would like to see in Paris while you're looking at dress shops.'

Curious, Patsy said, 'That sounds intriguing Maggie. What have you got in mind? Do tell.' Patsy liked the idea that at last Maggie felt at ease with expressing her own wishes and not standing on the side-lines. Mischievously, she did wonder if Maggie didn't want to come because she would have to wear something other than her cardigan!

Frowning, and slightly embarrassed, Maggie put her teacup down. 'That Louvre place is in Paris, isn't it? I wouldn't mind going there to see that Mona Lisa and taking a look at the Eiffel Tower.'

Smiling, Victoria agreed. 'That sounds lovely Maggie. Would you mind if I joined you or would I be intruding on your privacy? I also want to go to the Chanel shop.'

'I'd like that Victoria, what a lovely day out. I would be glad of the company, thank you.' Maggie smiled.

Patsy nodded; it seemed everyone had their plans, and it was good to hear. Listening to all of their days out reminded Patsy that she had a day out planned for herself, too. She would solve her mystery once and for all and drive up to the road where she had her accident and hopefully stop it haunting her. 'Well, that all sounds great. Anything special you would like to do Sheila?'

'I just want to go into the shops. Proper shops with designer labels. People waiting on me like I am not the scum of the earth and clothes that don't have a charity shop label. I never dreamed I would be in Paris choosing posh frocks; it's like a parallel life!' She laughed and took a bite out of her crusty bread.

* * *

They all rose early as the sun shone through the blinds and the smell of the roses in the gardens let off a perfume of their own. Standing barefoot in her red satin dressing gown, Patsy opened the cottage door and looked out at the flowers and the fields and the long driveway that stretched up to the chateau. Exhaling, Patsy felt at one with the world. The sun warmed her face as she stepped out and the ground felt warm under her feet. Pushing Larry to the back of her mind so as not to spoil her morning, she could hear a noise inside the kitchen.

Wandering back in, Victoria handed her a cup of coffee, looking concerned. 'You look miles away Patsy. Almost daydreaming. Anything I can help you with love?'

'No thank you Victoria, I'm fine. I'm just musing. This is a beautiful place and it smells of summer and fruits; no wonder Paul looks so well. I'm going to sit out here for a while and drink in the ambience, but we must all go to the chateau and see it after breakfast.'

Sheila stumbled into the kitchen with her pyjamas on. 'For Christ's sake, those bloody dogs. They woke me up at 5 a.m. barking and those blokes didn't help shouting from their trucks. Look, I've bags under my bloody eyes!' she moaned and slumping into a chair, grabbed the coffee pot.

Maggie smiled at Victoria. 'Those dogs barking means truffles doesn't it, and truffles mean money!'

'Well said Maggie. That means they've found something and that means money for us. So firstly we must go and see Paul, but after that we will drive into Paris.'

Satisfied, Patsy excused herself to shower. She didn't want to say anything to the others, but she wanted to be alone to drive past that field. It was like a magnet pulling her back there.

As they all drove up to the chateau, none of them could hide their feelings. They were in awe of the place. The hedges outside had been dull and unkempt under Karen Duret's hand, but Paul had had them ornamentally shaped into balls. They were awesome.

Inside the chateau, the cool shade of the marbled hallway greeted them, making them shiver for a moment. The huge chandelier hanging from the ceiling with its many crystals cast different colours on the beige walls. Slowly they walked down the hallway, taking in their beautiful surroundings.

Hearing them, Paul rushed forward. 'Mrs Diamond, you're here.' He beamed, throwing his arms in the air, and led the group through the chateau. The winding staircase in the hallway led up to numerous en-suite bedrooms, each with their own unique name. Paul looked at them all. 'The French builders came up with the names. Their supervisor has been magnificent with all of the added touches. Come into the ball room. It has been extended on the back. It would be ideal for a wedding and it leads onto the porch outside near the lawn,' Paul explained. 'I will show you the swimming pool, too. Your French friends insisted on it. It's in the shape of a number eight. Renting this out for functions will make you a fair packet, Mrs Diamond. Then, of course, there is the kitchen. It has everything a chef could ever want and again' – Paul hung his head a little – 'your French friends have given me some French cooking assistants to help with local delicacies. We have been practising but it's nothing I can't get the hang of.'

'My French friends?' Patsy was confused for a moment. She was so taken aback at how much the place had been transformed, she hadn't fully taken in what Paul was saying.

'He means the Milieu,' Sheila whispered in her ear. 'They said they would take an interest in the place and it seems not only their own builders but some of their own chefs as well.' She shrugged. 'At least they haven't undermined you and made them Paul's superiors.'

Without thinking too much about it, Patsy reached up to Paul's huge bulk and kissed him on the cheek. He looked very French with his white apron and blue-and-white checked shirt stretching over his bulky frame. 'You've done a fantastic job Paul. Show me the restaurant.'

Even Victoria let out a gasp when she saw it.

'I've based it on the Savoy in London, Mrs Diamond. I used to work there many years ago...' He trailed off.

'I understand Paul. When do you think we will have out first booking?' asked Patsy.

'We are still adding the finishing touches, but your French friends have already started to advertise it. They said if they have royalty to stay here, that will make others want to follow in their footsteps.'

Confused, Victoria stepped forward. 'I didn't think the French had royalty any more?'

Unexpectedly, Maggie chipped in. 'Not in charge of the country like our monarchy, but there are still bloodlines and they are still royalty, you can't deny that. During the revolution, all their families were guillotined but yes there are some and they are respected in France now.'

Raising their eyebrows, they all turned to Maggie. Sheila spoke first. 'Well Maggie, there is more to you than meets the eye, isn't there?'

'So,' Patsy said nonchalantly, 'my French friends think people will be impressed by a nobleman who isn't recognised in his own country? Well, I suppose they know what they are doing.'

'Well, we've had the tour and the history; can we do some shopping now?' Sheila moaned. She couldn't deny the beauty of the chateau and its huge balconies, with ivy and flowers climbing up the outside of the walls, but Paris and its shops seemed something much more interesting and she was itching to leave. After they waved their farewells to a very proud Paul, Patsy drove off to Paris.

15

A KNIGHT IN SHINING ARMOUR

Sheila sat in a dress shop. She was given a glass of champagne and models paraded the gowns before her. It was fairy land to Sheila. The only problem was that she liked all of them.

Patsy made a face and gave her a knowing look. 'Pick one Sheila, these poor women are walking up and down; they must be tired. This is Louis Vuitton and Hermès, not to mention, Chanel. For the rest we will go to Galeries Lafayette. It's the biggest department store with everything you could imagine.' Patsy had been to Paris many times, but seeing Sheila's delight made it extra special. It was like a child meeting Father Christmas.

'Dior,' said Sheila at last, 'that's the one I want Patsy.' Sheila blushed. She looked almost girlish and starry-eyed. 'Do you think I will look like that model in it?'

'You'll look better Sheila, and I am going to style your hair. You will be a princess in Paris. Even if they aren't recognised by everyone...' Patsy laughed.

Patsy waited while they measured Sheila and layers and layers of material fell to Sheila's ankles. A foggy grey silk tulle was draped over her, with an overlay of scallop-shaped petals, full of pearls and beads, and sequins adorned the bustier top. It was indeed beautiful and almost brought a tear to Patsy's eyes.

'What about you Patsy, what are you going to wear?'

'I'm wearing Vivienne Westwood – a little bit of outrageous glamour for me. Black velvet with a sweep train. Gold embroidery at the bottom reaching up to the waist. I've already seen it and I'm in love with it. The V-neck and the low back means I need a light tanning though.'

'My God, you kept that quiet. Can we get that in Paris?' asked Sheila.

'Sheila, it's Paris and I know exactly where to go. Come on.'

After all the fuss of being measured by many assistants and champagne after champagne, Sheila was quite heady with it all. 'Patsy, I've just heard how much that dress is going to cost – it's a small fortune!'

'You're worth a fortune Sheila; I wouldn't care if it was double. It's worth it to see the look on your face. You will be the belle of the ball. My treat for my sister.' Patsy stroked Sheila's face gently. Never in her life had she had a friend like Sheila. For once in her life, Sheila was serious. There was no flippant remark or joke only a tear in her eye after Patsy's sentiment.

Bags and bags of shopping later and a lunch sat out on the streets of Paris made it a special day until Sheila stated the obvious. 'Aren't we supposed to be looking at wedding dresses, Patsy?'

Gulping the last of her wine down, Patsy smiled. 'Indeed. Which means I will have to come back to Paris for a fitting. What will Larry know if it's from Paris or Primark. Since when was he a designer? Don't worry, I will come up with something. Come on, there is somewhere I need to be.'

Puzzled, Sheila picked up her new Chanel bag. 'Where are we going?'

'On a mission. We've done what you want, now it's my turn. It's something that's been bothering me, but I want you to keep quiet about it.'

'This sounds intriguing, but I feel I know what it is. It's that white horse business, isn't it? I saw your face the other day. Are you okay?'

'I want to go down that other road where I crashed. I just need to look.'

'At what? I don't understand. But if you want to go, then I am going with you.'

Patsy couldn't drive quick enough, even though Sheila told her to slow down, especially after they'd had a couple of glasses of wine. Trying to find her way, Patsy drove up and down country roads, miles away from the road to the chateau. As she drove along some open fields, she suddenly spotted a white horse and her heart skipped a beat. 'That's it, Sheila. The white horse.'

Bewildered, Sheila let Patsy go on her wild goose chase. She had been talking about this for a while now, but obviously she needed to prove to herself that it wasn't a dream.

Patsy stopped the car in a layby. 'Look Sheila, there he is.'

Sheila looked up towards the sunset; in the middle of it was the silhouette of a man on a white horse. He was riding fast and shouting for the horse to go faster. His shoulder-length black hair flew back in the evening breeze. It was almost picturesque with the sunset behind him.

They both turned and stared at each other, neither sure what they had just seen – it was like something from a novel. 'Come on, we're following them.' Without a second thought, Patsy drove on, while watching the horse to see where the journey would end.

'Steady on Patsy, this is a dirt track; who knows what's coming around that corner.' Sheila paled when she saw the speed Patsy was driving at. The rider and the horse seemed to slow down and then suddenly disappeared from sight.

'Is there any way we can get closer do you think?' asked Patsy.

Near a hedgerow, Sheila spotted a narrow lane. 'Look down there, Patsy, there's a tractor. If that can get down there, then so can we; follow that path.'

Driving slowly, trying to save her suspension as the car bounced around on the dirt road, they saw a sign. Instantly Patsy smiled and turned to Sheila. 'For crying out loud, why didn't think of that?'

'A bloody stables! It's a riding school or something. Go on Patsy, follow it down. Might as well take a peek while we're here.'

The more their car bounced around, the more Sheila started to panic about them getting stuck, until Patsy stated the obvious that there was a tractor on hand if they did. The huge stable towered above them. People were milling around in uniforms with different horses, guiding them back to their stables with blankets covering their steaming backs. It all seemed very grand.

'Christ, Patsy, this place is cleaner than my house, considering it's full of horse shit!'

'Shhh, they might hear you.'

Behind them they heard galloping, almost like a stampede. As they turned their heads, a white horse with its rider reared up on its back legs, almost like magic. The horse was breathing heavily but Patsy and Sheila looked at the rider as he slipped out of the saddle. He spoke to a groomsman in French, who hurriedly came up and took the horse away.

'My God,' Sheila whispered. 'Well, we've found the Lone Ranger, without the mask. Where the hell is Tonto? Is that your man, Patsy?' Gobsmacked, Sheila couldn't help but stare at the rider.

'Lift your jaw up Sheila; you're spoken for.' They both stared in awe. The man was possibly mid-forties, and his shoulder length, black wavy hair clung to his forehead with sweat and the heat of the day. The white shirt he was wearing was unbuttoned, almost to his stomach, displaying a healthy tan and a hairy chest. He was panting, but laughing with the groomsman, as he slapped the horse's backside.

'He can slap my arse any day... Okay Patsy, just window shopping, there is no harm in that but he is gorgeous. Christ, forget the Lone Ranger, its Antonio Banderas as Zorro.'

'Antonio is Spanish, Sheila, but I'm pretty sure by that accent he's French,' sighed Patsy. 'I'm sure that is the man who pulled me from the car. I'm sure of it, Sheila,' she stressed. 'I just have to find out why he never let himself be known. Surely, even in these parts, he would be classed as a good Samaritan. The man saved my life.' Patsy undid her seatbelt.

'Where are you going?' asked Sheila.

'I just want to satisfy my curiosity. I thought I was going mad, but he's real.' The more Patsy looked at the man walking around the stables talking to people, flashbacks of that fateful day came back to her. It was that man, she was sure of it.

Sheila shrugged and craned her neck to look around. 'Christ, where has he gone now? Maybe he is Zorro,' she laughed, trying to make light of the situation. 'Well, he can only have gone into one of those stable. There isn't much else around here, is there.'

'Are you coming Sheila?' Patsy asked. She didn't care whether Sheila did or not. She was impatient to meet this man, though, to be honest, even she didn't know what she was going to say.

'I'll sit this one out and look after the car. Be careful; if you need me shout or something,' Sheila said, but it was too late, Patsy was already marching ahead, putting her head over the tops of the stables to see if she could see her mystery man.

Patsy wandered around; each stable had horses in their stalls, but she couldn't see the man anywhere. Her curiosity was roused by the sound of running water. Walking deeper into one stable, she looked around, but couldn't see anyone. She took off her sunglasses and peered into the cool darkness of the stable more closely. Her heart was in her mouth, just waiting for someone to jump out at her, or scold her for being there. But, intrigued, she followed the noise. When she located the source, the sight she saw in front of her made her jaw drop and she found herself almost salivating.

There was her man, stripped to the waist. Spying him unnoticed, her gaze started from the bottom and slowly moved up. Patsy looked at his mud-splashed, now-wet black riding boots that came almost up to his knees. Following on from them were tight black low waisted trousers that were damp and clung to his legs. Patsy felt hypnotised as she watched him, ignorant to her presence, almost bent in half with his head under a running tap in the stable. Mesmerised, Patsy looked on as the water ran down his muscley, statuesque body; his thick black hair flicked back and forth as he swayed his head from side to side underneath the gushing water. Rooted to the spot, Patsy couldn't take her eyes off him. At last, he stood upright, and with his hands pushed his wet hair from his face. The water ran down his back and soaked his trousers even more.

He looked almost naked, and Patsy could see every outline of his shapely body. Her mouth was dry and her heart was hammering in her chest. It was the sexiest thing she had ever seen and she felt like a peeping Tom looking through the keyhole, but couldn't help herself. Patsy could feel her own body tingling as she watched the erotic scene before her.

He picked up a small towel and rubbed it through his hair, until he eventually stopped. Opening his eyes, he saw Patsy stood in the corner, almost hidden behind a haystack. Putting the towel around the back of his neck, he grinned and walked towards her.

Stunned that she had been seen, she nearly tripped over herself, trying to leave.

'I'm sorry,' she stammered. 'I'm in the wrong place.' Her face burnt with shame and embarrassment. She had been caught spying on this man.

'You're English, oui?' he asked as he walked towards her.

Moistening her lips before she answered and blushing to her roots, she nodded. 'Yes. I'm sorry, I think I've come in the wrong way,' she stuttered. Apologising again, she turned to leave.

'Wait, mademoiselle. There is no need to run, I don't bite.' He grinned. 'How long have you been standing there?' Raising one eyebrow, he smiled and took her hand, kissing the back of it. 'Did you like what you saw?' He grinned, teasing her and flashing a perfect set of white teeth.

Patsy felt the urge to reach out and stroke the damp hairs on his chest but resisted. Just watching him had roused feelings in her she didn't know she had. Although, she could sense this man's arrogance. He knew he was handsome and was obviously used to flirting with women and knew the extent of his own sex appeal, but that didn't stop her imagining herself in those muscly, wet arms and running her hands through his mane of black hair. Dismissing it from her mind, she apologised again, ignoring his question. Because the truth was, she had enjoyed watching him innocently cooling himself down half naked under the tap. The way he had thrown his head back as the water ran down his body, soaking his trousers and leaving nothing to the imagination had ignited a need deep inside of her.

'I had a car crash here not too long ago.' Stumbling over her words, Patsy tried giving some kind of explanation as to why she was here.

'That doesn't sound good, but why retrace your steps? What

are you looking for?' The smiling mask fell and he was more serious now.

'I don't know' – Patsy shook her head – 'but I think it was you that dragged me from the car. In fact, I know it was you.' Feeling more assertive, Patsy looked him directly in the eye. That well-chiselled face and those dark eyes seemed to flash in her memory. The slight bits of grey mingled in with the black at his temples made him more attractive. Even though she was looking at her saviour, her mind wandered off into the recesses of her memory. Then it struck, almost like lightning. 'You kissed me, I remember now. You leaned over me and kissed my lips.' Reaching up, Patsy touched her own lips and traced them with her finger. 'It was you, wasn't it?'

The man shrugged. 'Was it? I don't know. But you seem to be sure and that is what matters, isn't it? So, what are you hoping to achieve by retracing your steps with all of these memories?' Frowning, he paused, waiting for an answer.

'I don't know Mr, erm...'

'Philippe, my name is Philippe. And yours?' he asked.

'Patsy, Patsy Diamond.' Still unsure of herself, she held out her hand to shake his. She knew she was right, but he was giving no indication that he remembered her. Surely, you would remember saving someone from a car crash? she thought to herself.

'Well, Phillipe,' she said, 'I think my gut instinct is right, so thank you. I suppose that was what I wanted to say.' She smiled. 'I had better go now; sorry to bother you while you're working. You need to tell your boss to buy a shower and then you wouldn't have to wash in the stables near the horses,' she laughed.

Frowning, Phillipe looked at her for a moment before laughing. 'Yes, my boss. I will tell him what you said. Tell me, do you like to ride Patsy?' The mischievous twinkle in his eye made Patsy smile at his underlying innuendo.

'I don't ride Philippe. Never been on a horse in my life. Maybe you could teach me some time.'

'I would love to teach you to ride. To show you how to mount a horse and squeeze it with your thighs to steer it in the direction you want.' He winked.

Patsy knew he was toying with her, but she liked it. He was as charming as he was handsome and it had been a while since someone had flirted with her in this way. With each grin, there was another innuendo; it was as though they were having two conversations.

'My friend is waiting for me in the car outside,' she explained.

Philippe reached forward and touched her chin, tracing his finger down towards her cleavage. Patsy's passion had reached new heights, and she didn't care about anything else. She desired him, her pulse was racing and her heart was beating fast. This was pure lust and she wanted him. Reaching forward she pulled his head towards her and kissed him.

Instantly, he returned the kiss and it became more ardent as his hands roamed over her body.

'Then, we must be quick,' he whispered in her ear. His hot breath made her tremble and her nipples hardened under his touch.

She unbuttoned her dress, while watching him undo his trousers. She didn't take her eyes off him for a second and was more than ready for him when he laid her onto a haystack and moved between her thighs, thrusting himself into her, making her moan with ecstasy. She clung to his damp body and the nearness of him. Overwhelmed with passion, they writhed in unison. The heady scent of him added to the ambience, making Patsy feel quite lightheaded. She could hardly breathe and gasped for air, wallowing in the force of Philippe. Her body ached and trembled, like a volcano building up inside of her until she could bear it no longer and cried out, as her orgasm seemed to go on forever. With one last thrust, Philippe threw his head back and let out a slow moan. Both of them were panting, trying to gulp air into their lungs. It had been feisty and passionate and over way too soon.

Lying side by side in the haystack as they tried to control their breathing, Patsy closed her eyes, savouring the moment, while trying to compose herself. 'I should go,' she whispered through breaths.

'Your friend. Are they male or female?' he asked.

Turning on her side to face him and leaning on her elbow, she smiled and took a piece of straw out of his hair. 'Does it matter? They will wait, but, for the record she's female.'

'Will you come back?' His voice was low and husky, as he stroked her hair. His huge brown eyes bore into hers, waiting for an answer.

'Probably not. I think I have said my thank you properly.' She grinned. 'Do you want me to come back?' she asked with bated breath, hoping that he did.

'Only if you're passing Patsy, *ma chérie*.' Kissing her hand, he stood up, and started dressing himself. Patsy marvelled at his firm body, but she also felt sad. He hadn't expressed a wish to see her again. She realised it had simply been a spur-of-the-moment thing.

Standing up, she started dressing, feeling almost embarrassed and awkward in the cold light of day. While she dressed, she wondered what had possessed her to do this. But deep down she knew the answer. She'd fancied him the moment she had seen him. His display of eroticism with the water had captured her imagination and turned her on, to such an extent she couldn't stop herself. Every speck of common sense and reasoning had left her in that moment of madness.

Smoothing her hair down, she felt lost for words. 'I have to go,

Bye, Philippe.' She was about to turn when Philippe pulled her back towards him.

'That is not how the French say goodbye after passion.' Sweeping her up in his arms, he kissed her so ardently, she almost felt faint. And when he her let go, she was breathless. 'Au revoir, Patsy.'

Reluctantly she walked away but turned around to take one last look at him. Out in the courtyard, there were people milling around, getting on and off horses. Patsy almost giggled to herself when she saw them, wondering to herself what they would have made of her and Philippe in the haystack if they had walked in!

'Where the bloody hell have you been? I've been in and out of this car. You've been gone ages. Did you find him...?' Sheila slowly took off her sunglasses as Patsy opened the car door. Sensing a difference in her, Sheila knew her gut instinct was right when she saw Patsy's starry-eyed, carefree manner.

'Oh my God, you did, didn't you? Have I been sitting here, while Zorro has been practising his horse riding on you?' She laughed. 'Don't deny it, Patsy. You've got straw in your hair and that stupid grin on your face says, that's the best orgasm I've ever had! I want details Patsy. After waiting patiently, I want to know everything that happened. I've had some quickies in my time, but yours didn't have time for an introduction,' scoffed Sheila disbelievingly.

'His name is Philippe.' Even she had to admit to herself, it was all a bit quick. 'There, we had an introduction.' Patsy grinned. She was bubbling with excitement and couldn't stop herself from smiling.

Sheila grinned. 'Okay then, was he any good? Or is that a stupid question, seeing that dreamy expression on your face?'

'He was fantastic Sheila. Absolutely fantastic; my body hasn't recovered yet. Come on, let's get back; I need a very large glass of wine.'

'You need a shower; you stink of horse. How did you end up having sex with the stable boy that quickly?'

'I don't know, it just happened, and he's not a stable boy, he is very much a man, believe me.' Patsy gave Sheila a knowing look and they both burst out laughing.

'Are you seeing him again? Is he married?' Sheila fired question after question at Patsy who sadly had no answers for her.

'I don't know, we never discussed it. He said if I was passing by, to drop in.' The smile left Patsy's face when she realised how hollow that sounded. It was the brush off she had said to people herself just to get rid of them.

'So will you be popping by then, Lady Chatterley?' pushed Sheila. 'Do we get another chapter?'

'I doubt it. I've had my moment of madness. Found my man on a white horse and proved to you that he existed. He probably does it all the time with tourists, and I was just another easy lay. Albeit it, a very nice experience and I'm an adult. There is nothing more to discuss.'

'Just out of curiosity...' Sheila grinned. 'Apart from riding horses, is he hung like one?'

'For God's sake Sheila, that's disgusting!' Thinking about it brought the smile back to Patsy's face. 'But actually, he is.'

16

DANGEROUS LIAISONS

Victoria and Maggie walked into the cottage the next day, laden with bags and parcels. 'We're back,' shouted Victoria as she struggled through the door. 'Where's Patsy? Is she at the chateau with Paul?'

Tongue in cheek, Sheila lied. 'Oh, she just had some things to pick up and I wanted to stay in, chill out and sunbathe.' She knew exactly where Patsy was and it wasn't at the chateau. She had been itching all morning, trying to find excuses to pop out on her own, until in the end Sheila had burst out laughing, and teased her. 'Patsy why don't you just say you're going for more riding lessons? I take it you're going to accept his invitation to pop by?'

'Oh, bugger off Sheila, I just fancied a drive. I told you yesterday that was just one of those things. He probably won't even remember me; I don't exactly look my best.'

'Go on lassie, have some fun while you can. Let's face it, all you have across the Channel is a blackmailing lawyer awaiting you. Don't let that Philippe's boss find you scaring the horses though!'

Grateful for Sheila's understanding, Patsy almost ran out to her car and within seconds was driving up the winding road to meet her knight in shining armour. When she arrived, she'd gone to the same stable they were at yesterday, but he wasn't there. Disappointed, she walked over to a man brushing one of the horses down. 'I'm looking for Philippe?' she enquired.

The man looked at her quizzically and Patsy could see that he didn't understand English well, but he clearly recognised the name Phillipe. He imitated someone riding a horse and Patsy's heart sank. Phillippe wasn't there and why should he be? He was always out on horseback, and they hadn't made any special arrangements.

Walking back to her car with a heavy heart, she drove back to the chateau. She knew Sheila would laugh or make some jokey comment, but she wasn't in the mood. Phillipe had haunted her dreams and given her a sleepless night.

Driving back along the winding country road, Patsy cursed herself for not making some formal arrangement, but she hadn't wanted to seem too eager. Suddenly she thought she heard her name being called and she looked up. The slight breeze ran through her hair in the open-topped car, and she presumed it was the wind making a noise. At either side of her were hedgerows and she could see nothing but the road in front of her, yet again she heard her name being called. Her heart skipped a beat – racing beside her behind the hedge she could hear galloping! Pulling over, she looked around, but could see no one. Again, she heard her name and knew exactly who it was. Looking around, she didn't know where to go and could only presume she would have to drive back to the stables. But then, as if by magic, she looked around and saw Philippe's white horse flying through the air over the hedge and onto the road. Steering it to come to a halt, he stopped before her.

'I thought it was you,' he panted. Sweat appeared on his brow and the horse was breathing heavily as he soothed it. Patsy stood here mesmerised, her stomach doing somersaults as he jumped off the horse and approached her.

'I just thought I would go for a drive. It's such a beautiful day,' she lied, failing to tell him that she had just been looking for him at the stables.

Taking the horse by the reins, he held his hand out. 'Walk with me; there is a stream nearby and I can give the horse a drink. I think she's earned it, don't you?' He grinned.

Blushing to the roots, Patsy averted her gaze. Taking his hand, they walked around the corner, which was more of a dirt track and not made for cars. Further on, as they entered a field, she saw the stream. Philippe let go of the horse's reins and instantly it trotted towards the cool water.

'I'm disappointed you weren't coming to see me, Patsy.' He grinned and squeezed her hand, while leading her to a nearby tree for shade. Taking her chin in his hand, he kissed her gently. 'You give a man sleepless nights, Patsy,' he whispered and nuzzled her neck.

Trembling at his touch, she placed her arms around his neck in a sweet, passionate embrace. As they tore at each other's clothes and stood naked, shaded only by the tree, Patsy could feel the warm sun on her body. She ached for him and could feel his own arousal. Melting into each other's arms, they made love. This time, it was slow and every fibre of her being tingled as he stroked and teased her body with his hands and tongue. She felt like a volcano about to erupt as he entered her. Her mind spun, and the ecstasy she felt was out of this world. All she could do was moan and gasp with pure pleasure as both of them, hungry for each other's bodies, writhed together until at last her body shook and trembled as she reached her peak.

Afterwards, they lay there in each other's arms, at one with the world and contented. Patsy knew she would remember this

moment for the rest of her life. The warm sun, a handsome
man making love to her in a field as a horse gently lapped up
water from the stream. It was what fantasies were made of.
Nuzzling closer and kissing his arm, she noticed a tattoo on his
shoulder. 'That's a nice tattoo, I didn't notice it before. It's
unusual for a man to have a small flower emblem on his shoulder. Don't they usually have skulls or dragons?' She smiled
contentedly.

'It is the fleur-de-lis; it has a strong cultural and historical
significance in France. The white fleur-de-lis means purity and
the purple which could be a lily or an iris, represents leadership.
Mine is purple on a white background, as you can see.'

'It's pretty, with the three petals shaped like that. Maybe I will
get one for myself.' She smiled and traced her fingers around the
tiny tattoo emblazoned on his shoulder. 'So you're a pure leader
Philippe.'

Lying in his arms, with her head on his chest, all her cares
seemed to disappear.

'So, tell me Patsy, why are you in France?' Philippe asked while
he stroked her hair.

'Just business. I have a chateau we're converting into a restaurant... although,' Patsy faltered, 'I'm supposed to be buying a
wedding dress.' Mentally, she cursed herself for saying that at a
moment like this. What a stupid thing to say. She expected him to
jump up or say something angry, but he didn't. He carried on
stroking her hair soothingly like you would a child.

'You don't sound very happy about it. Aren't women normally
pleased to be buying a wedding dress? You must be very much in
love if you're getting married.'

Again, Patsy cursed herself and waited for the obvious punch
line. Of course, he was going to ask her why, if she was so in love,
she was lying naked in a field with a stable hand. It seemed

incredible even to her. She felt she owed him some kind of explanation, otherwise it didn't seem right.

'Oh, it doesn't matter if I tell you Philippe. We'll probably never meet again after I go home,' she sighed and held him tighter. 'I've done some wrong things lately, some would say bad things. My life has spiralled out of control in one way or another. Stupidly I had an affair with my lawyer; I liked him, don't get me wrong,' she explained, 'but now he is blackmailing me into marriage.'

'Why would he blackmail you? Personally, I only want willing women, not forced ones.'

'Larry doesn't care. He has damning evidence against me that could possibly put me in prison.' Patsy raised her head and looked at him. 'I don't know why I am telling you this I really don't. Sorry...'

'Why apologise? You obviously need to get it off your chest. Is it money he wants? Or you?' he asked. His voice was calm and unemotional. For a moment, Patsy felt his disinterest as though he was listening but dozing off in the sun after their love making. She felt as though she were just talking aloud, trying to sort it out in her mind.

'Both, I suppose. I'm not a poor woman, just a stupid one. I should marry him and make his life hell, but the very idea of it makes me feel sick. I hate the manipulation and he likes the power and control it gives him over me I suppose...' Patsy trailed off, closing her eyes. 'Never mind all that. What matters is the here and now and for now I am happy and content. To be lying with someone who doesn't want anything from me.' Smiling, she kissed his chest.

'Oh, I wouldn't say that Patsy.' Philippe turned towards her and kissed her. Lying her on her back, she felt the strength of his body as he possessed hers, and again, in the warm sunny afternoon, he made love to her, and she savoured every moment of each tender kiss.

'Come swim with me Patsy. Over there in the stream.' Standing up, Philippe pulled her up to meet him.

Confused, Patsy looked around. 'What? You mean in the stream your horse is drinking out of?' She laughed. 'You've got to be joking! What's in there apart from bacteria? No way Philippe, I value my health.'

Ignoring her, Philippe pulled her along until she stood at the side of the water. He stepped forward and waded into the shallow stream. 'It's a spring, a clear stream. Do you think I would poison my horse?'

Nervously, Patsy dipped her toe into the water. It felt warm and as she looked down into it, she could see that it was clear, because she could see the stones and pebbles along the bottom. 'What about fish?' she asked pensively.

Cocking his head to one side and raising one eyebrow, he put his hands in the water, cupping them together he splashed his face with water. 'Where there is water, there is fish. Do you trust me, Patsy?' Holding out his arms, he beckoned her.

She looked into his brown eyes, as they captured hers. 'I don't know why, but I do trust you Philippe. After all, you saved my life once, didn't you?' Patsy waded into the stream until she was waist high. The warm water felt good against her bare skin, and soon Philippe was splashing her playfully. They were laughing and splashing around like children and as he held her in his arms, they kissed. Patsy's head swam with happy thoughts. She had never felt like this before, never. She would never have imagined that she would be swimming naked in a stream in France with a complete stranger; it was wrong, stupid even. She knew nothing about him, but she didn't want to know anything about him that would muddy the waters. For the moment, ignorance was bliss.

This was a mad holiday romance and for a few hours she was plain old Patsy the hairdresser again, free from responsibilities. Philippe's calmness made her feel safe, although she knew Sheila would probably warn her he could be a serial killer!

After they went for a ride on his horse, Patsy said goodbye to him and then hurried home and almost threw herself through the cottage door, much to Sheila's amusement. Almost gasping for breath, Patsy looked around the kitchen. 'Where is everyone Sheila?'

'Taking in what's left of the sun and drinking wine on the veranda. More to the point, where have you been? Sheila laughed. 'I take it you passed by the stables and found him then? Go upstairs and change Patsy, you look a big dishevelled. What have you been doing? Well, apart from the obvious, of course.' Sheila carried on taking a new bottle of wine out of the fridge, while nonchalantly enjoying Patsy's flustered appearance.

'Oh Sheila, we went swimming in a stream and then he took me for a ride on his horse.' Patsy sat at the kitchen table with her head resting in her hands and sighed. 'I've never ridden a horse before, but it was lovely just sitting behind him, holding him. Oh Sheila…' Patsy sighed again.

'Don't, "oh Sheila" me when it all goes tits up lassie and it's home time. You're coming back to earth with a bang, so be prepared,' Sheila warned. As much as she was pleased Patsy was enjoying herself, she was concerned. It would all be over too soon and she would be back to reality with Larry. But the dreamy expression on Patsy's face told her this was something else.

'I'll go and get changed; where did you tell them I've been? Did you make my excuses?'

'Yes, I've covered for you lassie. I thought they wouldn't believe the truth anyway, so I told them you had business in town – will that do?' Sheila looked on apprehensively as Patsy bounced up the stairs to wash and change. There was something different about Patsy, she could see that. She was glowing, but, then all couples glow in the honeymoon period, don't they? Sheila wandered out to the patio area to join the others.

Looking up, Victoria smiled. 'Was that voices I heard Sheila? Is Patsy back?'

'She is, but she's popped upstairs to freshen up. I've brought her a glass out. It looks like she's had a long tiring day,' Sheila remarked, very tongue in cheek.

Each of them basked in the late afternoon sun, and watched as the sun went down. The place was idyllic, and even Maggie agreed it was the perfect setting for a couple to get married, or even spend their honeymoon, which surprised everyone.

Taken aback, Sheila laughed. 'Maggie, I didn't realise you had a romantic side to you.'

Still with her black cardigan hanging over her shoulders, considering how warm it was, Maggie glared at Sheila. 'You don't know how many sides I have to me Sheila, so mind your own business!' she snapped.

Victoria changed the subject by telling Sheila about their travels, until eventually Patsy joined them. 'You look worn out, Patsy. You need to have a day to relax while we're here.'

'Yes, you're right Vicky, I've told her to lie back and put her legs up while she's here. It will do her the world of good.' Sheila cast a furtive glance towards Patsy and they both started giggling.

Seeing that Victoria was puzzled, Patsy nodded. 'I will Victoria, there is no need to worry. It's just nice being here in the sunshine with friends.' Patsy raised her wine glass to toast, 'To friends.' They all echoed her words as they chinked their glasses together.

Maggie shook her head. 'Sheila has been boasting that her evening dress is going to be ready tomorrow afternoon, before you go to that ball tomorrow night. That's impossible! Surely you have to have lots of fittings for these things?'

Patsy swallowed her wine and shook her head. 'You forget Maggie, these are professionals and if you pay the money they will work through the night. Sheila will look the belle of the ball.'

Seeing Sheila's elation, Patsy felt it would be the best money she had ever spent. Just seeing the excitement on Sheila's face made it all worthwhile.

'Well, me and Maggie have also been shopping in Paris. It's not just for you young women, you know,' Victoria scoffed.

Swiftly turning towards Maggie, Sheila couldn't help herself. 'Are you telling me you have bought a new designer black cardigan? Are you going to leave the one you always wear in your will for me when you die!' She laughed.

A wry grin crossed Maggie's face. 'Maybe, maybe not,' she replied secretively and smiled at Victoria.

Patsy's phone burst into life and looking at it, she saw that it was Larry, which made her heart sink. 'You answer, Victoria. Tell him I'm in the changing rooms at a store. He'll believe you.' Seeing Victoria's apprehension, she looked again at her pleadingly. 'Please.'

Doing as she was asked, Victoria gave Patsy her phone back. 'You're going to have to speak to him sometime, Patsy.'

Patsy pulled a face and shook her head. 'No, I don't. Anyway...' She hesitated. 'I've decided to go ahead with Larry's plan B and let him go to the police with his stupid letter. Let them dig Karen up wherever she is. I've made up my mind and I will tell him when we get back to England. I am not hiding any more. It looks like I am frightened, and I suppose,' she argued, 'I was a little at the prospect of jail, but not any more. To be honest, I don't give a fuck! And I've promised myself that I am going to torture him before I kill him with my bare hands. I want to be the last person he sees before he dies. I want to see the fear in his eyes when I point a gun to his head. I want him to beg and cry before me like the coward he is.' Patsy's voice dripped with anger and everything she felt poured out venomously. 'Karma ladies. I believe in karma.'

Everyone around the table went silent and cast a glance at each other.

'Bloody hell lassie, you want a lot don't you!' laughed Sheila trying to break the ice. It was a tense moment, but looking at Patsy's stern face, she could see there was no talking her out of it.

'Well let's not let this spoil our trip, eh? We have our plans, we have sunshine and wine. Let's not let Larry spoil that.' Everyone smiled and nodded at Victoria's wise words.

'Oh, don't worry lassies, Patsy permanently falls into horse shit and comes out smelling of roses,' joked Sheila. Patsy heard her innuendo and burst out laughing. The others did likewise, but only Patsy and Sheila knew the in joke.

* * *

The following morning, Sheila was buzzing. 'We're going to Paris la la la, going to get my dress,' she sang, very much out of tune.

'Well, I hope they don't make you sing for your supper Sheila because you would starve,' snapped Maggie as Sheila got under her feet while she was trying to make coffee for everyone. 'Get out of the way, for goodness' sake.' Maggie brushed her off playfully as Sheila stepped forward and kissed her on the cheek just to annoy her a little more. Victoria caught Patsy's eye and smiled. They had never seen Sheila so excited, not even about her ring from Angus.

Although Patsy kept looking at the clock and wondering to herself if she could maybe slip away for an hour, she didn't have an excuse and she didn't want to offend Sheila. She just wanted to see Philippe once more before they left for England, but she knew it was impossible.

As though knowing what she was thinking, Sheila turned serious. 'Patsy, do you mind if we go earlier just in case they do need to make any adjustments? I don't want to leave it too late.'

Patsy looked at her under lashes and frowned. 'They have all of your measurements, Sheila. These are professionals, but if that's what you want?' She shrugged. 'It's only 10 a.m. and we don't have to pick it up until 2 p.m. but, I understand. You want it to be right.'

The wink and smile that Sheila gave her confused Patsy slightly, and for the moment she wasn't sure what to think as she got ready.

'You two ladies don't mind if I get Sheila from under your feet, do you?' Patsy asked.

Maggie and her sharp tongue were the first to answer. She liked bantering with Sheila, even though it always sounded like an argument. 'For God's sake, get her out of here, she is doing my wee head in. You'd think she never had a dress before!'

'I agree.' Victoria smiled. 'Put Sheila out of her misery and take her to see her dress. I only pray that they have finished it.' Victoria put her hands together in prayer.

Once Patsy started driving, Sheila told her to pull over. 'Right, Patsy. You have one hour to go and find your stud. One hour only, do you understand? No swimming, no horseback and dewy-eyed looks. I don't know when you will get the chance again, but I intend to enjoy myself tonight and I am not going to be able to do that if you have a miserable face on you. So, go on, drive up there and I will wait in the car. You only have one hour,' Sheila repeated and showed her watch to Patsy to confirm the time.

A beaming smile spread across Patsy's face. 'Thank you, Sheila. Let's just say if I find him, it's one for the road, eh?'

'I'm an old romantic lassie, but if you're determined to let Larry go to the police, it could be the last wee shag you have in a long time. So enjoy it Patsy, with my blessing. In fact, give him one for me!' She laughed.

Patsy's heart raced as she ran to the stables; this was her last goodbye, and with all her heart she hoped he was there. She put her head around the door to the stable she had found him in before and to her relief he was there.

The smile that greeted her made her heart beat faster. 'I wondered if you would come *chérie*. I've been waiting.' Standing up, Philippe opened his arms to her.

As they embraced, their lips met and their passion for each other took over. Instantly they were tearing at each other's clothes, engulfed with passion. 'I only have an hour, Sheila is waiting in the car,' Patsy whispered as he nuzzled her neck.

'Patsy, believe me, I have waited for you since yesterday; I doubt it will take that long.' He smiled and rubbed his nose against hers, making her heart race. And as he kissed her and led her to their haystack, Patsy trembled with excitement.

17

AN EVENING TO REMEMBER

When Pasty looked across at Sheila's transformation, she almost gasped. Before her stood a totally different woman. She looked elegant in her gown and her glowing tan heightened the colour, making her look glamorous. Such a world away from Sheila from Thistle Park estate. It was true: clothes certainly did make the man, or woman, in this case.

'You look absolutely beautiful Sheila. That was definitely the right dress for you, though God knows how we're going to get all those layers of underskirts in the car!'

Sheila did twirl after twirl in front of the mirror, gazing at herself. 'I don't give a shit Patsy. For once in my life, I look like a princess. I will never forget this moment and look at my hair. Thank you, Patsy, thanks ever so much.' Sheila walked towards her and held both of Patsy's hands. 'I would hug you, but I can't get close enough.' A tear almost brimmed on Sheila's lashes, and she sniffed hard to hold back the tears. 'Thank God I am wearing waterproof mascara.'

Victoria and Maggie walked in and the looks on their faces said it all.

'Now that was the look I was hoping for lassies.'

'My goodness Sheila, you look amazing!' exclaimed Victoria. Even Maggie managed a smile.

'Where have you been hiding yourself all of these years, Sheila?' she said. 'You deserve this. Every woman should have their moment, and this is yours.'

'You don't look so bad yourself Maggie. I do declare there are sequins on that black cocktail dress of yours, and I never knew you had legs. You're always in black trousers to match your cardigan.'

Blushing slightly, Maggie smiled. 'As I say, us women are entitled to their one moment in their life and this is mine.' Maggie wore a black cocktail dress, with black sequins dotted here and there, with matching court shoes. Patsy had spent hours doing all of their hair and to her own satisfaction, she knew no one could have done any better. She had even encouraged Maggie to put some make-up on and to wear her usual tied back bun down. No one in Glasgow would have thought it was Maggie.

Victoria wore a pink Chanel suit which highlighted her blondeness. 'When in Paris ladies, you have to wear Chanel.' She twirled, much to their laughter and enjoyment.

'Let's take a photo of us all, so we never forget it, lassies.' Sheila picked up her mobile and set the timer as they all stood there in their glory. 'I have to send one to Angus; he will never believe me if I describe it.' She laughed.

Hearing a car horn, Victoria looked out of the window. 'That's our car Maggie. Come on, get your sequined bag,' she emphasised, more for Sheila's ears than anyone else's and winked.

'I've ordered us a car, too, and it should be here any minute Sheila.'

'Thank God for that, but did you have to order such a big one? My dress isn't that big.'

Puzzled, Patsy looked out of the window to see a large white Rolls Royce pulling up outside the door. A chauffeur in uniform got out and opened the doors.

'I didn't order that...? I ordered a taxi. Who is that for?' Confused, Patsy walked to the door. 'Are you waiting for someone?'

The chauffeur frowned. 'Mrs Diamond, is that you?'

Dumbfounded, Patsy turned towards Sheila and shrugged. 'I swear I didn't order that.'

Sheila gave her a knowing look. 'It must be those Frenchies. Isn't it great to have friends in high places? Come on.'

* * *

'Everyone get down on the floor and put your hands above your heads!'

Four armed men wearing balaclavas ran into the Glasgow bank, shouting their orders and waving their shotguns in the air. The bank was nearly empty, only half a dozen people were in there, and it would be easy to control this crowd. One of the gunmen fired his gun into the air and shot at the cameras in the far corners of the bank. Another one ran towards the cashier's desk.

'Don't even think of pressing that button and raising the alarm for the police or you will be the first to die.'

Shocked and panic-stricken, everyone turned from what they were doing and saw the masked men.

'Down on the floor and let me see those hands.'

Afraid and shaken, people lay face down, although their eyes looked up to see what was happening. The gunman at the desk barked his order for the cashiers to move away from their desks and put their hands on their heads. Wide eyed with fear, the two female cashiers stood up and did as they were told. The gunman shot the plastic screens between them, making the two cashier fall to the floor, trembling and crying.

'Don't shoot us please,' one pleaded as tears rolled down her face, 'I have two children. Please don't shoot mister.'

'Do as I say, and no one will get hurt. Do you understand?'

Nodding their heads, they sat with their backs to the wall their knees almost touching their chins and their hands above their heads. One of the gunmen jumped over the counter. 'What is the code for the cash register?' he shouted to them.

Hearing the noise, the manager came running from the back room with other bank workers. Looking around his bank, he saw everyone on the floor, shaking and crying. Seeing the blasted screen and his two cashiers trembling in a corner, he paled and looked at the men in balaclavas. 'Take what you need and leave.'

The gunman ordered him to start emptying the cash register and to fill the bag he threw at him with money. 'Get on with it and don't be a hero. The cemetery is full of them. I presume the police are on their way?' the gunman shouted, knowing full well that before the manager had appeared, he would have alerted the police.

One gunman stood beside the doors keeping watch and looking around with his gun in his hand, while another walked around the crowded floor. Larry lay on the floor and raised his head to look up at the gunmen. Shaken and shocked by the events, Larry spotted a mobile phone that a woman in front of him must have dropped in her haste to drop to her knees. Slowly he moved his hand along the floor to reach it, while watching the gunman walk around them with his back to him.

'Target!' one of them shouted, and suddenly a shot rang out a Larry was shot in the back of the head. Nearby, people screamed in panic and cried out as they saw the blood and tried moving away from him. The gunman walked up to Larry and kicked his body over so that he was flat on his back. His face was barely recognisable and his brains were almost hanging out. The carpet was crimson.

Frightened, people lay on the floor trembling with fear but dared not move or speak for fear of the same thing happening to them. The gunman ran his hands through Larry's jacket pocket and picked up his briefcase. 'Time to go,' he shouted. Police sirens could be heard in the distance and the four gunmen quickly backed away while pointing their guns at the crowd of people. Running out of the bank they jumped into an awaiting car and sped off.

Moments later, armed police burst through the doors. Each of the police squad ran around the bank, just in case any of the robbers were still there.

'All clear,' they shouted. The bank manager almost collapsed as they ran towards him.

Ambulances and other police were swiftly behind, running in and helping the victims. Everyone was crying and panicking as they were helped to their feet. Then the police saw Larry and shouted the ambulance crew over to cover him. A nearby woman was covered in Larry's blood and fainted.

One of the policemen looked over at the manager. 'What did they get away with?'

'Just this cash register, maybe a few thousand, nothing more,' he stammered. He could barely string a sentence together and sat down.

The policeman could see the robbers hadn't taken much. Once the detectives arrived, the policeman walked up to them. 'It looks like a bungled robbery, although one man is dead. They didn't get much; only one cash register was opened.'

'But someone has been murdered officer, and that doesn't

make it a bungled robbery in my book.' Looking at the police officer with distaste, he walked away from him and spoke to a colleague. 'Forensics are on their way; don't let anyone touch anything and get the names of those people in the ambulances outside. I want to interview all of them. Do we have any idea who the dead man is?'

'Someone thinks he is a lawyer from around here. We will check his identification later and let the family know. It looks like whoever did this had been watching the place, because the place was almost empty.'

Nodding, the detective in charge walked away and looked around at the bank. It had been shot to pieces. Cameras were hanging from the walls and the ceiling had bullet holes in. The screen between the cashier's desk had been shot and there was a dead man with his brains blown out, but hardly any money had been taken. It was clearly amateurs with guns in their hands frightened to death themselves, possibly even a few drugged-up men from the local Glasgow estates. He would soon find them, he mused to himself. Even he doubted that they had intended to murder anyone...

* * *

'For crying out loud Patsy, my ringlets are drooping. We have been driving for two hours! I thought you said it was a local hotel?' Sitting in the back of the Rolls Royce that had been sent for them, Sheila was starting to get irritated.

'I don't know Sheila. What's the name of the place again? Let me look it up.'

'Carrots or Carrie.' Sheila fought hard to remember, but couldn't.

'Carreaux,' the chauffeur interrupted them and pointed as they turned into a driveway.

Patsy and Sheila both stared wide eyed and sat forward in their seats. They couldn't believe it. 'I thought you said it was a hotel, Patsy!' Sheila exclaimed. 'Oh my God, it's a stately home!'

'I presumed it was a hotel; where else would they have a ball?' Confused, Patsy tapped the chauffeur on the shoulder. 'Are you sure this is the right place? It looks like a palace.'

Nodding his head, the chauffeur continued driving down the long winding driveway. Every few yards there were lit torches nearly a mile high in the sky lighting the way. The outside of the house in all its splendour was lit up. They both sat there stunned, staring at the beautiful stately home before them. Other cars were pulling up and stopping before the long winding steps up to the main doors, where two doormen were stood in full livery awaiting the guests.

'Oh my God Patsy, I think I am going to faint,' Sheila whispered. 'What if I use the wrong knife and fork? Look at all those people and those beautiful gowns. I have never seen so many fur coats in one place.'

'Well, Cinderella, you have your gown and you're going to be the belle of the ball. As for knives and forks, they will just put it down to the fact that you're English,' Patsy laughed, while trying to hide the bubbling excitement inside of her. She was taking it all in her stride, but inside she had never seen or been to anything as grand as this. She was more than impressed.

'I'm Scottish, Patsy!' Sheila said indignantly. 'Here, I've googled it, Carreaux. It doesn't say who owns the house though.' Sheila was hastily scrolling down her mobile when Patsy told her to put it away.

'Pretend like you're used to this, like it means nothing to you. Nonchalance is the key Sheila,' Patsy warned her. 'I think we're being tested to see if we can cope in such surroundings. Well, we can, can't we?' Patsy was determined not to let the surroundings floor her, but Sheila's jaw was still wide open.

'I'm trying Patsy, I really am, but the last time I went into somewhere like this was a stately home exhibition and I had to pay to go in!'

At last, it was their turn for the car doors to be opened by the footmen. Patsy gave Sheila a warning glare and almost glided out of the car first, hoping that Sheila would follow suit.

As they walked through the large wooden doors, a man in a red bolero jacket announced them to the rest of the guests who were stood drinking champagne and entering into the usual small talk. Feeling awkward and embarrassed because they knew no one, they took their proffered glasses and stood to the side, looking around at everyone.

'Do you think Mr Darcy is here?' Sheila muttered under her breath and giggled.

'I know what you mean,' Patsy sighed. 'It does look like that, doesn't it?'

'Mrs Diamond, Sheila, how nice of you to come.'

They both turned around and saw Manne dressed in his tuxedo, followed by the others. In their usual fashion, they kissed the back of Patsy's and Sheila's hands. 'Before we go into dinner, we have something for you Mrs Diamond. You are one of us now and belong to our circle. This will protect you worldwide when you shake the hands with people of influence.' Manne looked at Jules and indicated for him to give Patsy the gift he spoke about. Jules took a leather-bound ring box out of his pocket and handed it over. 'We always wear it on the middle finger of the right hand, Mrs Diamond. If it needs altering, please let us know.'

Hearing the dinner gong, the men took Patsy's and Sheila's arm and walked towards the dining room, which again was huge.

_arge paintings donned the walls and ceilings. Sheila nearly fell
ver as she stared up at the painted ceiling and thankfully Jules
_as there to steady her.

As they entered the dining room, they both stood like statues.
_he dining table was the full length of the room and was filled
_ith silverware and candelabras, including an ice statue of a bird.
_veryone stood behind their chairs, and Sheila was about to pull
_ut her chair when Patsy stopped her. 'Wait,' she whispered.
We're waiting for the host; look at the chairs at the top of the
_able; no one is standing there.' Patsy bowed her head.

Suddenly the man in the red coat that had announced them,
_tood at the door, and called, 'Ladies and gentlemen, Viscount
_hilippe Carreaux and the honourable Lady Adele.'

Everyone turned to see the viscount enter the room. Dressed
_n a tuxedo, his black hair slicked back from his face and a brooch
_ith a coat of arms on the jacket pocket, he waltzed in with a
_eautiful tall, slim woman. Her long waist-length black shiny hair
_wept down her back and the simple red A-line red gown she
_ore with a swoop neck highlighted her slim waist and black hair.
_ler long diamond earrings almost touched her shoulders. Patsy
_aled and looked at Sheila; she felt sick, and her heart sank.

'Are you okay Patsy?' Sheila whispered, then looked up as the
_iscount sat down and everyone else's chairs were moved out by
_ootmen for the guests to sit down. 'Patsy what is it? You look ill.'
_rabbing Patsy's hand under the table, Sheila squeezed it hard to
_ring her out of the trance she was in.

Dazed and expressionless, Patsy squeezed her hand back.
_wallowing hard, she turned towards Sheila. 'My stable man,' she
_hispered. Patsy could feel herself trembling.

Good manners or not, Sheila reached out for two glasses of
_ine and handed Patsy one. 'Him? Your stable boy? Are you sure?'
_rowning disbelievingly, Sheila looked from Patsy to the viscount

at the head of the table. She didn't know what to think, but didn't want to make a fuss.

'Steady the Buffs, Patsy. Let's not be hasty; it could be his twin brother or something.' Sheila's attempt to make Patsy smile failed miserably. 'We can go if you want to, but personally I would brazen it out and wait until you can catch him on his own and give him a good mouthful. Bide your time; I am sure he is squirming just as much as you are – the dirty, lying bastard,' Sheila muttered under her breath.

Patsy gave a weak smile. Sheila had just said everything she was thinking. How could he not tell her who he was? She felt foolish and argued with herself that surely he would have known she was invited. Questions swam around in her head. Leaning forward slightly, she looked towards the top of the table at Philippe. She could see him smiling and chatting to people at either side of him. He must have had a sense of being stared at as he looked towards her. Their eyes met and seemed to lock for a moment and then without any kind of expression, or show of recognition, he turned away and concentrated on the person talking to him.

Course after course was served, but Patsy hardly ate a thing. She couldn't wait for it to be over so she could leave. She didn't want to spoil it for Sheila, so she put on a brave face and laughed gaily at the jokes of people sitting beside them making small talk. Furtively, she glanced at the other end of the table where the beautiful young woman Philippe had walked in with sat. Patsy had to admit it to herself that the woman was beautiful and perfect; that must be his wife. The very woman he had cheated on with herself. The thought sickened her. That poor woman sitting there talking and laughing with his guests was as innocent as she had been when Nick was cheating on her. They were both oblivious to the fact, and she was Philippe's bit on rough, just as Natasha had been Nick's. She almost felt sorry for the woman.

At last, it was announced for everyone to go into the ballroom. Everyone stood up and followed the sound of the orchestra playing. Manne and Jules stepped forward and asked Patsy and Sheila to dance. 'I don't waltz, laddie, but I'll give it a go,' laughed Sheila as she gulped yet another glass of wine down her neck. Sheila was heady with the alcohol and the ambience of it all and even Patsy had to admit it was out of this world.

'How do you know the viscount, Manne?' Patsy asked nonchalantly while doing her best to dance a waltz.

'He is family Mrs Diamond. "Our" family, if you know what I mean.' He smiled and said no more, leaving Patsy puzzled and confused.

After the dance, she joined Sheila again, who by now was so tipsy she was talking to anyone who would listen. Patsy wasn't sure who looked more confused. The French trying to understand Sheila's Scottish accent or the other way around. The thought of it made her smile and as she looked up, she saw Philippe standing alone at the far end of the ballroom.

Taking the bull by the horns, she walked towards him then realised he was standing with his wife. No longer caring, she tapped him on the shoulder. As he turned, he smiled and was about to introduce his wife when Patsy glared at him. 'Outside on the balcony now!' she snapped.

Marching ahead of him towards the patio area, she was surprised that he had actually followed her. As she turned around to face him, all of her pent-up venom and anger spewed out. 'How dare you tell me you worked at a stable when you are a viscount! And you're married, you bastard! Why didn't you tell me?' She couldn't help raising her voice and Philippe steered her by the elbow out of earshot of the ballroom.

'I never said, because you never asked if I was married. You presumed I worked at the stables, Patsy, I just never contradicted you.'

'Did you know I would be here tonight? I was invited by friends who say they know you and you are part of their circle – is that right?' Patsy spat out. Her face was red with anger from all of the things that had been bubbling up inside of her since she had sat down for dinner. His calmness angered her. The very fact that he made no excuses or apologised annoyed her even more. 'I have been beguiled and blinded by your charm.'

'I know what beguiled means Patsy, and you're wrong. I never charmed you with deception. And yes, I did know you would be here tonight; so what of it? We had a lovely time today and the days before that. As for my dealings with the Milieu, which is what you're implying, I don't deny it. Yes, I am a viscount, born and bred, but in France it doesn't mean anything any more. Since the revolution, my family were turned out, robbed of everything they owned and made penniless until they were guillotined. I am forty-seven years old Patsy, and I have made it my life's work to get back everything my family lost, one way or another – and I have. You're no better, you have dealings with them too and people in glass houses shouldn't throw stones. May I remind you Patsy, it was you that came looking for me, and when you found me, you came back looking for me again. I never forced you; I never deceived you.'

As he spoke, Patsy's anger rose to a pinnacle. She was lost for words and couldn't contain her anger any more. Impulsively, she raised her arm and with one huge swing, slapped him across the face so hard, he staggered backwards. Her hand stung and throbbed because of the force she had used. Once he'd steadied himself, he shook his head to bring his senses back and rubbed his cheek. Patsy looked at the bright red hand mark on his cheek as he rubbed it.

'I think you've made your point Patsy. I hope you feel better.'

Unexpectedly, he turned and walked away back to the house. Patsy stood there stunned. She didn't know what she'd expected, but it wasn't the cool calmness he had expressed. Most men would have shouted or screamed obscenities, but Philippe had done nothing and to be honest that made her feel worse. Standing there alone, she felt quite embarrassed. She knew she couldn't walk back into the ballroom after what had happened, so she started walking towards the front of the house. She wasn't sure which way it was and it was dark, with only flood lighting showing her the way.

'Patsy! Patsy, wait up!' Turning, she saw Sheila, trying to run towards her while holding up her dress with one hand and clutching a bottle of champagne in the other. Relief washed over Patsy when she saw her; she had wondered what she was going to do about Sheila or how she was going to get home.

'What happened?' Sheila linked her arm through Patsy's; she could tell Patsy was upset and put her arms around her. 'Here lassie, sit on these steps, and have a drink. What did he say?'

Heart wrenching sobs escaped Patsy as Sheila held her tightly. 'I always fall for the wrong men, don't I?' She sniffed. 'I'm a stupid woman, a bloody stupid woman!' Patsy scolded herself and wiped her eyes. 'I didn't expect me and Philippe to last; in fact, I had resolved myself into accepting it was over now the holiday was, but it's the lies and deceit I can't stand. Look at Nick, look at Larry but, for some reason, I thought Philippe was different, but, no, I am wrong again.'

'Oh wee lassie, don't worry about it. Have a drink of this, you'll feel better.' Sheila handed over the bottle of champagne and waited while Patsy took a huge gulp from it. 'Come on, let's find a car and hijack it; no one here will know the difference. Did you slap him?'

Nodding, Patsy smiled and took another drink out of the bottle; most of it ran down her chin. 'One great big whopper Sheila; you would have been proud,' she laughed.

'Good, because viscount or viscunt, I'd have punched him hard. What did he do when you slapped him?'

Patsy shivered slightly from the cool breeze and shrugged. 'Nothing, Sheila. He showed no emotion, nothing, just walked away.'

Sheila walked further on to where the cars were parked. 'So that's where they put all the chauffeurs. Come on, let's go and find one. I saw your man walk back into the house,' Sheila added, 'but he didn't go back into the ballroom, he went through another door. Probably soothing that red face of his by the sounds of it,' Sheila laughed.

Patsy laughed too. Now she thought about it, it was funny. She had gone berserk, with a strength she didn't know she was capable of, and hit him. 'It did make him stagger a bit; he almost fell on his arse.' Patsy laughed again and took another sip out of the bottle and passed it to Sheila.

* * *

Philippe stood in a small dressing room beside the ballroom and gazed into the mirror. His face was burning and he could still feel the sting of Patsy's anger. The red tell-tale mark on his cheek was fading but, he felt her anger would never fade. Bending over the sink, he washed his face, hoping to soothe the sting.

'That could turn into a bruise if you don't get any ice on it, Philippe.'

Turning, Philippe saw Manne standing there. 'Do you always creep up on people like this?'

Smiling, Manne sat down. 'It's been known, Philippe. I take it Mrs Diamond did that. I warned you; she has a hot temper. I have no sympathy for you.'

Ignoring his comments, Philippe dried his face. 'What I asked you to do... Have you done it?'

'I have Philippe, just as you requested. Although it wasn't our problem to fix.'

'It was our problem. It came back to Karen Duret and her stupid, greedy husband, and that would have led to us,' Philippe snapped.

'I am older than you, Philippe, and I don't wish to sound condescending, but why do I feel there is more to this than meets the eye?' Manne put his hand on Philippe's arm. 'It wasn't your fault that day when she was in the car accident. You did what anyone would and saved her. She came in search of you Philippe but, you didn't have to encourage it. You should have dismissed her, but instead, I feel you may have sailed very close to the wind. You are mixing business with pleasure Philippe and we never do that. Business always comes first – that was your father's motto.' Manne patted Philippe's arm and was about to walk away, when Philippe stopped him.

'Fate is full of accidents, Uncle. I never asked for this and you're right, I shouldn't have encouraged it. Mrs Diamond didn't deserve it, but her troubles are our troubles now. We are all Milieu and that means family. I'm just glad everything is sorted out now.'

'As you ordered Philippe... Are you okay, my boy?' Manne softened his tone somewhat and frowned. 'Maybe tonight was a bad idea.'

'No, you're right, Manne. I have been a fool, but it's been a long time since I have been seen anything other than Viscount

Carreaux. It was nice for a while to be a stable hand without penny. Women and gold diggers throw themselves in my path their fathers encourage it; God knows they do – but Mrs Diamon didn't care if I was a rich man or a poor man and that is somethin for me to keep. Let's go and have a drink; we have guests waiting.'

'Have some ice in your drink and suck it slowly to ease th pain in your cheek. Everything is in order, Philippe. The proble has gone away. As for you and Mrs Diamond, why do I feel the are just beginning?' Manne laughed and walked ahead, back in the ballroom.

18

ULTIMATE SHOCK

'Did you have a nice time last night girls?' Victoria asked over breakfast. 'We did, didn't we Maggie? It was lovely and we took lot of pictures of the Eiffel Tower – look.' Victoria passed around her mobile phone while Patsy tried to muster up the excitement required.

'You seem very quiet today, Patsy. I expected a lot more gossip this morning?' Maggie asked.

Sheila butted in. 'Too much champagne Maggie and a late night all adds up to hangover. I do like your photos though; it does look like the Blackpool tower, but I haven't been to Blackpool either so I wouldn't know.' Sheila rambled on, describing the mansion they had been to, while trying to save Patsy from their questions. 'What time are we leaving for the airport?' asked Sheila.

'The car is booked for midday, but I want to call in on Paul first.' Patsy's short answer was more like a snub and she cursed herself for it. But she couldn't help it. She wasn't up to small talk but had to do her duty by Paul. She just wanted to get home; suddenly France had lost its appeal.

Maggie and Victoria sensed there was something wrong and excused themselves to pack. As Sheila and Patsy sat across the breakfast table, Sheila decided to take the bull by the horns and speak the unmentionable. 'We don't leave for the airport until midday. Why not go to the stables and make your peace with Phillipe? Be a grown-up Patsy and have some dignity. Say goodbye, shake his hand and thank him for a nice time. Look at you, you're miserable and it will just play on your mind. Trust me, you will wish you had.'

'Oh for God's sake Sheila, let it go; you're like a dog with a bone. Last night you were going to hang, draw and quarter him, and now you think I should go and say goodbye. Shall I say goodbye to his wife as well? Maybe we should all take tea together!' Patsy snapped. She was about to get up from the table, when Sheila stopped her.

'Lassie, don't be stubborn. I know you like him, maybe even more than like him. Don't end on bad terms. You're both adults, you've had a bit of fun on the side; why make a mountain out of a molehill? At least this way, if you bump into him again – and you will,' Sheila stressed, 'if he works for the Milieu – you don't have to be embarrassed or cross the road to avoid him. Put your big-girl pants on and stop acting like a love-struck teenager!'

Patsy knew Sheila made sense, but all kinds of questions went through her mind. How could she pop by nonchalantly and say hello and goodbye? She would be the last person he would want to see. But, again, she mused, Sheila was right; it seemed they could end up working together in some form or another and it was better to do it with a clean slate and no skeletons in the cupboard.

'I can't go with Maggie and Victoria in the car. I don't want them to know about him or what I have been up to.'

'Well, you've just said you're going to see Paul. It might take longer than you thought. Go and get ready, see Paul, and then say your last goodbye to Phillipe.'

A smile appeared on Patsy's face for the first time that morning. 'Thank you, Sheila, you're like my fairy godmother. You're right, clean slate it is.' Patsy laughed and picking up a piece of toast, left the room singing.

After showing her appreciation again to Paul, Patsy made her excuses and left leaving a very happy, contented Paul in her wake. Taking a huge sigh, she drove up to the stables. They seemed different today and she felt nervous. Today she felt a sense of doom and now regretted going. Some things were best left and needed space and this was one of those things. She looked into the rear-view mirror and turned her head to look behind her. As clear as day in the sunlight, Phillippe was standing there, wearing his usual skin-tight black trousers and a pale blue shirt, open at the neck, showing the hairs on his chest. His black hair was worn loose around his shoulders, and his eyes met hers.

Getting out of the car, she walked slowly towards him, her heart thumping in her chest.

Frowning, he spoke first. 'Are you leaving?' he asked. Patsy noticed his voice was steady and calm, without a hint of anger or frustration.

'I was coming to say goodbye.' Patsy felt herself almost running as Philippe opened his arms to greet her. Embracing, they held each other tightly. All thoughts of last night disappeared from Patsy's mind as they kissed. A deep yearning for him engulfed her as their kisses became more ardent. Philippe led her to a side stable, where frenzied passion overwhelmed them both, without thought of the consequences. They wanted each other and for now, that was all that mattered.

Afterwards, Philippe was about to speak, but Patsy put her finger to his lips. 'Don't spoil this goodbye Philippe. I have to go.'

Adjusting her clothing and walking out of the stable, Patsy turned and took one last look around and then at Philippe who was still dressing. Her heart felt heavy and a feeling of pain washed over her. A feeling she had never experienced before. Even though she had loved Nick and been married for years, she had never felt like this. Philippe seemed to have the key to her heart, that unlocked all the passion inside of her and it had come flooding out unexpectedly and now it was to be locked away again. As she drove away, Philippe stood outside of the stable and waved at her forlornly. Tears spilled down her cheeks as she looked into the rear-view mirror and saw him disappear into the distance.

* * *

Back in London, Janine must have seen their cab pull up because she already had the door open to greet them. 'Hi Patsy; welcome home.'

'Where's Fin?' Patsy asked as she marched inside Janine's house.

Taken aback by Patsy's bad mood, Janine simply pointed towards the lounge. 'He's in there.'

Patsy marched into the lounge and surveyed the scene before her. Fin was lounging in an armchair watching television, with his plastered leg resting on a pink, tasselled pouffe.

Calmly, Fin looked up at her. 'Welcome home, Patsy. I think you should sit down and take that look off your face because wherever you have been they obviously don't have newspapers or internet.'

Puzzled by his statement, Patsy sat down on the sofa, while everyone else stood in the doorway waiting for Patsy's outburst. All the way home Patsy had snapped and snarled at them, irritated by everything.

Once Fin saw that she was seated and looked quite calm, he began. 'Larry's dead.'

Shocked, all of them gasped in unison, not quite taking his words in. Patsy paled and looked across at him; she couldn't believe her ears. 'Larry? You mean our Larry? The Larry I am supposed to be marrying?' She couldn't believe what Fin was saying. 'How, when?' she stammered, looking at Fin for answers.

'Some gunmen held up a bank in Glasgow and Larry was in here and he was shot dead. He was the only one to have been harmed and apparently the robbers got away with hardly anything. They are saying it was a robbery gone wrong, but they have a dead body on their hands. Apparently, they blew his head off with a shotgun...'

'When was this?' Patsy asked calmly, but already Sheila was googling the local news reports to find it.

Fin filled her in on as much as he could. 'The police aren't giving much away; they say they are making enquiries. To be honest Patsy, I wondered if you had anything to do with it. I even wondered if you had brought Freddie in on the deal and not told me about it. Well, have you?' he asked seriously. Fin's face was set in stone; he didn't like the idea that Patsy had gone behind his back and organised something like this without telling him. They were supposed to be work mates, family even.

Patsy held up her hands in submission. 'I swear Fin, I know nothing about it. Look at my face, do I look like I knew about it?'

'No, but I wanted to see your face when I told you. I wasn't sure. You have been so angry about him... and Freddie, well, he was weird the last time I saw him...' He cast a furtive glance towards Janine standing behind them all. It was clear he didn't want to say any more.

'I wonder if the police will be in touch with you. After all, you're his fiancée. I presume his ex-wife already knows. Patsy, call it

coincidence or fate, but I find it strange that he was the onl
person hurt. Someone heard them shout, "Target," before the
shot Larry.' Fin cocked his head to one side and looked to Janine
'Is there any chance of a cup of tea Janine? My throat is parched.'

'Course there is! Sorry everyone, I'm forgetting my manner
and you've all had a long journey.' Janine walked out of th
lounge, while Maggie followed her, offering to help.

'Everyone knows that Larry uses that bank regularly, and h
always goes at the same time when it's quiet. He has said that i
conversation many times, hasn't he? He always banks the firm
cheques and payments. Someone must have been watching hir
Patsy and they knew who they were looking for. They went i
there on a pretend robbery to shoot Larry. Now my guess is, it's go
something to do with you.'

Patsy suddenly saw Fin through different eyes. Gone was hi
boyish charm and carefree ways, he was a grown man an
speaking to her as such. This was his serious side, a side sh
hadn't really been privy to until now.

'You think I have deceived you or betrayed our confidence
Fin, well you're wrong about that. I trust you with any dealings
have. Nothing has changed. As for Larry, I am as shocked as yo
are. No one knows about Larry and his blackmail – just us.' Pats
looked up at Sheila and Victoria for answers.

Sheila shook her head. 'Don't look at me, I haven't said a wor
to anyone, but I agree Fin, it's one hell of a coincidence that th
only person making our life a misery is dead.'

Once again, Fin looked at them stoney faced. 'You don't get i
do you? None of you have thought about it. I can't believe it hasn
crossed your minds. Fuck Larry, he had it coming, but where i
that letter?' Fin stressed. 'If the police find it, we're fucked… Actu
ally, Patsy, no. You're fucked, not me.'

Sheila put her head in her hands. 'Oh my God, lassies, th

police will go through all of Larry's stuff; it's procedure. Someone will find it.'

Once the penny had dropped, they sat there in silence until they were interrupted by Janine and Maggie with the tea. Putting on a brave face, Patsy thanked her and waited until Janine had plumped up Fin's cushions before leaving the room again. It was obvious to Janine they were having a serious chat and so she decided to make herself scarce.

As Fin's words sunk into her brain, Patsy knew she was doomed. There was no escaping this now. They would find the letter and investigate what James had written. Supposedly, Karen's body had been moved and destroyed, but there was still the question of that grave with no body inside it. How was she supposed to answer that? Especially with James's damning evidence pointing the finger at her.

Letting out a huge sigh, Patsy looked at all of them in turn. 'I don't know what to do, I really don't.' She almost felt like crying and was lost for words.

Sheila looked down at the floor, dumbfounded. There were no answers and for once even she was lost for words. 'All you can do lassie is ride the tide. See what happens, but in the meantime, I suggest you look like the heartbroken fiancée. Contact his ex-wife and son, tell them you have been in Paris looking at wedding dresses. God knows what Larry told anyone about you. My guess is that the police will go to the estates looking for the gunmen. They know someone on the Glasgow estates, will know someone bragging about a robbery in a pub. Or if they got some money, someone is out there spending what they don't usually have. That's what the police are looking for. As yet, there is no reason for them to think Larry was the target as such. He was just in the wrong place at the wrong time. Look here.' Sheila showed Patsy and Fin her mobile. 'It says here they think he was a have-a-go hero and one woman saw him reach for a mobile phone. They will want to know if he had enemies; fuck, he's a lawyer putting people behind bars – of course he has enemies. But let's not do anything rash yet.'

For the first time since they'd arrived, Fin smiled. 'I'm just glad my leg is in a plaster cast and I am in London with a hospital as my alibi, or they would have been knocking my door down by now. So as much as I hate to say it, I am thankful to the guys that did this to me,' Fin laughed.

Sheila passed around the cigarettes. 'Too bloody right Fin, you and me both. They would have done a dawn raid by now and smashed the door in... Oh how I miss the good old days, not!' She laughed.

Fin turned towards Patsy; he could see she was deep in thought. 'You need to go back to Glasgow, Patsy.' Fin stretched out and put his arms behind his head. 'I think I might stay here for a while.' His infectious grin made them all smile and Sheila threw a cushion at him.

'We still have things to talk about Fin. Like, what happened to you that night and what was Freddie doing there?' Patsy sat forward. She hadn't had a proper chance to speak to Fin until now.

'I was taken to some old scrap yard. It turned out the men who took me weren't friends of James at all, they hated him.' Fin shrugged. 'Anyway, they wrecked your salon because they believed the money would still be there, but Janine had moved it, hadn't she?'

Patsy nodded. 'Carry on.'

'They knew I worked for you, and when I didn't give them the information they wanted, they decided a good beating would get rid of me. This boss guy, all dressed up to the nines, was called Mr Duke and apparently he ran things in that part of London. Loan hark, protection, prostitution, you name it. I was crouched down on the floor with my head down waiting for another kicking and through the slits of my eyes all I saw was his shoes. When I managed to look up, I saw the well-dressed bloke, but standing beside him was Freddie. Seeing him, I knew my days were numbered. I was dead meat. Mr Duke instructed Freddie to finish me off and then said he was going to get rid of you next.' Raising one eyebrow, Fin gave a wry grin. 'I must have done something right in a past life lassies, because Freddie took out his gun and when Mr Duke told him to shoot, he turned and put the gun to Mr Duke's head and fired. Straight through the bloody head. It's weird though. That Mr Duke must have told Freddie he wanted Patsy Diamond dead, so why did Freddie go along with it? Do you think he intended to kill him all along? After all, it was a secure place, with only a few of Mr Duke's men there. Anyway, out of nowhere, all Freddie's mates appeared and it was mayhem as they shot everyone. I remember Freddie telling someone to dump me at a hospital, which they did. They took my wallet and put my driving licence in my pocket, but the words that stuck with me more was what he said about that Milieu gang.' Fin laughed to himself. 'I didn't think that Freddie was frightened of anyone or anything, but he wouldn't cross them and kill you. He knows you're doing business with them, and that his head would be on a plate. So he took the best option and killed the guy who wanted you dead. Could be worth brownie points I suppose,' Fin laughed.

'True,' Patsy mused. 'The first time I met the Milieu, Freddie was there. He obviously knows them very well. It seems like Mr Duke chose the wrong mercenary when he asked Freddie to kill me and you Fin.'

Sheila let out a low whistle. 'You are one lucky bastard Fin.'

Smiling, Fin nodded. 'Do you know, that's exactly what Freddie said to me that night.'

19

UNSETTLING TIME

Spending time with Nancy took Patsy's mind off what she had to do next. She would drive back to Glasgow tomorrow and play the heartbroken fiancée just as Fin had suggested. Victoria popped her head around Nancy's bedroom door. 'It's nice of your parents to let us all invade their home again; it's getting to be a habit.' She smiled. 'Well, little lady, what are you all dressed up for?' Victoria knelt down so that she was face to face with Nancy and kissed her on the cheek.

'These are my tap shoes and we're doing a show tonight. I'm dancing on the stage.' Nancy grinned and did a twirl, showing off her blue floral dress and shiny black tap shoes.

'I know darling and we're all coming to watch you. Grandma Emma has arranged our seats. I'm going to be cheering you on.' A wide grin spread across Victoria's face as she stroked her grand-daughter's hair. 'You're a beautiful princess, Nancy Diamond, you really are.' Patsy watched as Nancy flung her arms around Victoria and they hugged. It was heart-warming to see Nancy and Victoria bonding.

Leaving them to it, Patsy went downstairs. Her father was

atching the local news, while Sheila, Maggie and her mother
ere chatting away in the dining room.

'Where is the wee lassie? I thought you were getting her ready
or this concert?' Sheila asked.

'Victoria managed to pop up to say hello and so I have left
iem to it.' Patsy smiled. 'Do I smell coffee?'

Emma got a cup and poured Patsy a cup of coffee. 'I'm so sorry
bout Larry love. It was all over the news. I know how you felt
bout him, but I'm presuming you must feel a little sad the way he
as murdered. You liked him once.'

Patsy spied the look of concern on her mother's face and
ached out, squeezing her hand. 'I'm fine Mum. It's tragic, but it's
ot the first man in my life that has been shot, is it, and a lawyer at
iat.' Shaking her head and waving her hands at the others
round the table, Patsy apologised. 'Sorry, sorry bad joke. Maybe
iy way of coping. Mum you're a softie and I love you for it, but
t's not forget what Larry was doing to me – he was blackmailing
ie, so why should I feel pity? He was probably blackmailing
ome other poor bastard and that is why they shot him!'

'Maybe I am soft Patsy, but I don't wish death on anyone. It's
ad karma and he has left a young son behind. I know what he
as up to and I also know you would have sorted it, but I suppose
m just looking at the other side if things.' Emma looked up, her
yes widening as a thought occurred to her. 'Did you have
nything to do with it? You and your friends?'

'For crying out loud, Mum, no I didn't. I've been in Paris.'
iobsmacked, Patsy looked around at them all. 'Why does
veryone think I had something to do with it? Bloody hell, I am
lad you're not the police; I'd be behind bars already! Believe me,
Mum, I felt like it, but, no, cross my heart, it was as much of a
hock to me as it was to you. Although, I admit I feel no pity.'

Sheila's head shot up. 'Christ Patsy, any lawyer that fancies you

in the future will think twice that's for sure!' Everyone laughed
'Seriously Emma, she's not bullshitting you. It's the truth,' stressed
Sheila.

* * *

They all clapped and cheered as Nancy and her troupe of tap
dancers took their bows and curtsied. Afterwards, they went for
burger and chips. As far as Patsy was concerned, it was
wonderful family evening with the people she loved. She was
dreading tomorrow, but after a long chat with the others she had
her plan of action. Her first port of call would be to drop every
thing off at her apartment and then she would make her way to
Larry's ex-wife's home.

She knew his son Paul and felt it was only right to go and see
him. Deep down Patsy felt if anyone knew anything about Larry
demise and the police investigations it would be them. She also
remembered Larry's sister who she had only met briefly. She had
never met his parents, and he had never really mentioned them so
that, as far as Patsy was concerned, was a dead end.

Suddenly her life seemed empty again. Victoria had left for
Dorset and Sheila had been dropped off in Edinburgh, while
Maggie had gone home to her flat. Patsy wondered if they all
felt a little deflated after their trip, too. It had been a wonderful
few days and they all glowed with tans from the French sun. A
fleeting thought of Philippe passed through her mind, and she
did her best to dismiss it. She wondered what he was doing
now, and if he was holding his beautiful young wife in his arms
the way he had her. Her heart sank. She couldn't express the
way she felt; after all, it had only been a few days and as far as
Sheila was concerned, a holiday fling, but Patsy didn't feel the
same way. Her feelings were stronger than that, although she

knew it was hopeless. He would never feel the same way about her.

Knocking on the door to Larry's ex-wife's home, Patsy felt nervous. She had expected to see a tearful woman open the door, but instead the woman seemed quite chirpy. 'You're Patsy; I wondered if you'd come. Come in and have a coffee – you've been on holiday, haven't you?' The woman left the door open and walked down the hallway towards the kitchen.

Following her, Patsy answered her questions. 'Yes, I've been to Paris. I was looking at wedding dresses actually...' Patsy almost bit her tongue; she didn't feel it was appropriate to say that to his ex-wife.

'Hi Patsy.' Paul greeted her with a smile, but she could see the dark circles around his eyes and his once-cheerful face seemed pale. Patsy remembered what her mother had said; no matter what she felt about Larry's death, he had left a young grieving son behind and for that she felt sorry.

'How are you, Paul? I'm sorry I didn't come sooner; I've only got back today.' Patsy opened her arms as the young boy burst into tears. She didn't know what to say. Paul had lost his father and he must be heartbroken.

His mum came forward and ran her hands through his hair. 'Come on Paul, why don't you pop upstairs and wash your face? Go on love.'

Patsy watched as the young boy wiped his tears away with the back of his sleeve and rubbed his red face. 'You'll say goodbye before you go, won't you Patsy?' he asked hopefully.

'Of course I will darling. I just wanted to see how you were. Your father was a very brave man, remember that.' Feeling like a hypocrite, Patsy gave him a weak smile as he went upstairs.

'I'm Wendy by the way. We've never been introduced.' Paul's mum held out her hand to shake Patsy's. 'It's good of you to come, considering how you must be feeling. How do you like your coffee?'

Patsy looked at the woman. Her brown hair was tied back in a ponytail, and she was dressed simply in jeans and a T-shirt. 'I presume you must feel much the same as I do; he was your husband, after all.'

Wendy put the mugs down on the table in the kitchen. 'Not really, Patsy. Of course, I'm upset because Paul is. He loved his father and it's crushed him. But I'm the outsider, a bit like you I'm afraid. You were his fiancée, but you have no rights, and I am just the mother of his son. The police said they would notify us when they are releasing his body so that we can arrange a funeral. I've contacted other family members of his that I know, but it really isn't my responsibility. His sister will organise the funeral.'

Surprised by Wendy's offhand manner, Patsy was intrigued. Apart from Larry telling her he was always working and never at home, he had never really said why his marriage had ended.

'Well Wendy, you seem to have everything in hand, and you're right, I am just a bystander.' Patsy took out her tissue and sniffed into it. 'I'm very upset, but I didn't want to come here trailing black cloth; I didn't think it would be fair on you both.'

'Personally, I am glad to see the back of him and I don't deny it. I am sorry Patsy, I know you loved him and you were going to get married, but, I wonder if you really knew Larry the way I did?'

Frowning, Patsy spied her over her coffee mug. The more Wendy spoke, the more she was intrigued. 'Larry never did say why you divorced. I don't mean to pry, it's not my business,' Patsy stammered. She was finding it hard to find the right words without sounding too nosey.

Wendy took a sip of her coffee and gave a wry grin. Standing up, she closed the kitchen door, so that Paul wouldn't hear them talking and sat down again. 'I have wondered what he had told ou, I admit that. Never speak ill of the dead, eh. But I admit it's hard not to. I loved Larry, I really did, but as time went on, he became a control freak. He ostracised me from my family and friends. I tried leaving him once, but he threatened to take full custody of Paul and being a lawyer, he would know how to go about it. I was afraid and couldn't stand the thought of losing my son. I was weak, I admit that.' She sighed. 'He held Paul over me for a long time, always threatening to take him away from me.'

Patsy looked on in silence as Wendy's eyes brimmed with tears. 'So he was blackmailing you to stay with him?' she asked tentatively. Stunned, she listened to Wendy's story and it seemed very similar to her own.

'He was very manipulating, but in the end I took my chances and left. I went to my parents and of course that was the first place he came with his threats. But this time I stood firm and got my own lawyer. I was told that the easiest way to get a divorce would be to admit adultery, so that is what I did. I slept with the first man I met. It wasn't an affair but, I kept it going for a week or so and it did the trick. As far as Larry was concerned, I was "soiled goods",' Wendy emphasised. 'He didn't want me any more and agreed to joint custody. He kept the house, I hardly got anything but, he has paid regular maintenance and done everything he is supposed to do for his son, and for that I am grateful. I often thought of meeting you and warning you, but I would only have looked like a bitter ex-wife. You would have found out in time Patsy. Sooner or later, he would have wanted to know where you were going every time you stepped out of the door. He was suffocating, but maybe you would like that. We're all different...'

'I'd already started to find that out,' Patsy blurted out. 'He was starting to monitor my every move. I'm not sure if I would have gone through with the wedding.' Feeling she had said too much, Patsy took a sip of her coffee.

Wendy gave her a knowing look. 'Just be grateful he was showing his true colours to you before you married him.'

Blushing, Patsy gave a weak smile. 'It doesn't seem right talking like this now he's dead. Apparently, he died a hero. Have they said if they've arrested anyone?' This intimate talk with Larry's ex-wife was proving to be more than Patsy had expected. It almost made her wish she had spoken to her before, although she doubted Wendy would have spoken so freely.

'No, apparently there are no leads. I think the police have possibly interviewed all of their best informers but have come up with nothing. I doubt they will ever find out who it was. But you never know' – she shrugged – 'something might turn up.'

Listening carefully, Patsy felt satisfied. The police had nothing to go on according to Wendy. 'Will you keep me informed of any updates and the funeral?' Patsy asked. 'As you say, I have no rights here, but I would like to pay my respects.'

'Thank you for coming Patsy, and I am sorry if I have spoken out of turn regarding Larry.'

'You haven't Wendy, believe me, you haven't, and if there is anything I can do for you and for Paul, please don't hesitate to ask me.' Opening her handbag, Patsy tore the back of her cigarette packet off and wrote her mobile number on it. 'Here, take this, call me if you need anything...'

'That's very kind of you Patsy, but it will all be in hand, I am sure of it. Larry would have made a will and I presume left Paul the lion share and something for his sister. I really don't know. His death was unexpected and he wasn't old. I presume his sister, Jenny, will check his paperwork, letters, documents and stuff to see if he had any special wishes.'

Patsy's blood ran cold. 'Maybe I could help her to go through all that, I've had experience since I lost my first husband and I know it's a mine field. I would be willing to help.' Not wanting to ound too desperate, Patsy was itching to be invited to go through Larry's letters, especially to find her own in there somewhere.

Wendy stood up and indicated it was time for Patsy to leave by collecting her coffee mug. 'If there is any more information, I will let you know, but it will all be down to his sister. Why don't you speak to her? I'm sure she would want to speak to you considering our pending marriage... By the way, before you go, don't forget to say goodbye to Paul as promised. I think he feels you're a link to his father.'

Nodding, Patsy walked away and up the stairs and knocked on Paul's bedroom. She knew which one was his by the drawing on the door saying, 'keep out'. It made her smile and she thought of the time to come when Nancy would do something similar.

Pushing the door ajar, she saw him lying on his bed with his headphones on, tears streaming down his face. Her heart went out to him. Whatever herself or Wendy thought of Larry, here was someone who loved and missed him. Sitting on the edge of the bed, impulsively she opened her arms as he hugged her tightly.

'You love him, don't you Patsy? We were going to be family, that's what Dad said. You were going to bring your daughter and live at the house and I was going to live there too.' He sniffed.

Stunned, Patsy listened to the innocent words of a child. This was the first time she had heard about this. It only confirmed what Wendy had said downstairs; Larry had told Paul he would not be living with his mother any more. She doubted Wendy knew anything about that or she would have said something. Patting Paul on the back and soothing him as he put his head on her shoulder, her mind swam. Larry had been a control freak, just as Wendy had said. It seemed everyone was well rid of him and even Paul had been released from his clutches in the future.

'I will be at the funeral Paul. Please tell your aunt Jenny to contact me and let me know. I don't want to interrupt her grief.'

'Have you cried Patsy?' Pauls raised his head to look at her.

'Buckets,' Patsy lied. 'It's amazing what good make-up ca
cover. Believe me, I feel just as bad as you. I was going to be you
step mum.' She smiled, trying to pacify the young boy. She kisse
his cheek and opened her handbag. Taking out her purse, sh
grinned and put her finger to her lips. 'I hear there's a new gam
out for the PlayStation; maybe that might help take your mind c
things.' Patsy thrust a handful of money towards him. Seeing th
half smile on his red face as he picked up the money made he
feel better. Standing up, she blew a kiss and left.

Wendy was waiting at the bottom of the stairs. 'Thank you fc
coming Patsy. I'll let you know when the funeral is. Good luck.'

Walking towards her car, Patsy gave one last turn and waved a
Wendy who was still standing at the door watching her leave.
felt odd, knowing just how Wendy felt about Larry. Little did sh
know that Larry's plan was to take her son away, after all. What
bastard, Patsy thought to herself and drove off.

Once back at her empty apartment, she looked through th
mail. There was nothing that couldn't wait. After the hectic coup]
of days she'd had, she felt deflated and bored. Her instinct was t
call Sheila, but she didn't want to impede on her time with Angu
and her own children, so she let them be. Suddenly Patsy fe
lonely. Pouring herself a brandy, she swirled it around in her golc
fish bowl of a glass and took a sip, while deciding to have a hc
bath and recharge her batteries. Going into the bedroom, sh
looked at her unpacked luggage and sighed. First things first, sh
mused to herself.

Once she had started, it didn't take long to empty her bag
Unzipping the leather cover of her evening gown she had worn t
the ball, she smiled at it. It was a lovely dress, but with its mem
ries, she doubted she would ever wear it again. At the bottom c
the bag were the shoes that she had absently thrown in, with the

matching bag. She took them and the bag out. Opening the clasp, she saw the ring box Manne had given her that night. She had forgotten all about it.

Sitting on the edge of the bed, she held the brown leather ring box and lifted the lid. Inside was a gold signet ring. It looked quite plain, but the centre piece was black onyx. Patsy put it on the middle finger of her right hand as Manne had told her to do. Holding her hand up before her, she looked at the gold signet ring with its black centre piece. Picking up a tissue, she rubbed the black onyx from where her finger had smudged it and felt it move. Her first thought was that she had broken it and taking it from her finger, she inspected it closer. The centre piece turned on a swivel. The other side of the black onyx showed what looked like a gold sovereign ring, and on closer inspection she saw it wasn't a sovereign head, but the fleur-de-lis. Patsy recognised it instantly and remembered it from the tattoo she had admired on Phillippe's shoulder. It was obvious that Philippe knew the Milieu but just how involved was he, she wondered? She didn't remember him wearing a ring, although she wasn't sure. But this stamp of the Milieu was emblazoned on his shoulder in full colour.

Patsy decided to put the ring back in the box. She didn't feel the need to wear it now. As she was about to close the lid, she noticed a piece of paper on the inside of the lid. Picking at the tiny, folded piece of paper, she managed to pull it out with her fingernail. It had been folded many times and as she opened it, her curiosity grew. Her heart raced and skipped a beat and she dropped the piece of paper as though the very touch of it had burnt her fingers. Taking a moment to compose herself, she picked up what was now an A4-sized piece of note paper.

She recognised it instantly; it was James's letter that Larry had used against her. As she looked at it more closely, she could see that it was the original and saw James's signature on it. But how did the Milieu know about the letter and Larry? She had never mentioned it to them.

Suddenly there was light in the darkness. Taking a sip of brandy to soothe her nerves, she looked at the ring box again. This proved that Larry's murder was not an accident. The bank robbers were members or friends of the Milieu and they had staged that robbery to kill Larry and his dirty secrets. Patsy wasn't sure what to do with it. Her first thought was to burn it straight away, but she wondered if she should show the others. Picking up her drink again, she gulped it back in one. Her hands were almost trembling as she read the letter again. James had left damning evidence against her and in the wrong hands she would definitely have been arrested and possibly charged with something, even murder. The thought of what might have been made her blood run cold.

Soaking in a foamy bubble bath with a glass of wine, Patsy hoped that all her troubles would be washed away down the plug hole with the dirty water. Allowing herself time to lay back and relax in the scented water, she closed her eyes and listened to the music in the background. She felt relaxed and warm as her mind wandered.

Allowing herself a few moments of indulgence, she thought of Philippe. Though she dared not admit it to anyone else, she missed him. As she inhaled, she could almost smell the scent of him, as if he were right there with her. Sadly, she knew it was time to let go. Sheila was right, it had been a holiday romance, not even an affair. A few days of sex. She consoled herself with the fact that he was married and a cheat, and if he would cheat on his wife with her, then he would cheat on her with another woman. She was best out of it.

Suddenly sitting bolt upright in the bath, Patsy pushed the soapy water from her hair and face as a thought crossed her mind.

'Phillipe!' Her heart was pounding, and reaching out for her glass of wine, she gulped it down. Lying back in the bath, she thought about that day with Philippe in the field. They had lain in each other's arms and she had told him about Larry blackmailing her. He hadn't seemed to be listening while she'd bared her soul to him. But now she remembered, clearly. Fin had asked her who else knew about Larry and she had said no one outside of their circle, but she was wrong. She had told Philippe.

Getting out of the bath, she put on her robe and decided to telephone Fin and tell him what she had remembered. As she picked up her mobile, it rang. Smiling with relief, she saw that it was Sheila. 'Sheila, why are you ringing? Don't get me wrong, I'm glad, but shouldn't you be snuggled up to Angus?'

'Angus has been called out to cover someone and do a shift, so he's gone. The lassies are in bed and I've ordered a takeaway for one, so I thought I would give you a call while I am waiting. I have big news for you!'

'News?' Patsy laughed. 'Well, I hope it's good news; I could do with some.'

'I googled your Philippe Carrots, or whatever his name is, and on Google it had pictures of the ball we went to. Well anyway, that beautiful woman that was with your carrots is his daughter! Now that's taken the wind out of your sails, hasn't it? He hasn't lied to you Patsy, he's not married.'

'His daughter?' Patsy shouted. 'Oh my God. Well, how old is she?'

Sheila was laughing down the phone. 'She is twenty-six years old and he's a widower! You thought he was a dirty old man with a young wife. Nope, that honourable Lady Whatshername is his daughter. Now put that in your pipe and smoke it!'

Patsy didn't know whether to laugh or cry. Philippe hadn't lied to her or cheated on his wife. Relief washed over her. He may not want her, but at least now she knew the truth and sorely regretted her outburst that night.

'I love you and Google!' Patsy shouted down the phone. 'Actually, I have some news for you. Sheila, did you say you're alone with the girls in bed?'

'I am and before you ask, I have ordered takeaway for two, I was just waiting for you to take the hint,' Sheila laughed. 'See you soon.'

Bouncing with happiness, Patsy got dried and dressed in a matter of minutes. Picking up her car keys, she smiled. Philippe had a daughter! That made her feel a whole lot better. There may be no chance for them, but at least he hadn't used and lied to her like Nick and Larry. Maybe third time lucky, she mused to herself and that made her feel a whole lot better.

20

THE WAY FORWARD

Over the next few days, it was business as usual. Patsy oversaw the drug deliveries and Fin had increased the mobile van shops round the local estates and although a lot of protection was needed, profits were soaring. Patsy's biggest satisfaction was the ice-cream business she had acquired. That really was the jewel in her crown. It had cost her next to nothing for all the vans and stock and now, some of the Albanians were working for her, having turned on their own bosses.

They had all been given a trial, but they had all worked hard and caused her no trouble. The profit margins were just as they should be and they were glad of the work. The men were grateful, and Patsy paid a proper wage for their hard work, which surprised the Albanians. Patsy paid them the legal minimum wage, which was more than they had received from their own countrymen. For that gesture alone the men worked harder than normal and never let her down. Those ice-cream vans were out from dawn till dusk selling mild drugs, cocaine, meth and speed, and cleaned every night at the warehouse. On top of that, at Fin's suggestion, Patsy gave them a staff discount on groceries from the mobile shops and

ice-cream vans. Fin had said that knowing they got a discou
would stop them from stealing and he was right. Fin also pointe
out that their wages were going straight back into Patsy's pocke
Fin's business brain amazed her sometimes. Everything was i
order and everyone was making money and that was wh
mattered.

Bernie had Mr Duke's contact book that contained all of h
business associates and people that owed him money, whic
saved her a lot of leg work. She had everything in order down i
London, and had sorted out accommodation and seemed ve
happy with her fresh start. She had also come across a 'cook
which was the term used for someone who made drugs, and
supplier Mr Duke had used, and passed that on to Fin to loo
in to.

Knocking on Maggie's door, Patsy waited. 'Maggie, I hope th
isn't inconvenient. There is something I would like to ask you.'

'Come in, Patsy. I've seen you out and about and was going t
pop around and see you. I'll put the kettle on.' Maggie ushere
her into the lounge, but Patsy stopped her before she could wa
away.

'Wait Maggie, you know Bernie is still in London and will b
staying there. My problem is that she kept an eye on Leandra an
the girls back here. Now I know you're not a bouncer, Maggie
Patsy laughed, 'but I would still like someone to keep an eye o
things and keep me informed. Leandra and her girls are ni
enough, but I want no trouble; things are going along smoothly.'

Maggie started to laugh. 'You mean I am to be in charge c
them like their madam, Patsy?'

'That's an old-fashioned word Maggie, but, if you like. I wa
someone the girls can go to if they have any concerns. I want yo
to be my eyes and ears Maggie – that is, if you want the job. An
trust me Maggie, it pays well.' Patsy grinned.

'I am more or less doing that anyway Patsy, so I might as well get paid for it. But if muscle is needed, who do I call upon?'

'I'll sort that, I just wanted to know your slant on things first. I am going to London tomorrow; the salon is finished and I want to be there at the grand re-opening. I believe you're going to Dorset to stay with Victoria? Well, why don't you drive down with me and see Fin and go from there to Dorset?'

Smiling, Maggie nodded. 'It would be nice to see that young fool Fin and see how he is getting on. I would like that Patsy, thank you.'

Declining her offer of tea, Patsy left. That was just another box ticked off her list. Madam Maggie, who'd have thought it, Patsy laughed to herself.

* * *

'Well, I must say Fin, you're looking miles better! It must be all that care you've had from Janine.' Patsy winked, but it was true; Fin looked very well indeed. His face was still bruised and apart from his leg in plaster, you wouldn't know the pain and torture he had been through.

'I take it Sheila isn't with you?' Fin asked. 'Otherwise she would be making some smart arse comment about me looking clean and tidy.' He grinned.

'No, just us. Maggie thought she would look in on you first and Victoria is driving her down to Dorset after this visit.'

Blushing, and slightly embarrassed, Maggie nodded. Maggie hated emotion and admitting that she had gone to see Fin on purpose embarrassed her. 'I also came for the re-opening of the salon.'

Fin smiled. 'Thanks for that Maggie; here was I thinking you cared!'

'Where is Janine, Fin?' Patsy asked. 'Has she gone to the salon?'

Seeing Fin nod made her pull up a dining chair and sit beside him. Opening her bag, she took out the ring box Manne had handed her the night of the ball. 'Here, take a look at this.'

Taking the ring box, Fin opened it. Patsy had already told him about it, but she wanted him to see it as she had found it.

'That's some big shit Patsy. If ever I piss you off, give me the chance to apologise before you go telling other people you hate me, especially the people who gave you this ring.' Even though Fin was joking, the seriousness in his voice was apparent. She had made an idle comment about Larry to Phillippe only to find out that two days later he was dead.

'I wanted you to see the letter Fin. Do you think there are copies?'

'That's the million-dollar question Patsy, but honestly I would say no. Surely whoever is going through his stuff would have found it by now. Don't forget, he was also up to his neck in it. He should have handed that over to the police the minute James killed himself. Okay, nothing is going to happen now. There is no proof either way. They are both dead and cannot answer the questions. The police possibly would dig up the area that James is saying Karen is buried, but we know she isn't there and if they find Karen's empty grave, what has that got to do with you? There is no evidence or body Patsy. Burn it. Burn it now.'

'I thought you would say that Fin, and I agree, I just wanted you to see it first.'

Fin hobbled up onto his crutches and led the way to the kitchen. Fin took out his lighter and set fire to the letter over the kitchen sink. 'RIP James and Larry, you two-faced, lying bastards.'

Everyone watched the letter burn and when Fin turned the

tap on, ashes floated down the drain. Patsy felt it was like a great weight off her shoulder. It was gone.

'The police have released Larry's body and the cremation is next week. They are expecting me to attend.'

Fin nodded. 'And you will Patsy. You have to. See this through to the end. We've just cremated him, anyway. But you're his grieving girlfriend and you have to be seen as such. I've been watching the news regularly; there are no updates on that bank robbery, so, unless something turns up it will be shelved unless there is new evidence.' Fin hobbled outside for a cigarette and Patsy walked into the lounge to where Victoria was sitting quietly. She looked pale. 'Are you okay? You seemed to have had a funny turn?'

'It was as though someone just stepped on my grave. Fin standing there being all serious. His green eyes flashed at me. Jesus Patsy, it was Nick. He is Nick's half-brother, but sometimes you'd think he was his full brother. Even some of his mannerisms. Don't you ever see it? I'm glad we all found each other. Fate is a strange thing.' Frowning, Victoria looked at Patsy.

Patsy looked down at the floor and closed her eyes. 'Yes, Victoria. Sometimes for me, it's his laugh. Now and again he throws his head back and has a deep throaty laugh, just as Nick did. I agree it's strange sometimes. The other week he called me by my name and the hairs on the back of my neck stood on end. I could have sworn I was in the room with Nick...' Patsy trailed off.

For a moment they were silent, as though reminiscing. As Fin entered the room again, they both painted a smile on their faces.

After a moment, Victoria spoke up. 'Fin, I know this is an odd question, but when we tried to find you at the hospital, if it hadn't have been for Sheila, we would never have known your name was William Finnigan. Why have you never said?'

Fin looked up at Maggie. 'You know why, don't you Maggie?'

Maggie nodded sadly and sat down as Fin carried on talking. 'As you already know, Billy Burke was my dad. I didn't want to be known as William or Billy. Finnigan was my nan's name. She brought me up after my mum dumped me on her doorstep. After she died, I didn't change it. Everyone has always called me Fin. I suppose people think it's my first name, but, in my game, what does it matter? I will always be Fingers Fin.' His laugh was hollow and serious and covered many emotions.

'Well, if you would like, I would like it if you called yourself Diamond. You're family Fin, but it's up to you. You were Nick's half-brother. I understand, you're close to your nan and would like to keep the name, but as I say, it's up to you...' Realising she had blurted out her feelings, Victoria stopped.

'You class me as family, Victoria?' Frowning, Fin looked around the room at them all. 'I've never really had a family, although, I suppose we are, even without the Nick connection. We're all we have, aren't we?' He smiled.

Victoria stood up and walked towards him, kissing him on the cheek. 'You are family, Fin. I know you would always be there if I needed you... like a son.'

The room fell silent and Victoria walked back to her chair and sat down. She felt her emotions had got the better of her and she had said too much.

'I could call myself Fin Diamond. That way, I still keep my nan's name. She loved me, in her own way.' He shrugged and looked at Maggie.

'You're my blood Fin. I didn't know anything about you, until it was too late. But you're still blood and I think it would be nice if you kept your nan's name, but I think you could do with a fresh start and Fin Diamond sounds good.' Maggie smiled as though giving him her blessing.

'I'll sort that as soon as I can then. Thank you. It's been a long time since I have been part of a family.'

Patsy and Maggie looked at Victoria, who seemed happy once she had agreed. She was still a grieving mother and suddenly, in whatever form or fashion, she had a son back. But even Patsy had to agree that for all of Fin's faults, and there were many, he was a nicer man than Nick.

'I'm going to take Janine out for a meal on Friday. She's been really good to me.' Fin blushed.

Patsy smiled. 'Is she your girlfriend then Fin? Are you and er... together?'

Fin scrunched his lips together, as though toying with his answer. 'If you mean have we been up to naughties, then no. She's looked after me and that's it. She's done just as you asked.'

'Ooh, sounds like she's biding her time. And for the record Fin, I never asked her to look after you, she volunteered.' Patsy gave him a knowing look and watched the smile appear on his face.

Speaking freely, Patsy asked if there had been any repercussions from the pub shooting that nearly saw them all killed.

'They are running scared, these southerners. The other side of London doesn't care if you want to take over the patch as long as it isn't their turf you're after. But hearing how that pub was blown to bits with a machine gun, the word on the street is that the boss of these crazy people is a woman who fears no one. They are more afraid of you than you are of the police, too. Bernie isn't making their lives any easier. Believe me Patsy, they say men are evil, but angry women are much worse!'

They all burst out laughing when they saw the horror in Fin's eyes. 'Well, behave then Fin, or we'll set Bernie on you,' Patsy laughed. 'I am going to pop to see if she's around. I will leave you to it Fin, and enjoy your evening. Don't forget to wash behind your ears love.'

Standing up, Patsy kissed him on the cheek and walked towards the front door with the others in tow.

* * *

Patsy and the others were quite surprised when they entered Bernie's flat. It might have all been furnished from the local charity shop, but it was homely and it was clean.

'How are things, Bernie? Anything to report?' Patsy asked Bernie sat at the kitchen table in a white vest and black tracksuit bottoms. Her breasts seemed to hang well under the table and she was sat there eating a large fry up of eggs, bacon and beans. Even the way she shovelled the food into her mouth slightly scared Patsy. Looking up at Victoria, Patsy could see her and Maggie disgust, as Bernie spoke with her mouth full. It was like looking at the inside of a washing machine.

'Money I've collected is under the mattress Mrs Diamond. Been wondering what you wanted me to do with it. They are all running scared down here of that Scottish Diamond woman that's what they call you. But they hated that Duke laddie more than they fear you,' Bernie added, while shovelling another forkful of baked beans into her already full mouth. Patsy liked Bernie's matter-of-fact ways. You knew exactly where you stood with a woman like her on your side.

Patsy sat down at the table; she felt awkward in her cream trouser suit, in case some of Bernie's baked beans came flying out of her mouth while she spoke. Bernie pointed her fork in Patsy face. 'That is why so many people like working for you Mrs Diamond. You have given them their lives back. I wouldn't cross you because you're a hard-faced lassie, but you're good to your employees and respect gains respect, doesn't it?'

Patsy tried hard to make sense of Bernie's thick Scottish accent, but she realised somewhere in there was a huge compliment. 'As long as people don't think I'm a pushover Bernie, because I am not,' she reminded her.

'I ain't flattering you, lassie. They know you're no pushover. You like hurting people; I saw the look on your face when you killed that landlord. Got balls you have, and they know it. You might look like the sweet lady in your posh suits, but you like to get your hands dirty. You've got a taste for blood Mrs Diamond.' Bernie winked.

Patsy couldn't help laughing and looked up at Victoria and Maggie who were smiling in agreement. 'Keep what money you've collected so far Bernie, put it towards the rent and setting yourself up somewhere new if you want to. If you drive, get a second-hand car or something for now. I can't have you walking everywhere, it doesn't look right. If you need me, call me. See you soon Bernie.'

Bernie held out her arm and clenched her fist. Patsy had seen this before with Fin and his friends and held hers out and pushed her fist against Bernie's. That was their handshake.

As they walked back to the car, Victoria shivered. 'She scares the shit out of me, and I don't usually swear.'

Patsy laughed and turned to Maggie. 'She scares the shit out of all of us. Thank God she's on our side and I'm not her type!'

21

LOVE IS IN THE AIR

'We could have got a taxi Fin; why on earth did you struggle on the bus?' Freezing in her flimsy summer dress, Janine rubbed her hands together and blew on them.

This was her night out with Fin, and already she was regretting saying yes. When he'd said they would go for a meal, she had envisioned all kinds of a romantic evening, but standing at the bus stop hadn't been part of any of them.

Janine had curled her pink hair and worn a cream-and-beige summer dress with thin straps. Her matching high-heeled sandals were now hurting her feet.

She knew Fin still had his leg in plaster, but the top half of him left a lot to the imagination. Even though she had bought him a shirt, he had worn a T-shirt and a denim jacket. His jeans were cut up one leg to make room for his cast, but Janine felt disappointed.

'I should have booked somewhere; you don't know the restaurants around here.'

Fin hobbled along on his crutches, looking at the restaurants along the side of the road. He stopped outside a steak house. 'This looks good, we'll try here.' He smiled.

Linking her arm through his, Janine's heart sank. There were a hundred restaurants down this high street and he had chosen a steak house.

'Look at that, it's two for the price of one steak night.' Fin beamed and stood in line, waiting for a seat.

'There are better places around here Fin. Why don't we go and look at those if they haven't a seat here?' Janine prompted, but just as she said it, the waiter held out two menus and offered to take them to a table. It was rowdy with kids running about.

Trying to make the best of it, Janine smiled and looked at the menu. Fin ordered prawn cocktails for starters followed by their two-for-one steak, which was so tough Janine had trouble cutting it. Fin picked his up with his hands and bit into it. Once he'd polished off his lemon cheesecake and wiped his mouth with his napkin, he blew his nose on it. Janine looked around as others stared at them. She wanted the ground to swallow her up. Fin told her funny stories which made her laugh and overall she enjoyed the evening.

When the waiter brought the bill, Janine saw the worried look on Fin's face. 'What's the problem Fin?' she asked.

'Can you pay? I've forgotten my wallet.'

Janine nodded, and wondered if that was the reason Fin had chosen somewhere cheap because he couldn't afford it. Janine took out her card and paid the bill. Her heart sank again, when she remembered her earlier fantasies about her romantic evening out.

As they walked out of the restaurant, Janine resolved herself to walk with her aching feet to the bus stop, but Fin hailed a taxi. She was pleased he had, because her feet hurt and it had started to rain. Her once wavy hair now hung like rats' tails in the rain and her thin summer dress was drenched, leaving nothing to the imagination.

'Crikey Janine, hurry up. It's started to rain so hard, even the fish would drown.' He grinned. Once in the taxi, Fin smiled and reached into his pocket and handed Janine a wad of notes. 'Sorry about that. It's my first jaunt out and people will have heard I've been staying with you, especially the police who have been sniffing around since I was in hospital. I wanted to take you out but safety first, eh? Why would some Scottish tourist without a pot to piss in staying in a hostel go somewhere expensive and pay the bill? Especially as my wallet was stolen!'

Janine burst out laughing. 'I suppose that makes sense. Frowning, Janine made a face. 'Do you think they've been watching you?'

'I doubt it, but there's no harm in being careful, is there? I only deal in cash, no cards. Ex-con.' Fin shrugged and blushed. He didn't know how much Janine knew about him, and while he had been sat in her lounge, he'd wished himself a better man and worthy of her. He knew this was her act of kindness for Patsy and he didn't stand a chance. He'd never met anyone like her before. She had been to college and had a good steady job as a hairdresser. She didn't do drugs and didn't even smoke which was why Fin always went outside if he felt like a cigarette. He liked her a lot and they got on well, and for once in his life he felt truly ashamed of the way he had lived his life. He was punching way above his weight with Janine and he knew it.

'I know you've been in prison Fin, Patsy told me. And I know you work for her, but that doesn't bother me either. I've been working for her as well, in more ways than one. How do you think I could afford the mortgage for my house? And next time, if that is your plan, tell me and then I'm prepared for it and won't wear stupid shoes,' she giggled.

'Next time?' Fin asked hopefully. 'Is there going to be a next
time?'

Janine looked at him from under her lashes and smiled as the
taxi stopped.

* * *

The re-opening of Patsy's salon pleased her immensely. It was
overdue a makeover and this had given her a good excuse to do so.
Everything is half price, Janine. I don't care what they want, they
can have it. Get some of the other staff to keep the tea and coffee
flowing. How did your meal with Fin go? You haven't mentioned
'

Janine sighed and put on a face. 'Well, not what I expected. I
paid the bill at that awful steakhouse on the high street, but he
did pay me back. I thought he might try his seduction technique
but, no. I don't think he fancies me, Patsy... Never mind...'

Patsy stared at her, wide eyed. 'Fin never made a move? It's not
my business, and I don't really know that side of him, but I
thought he would have been like a ferret up a drainpipe. In fact, to
be honest Janine, I thought you already were, well, you know.'
Patsy grinned.

'No Patsy, a kiss on the cheek while I help him get settled for
the night, but that's it,' Janine explained, as she folded the towels.
'But he's honest Patsy, unlike some of the other blokes I've known.
What you see is what you get.'

As Janine walked away, busying herself with last-minute
touches to the salon, Patsy thought about what she'd said. Fin was
being the gentleman, or he felt it wasn't worth pushing his luck in
case of rejection. Musing to herself, she felt it was time for Aunty
Patsy the matchmaker to come out of the cupboard and have a
word with him.

* * *

'Did you know the week after next is half term lassie?' Sheil shouted down the phone to Patsy.

'I did, why do you ask?'

'Well, I was thinking of doing something with the girls. Mayb go away for a week, that's why I'm asking.'

'Sheila, why do I sense something behind this?' Patsy couldn hide her suspicion. It wasn't like Sheila to volunteer a holida 'Where were you thinking of, somewhere by the coast?'

'Kind of, I was thinking of that lovely cottage in France, wit all that space and sunshine. I was also telling Angus of an oppo tunity well missed. There I was buying ball gowns and I cou have been looking at wedding dresses!' And don't forget, there the grand opening of the chateau. Paul already has tables booke at the restaurant; maybe the owner should be there?'

'I don't want to go back there,' Patsy said hesitantly. 'I'm n ready to go just yet. Anyway, I have just heard Larry's funeral next Wednesday, so I should show my face there...'

'Paul would love it if you went and I think you need to fa your demons. You can't avoid Viscount Carrots forever lassie.'

'It's Carreaux Sheila! You and your bloody carrots. If I ever d see him again, I'd be afraid of slipping up and calling him carrot Anyway, I don't want anyone thinking I slept with someone call Carrots,' Patsy laughed. 'No, I will go anywhere else; you cou even come to my parents' villa in Greece, but I'm steering we clear of France for now.' Everything was running smoothly in h life at the moment. Her Diamond empire couldn't be better, an the money was rolling in. Larry had been her last problem solve and she didn't want to muddy the waters.

Sighing, Sheila couldn't help herself. 'We talked about this. H never lied to you Patsy, and that gorgeous woman with him w his daughter. Och, lassie, I worry about you. You're like a nomad wandering around from place to place.'

Patsy was touched by Sheila's sentiments and to be honest, she felt that way sometimes. At the moment she was living in a flat above a very busy community centre with people coming and going all the time.

'I'm coming back in a few days for Larry's funeral, so I will see you then. In the meantime, I have to sort out Fin's love life. I need to find out if he's interested or not, for Janine's sake as well as mine. I can't stand looking at her miserable face all day,' Patsy laughed.

'As for Janine's miserable face, well, that is exactly how I feel about you. Think on what I've said, and we'll catch up properly when you get back.'

Patsy was about to retaliate but Sheila had quickly ended the call so she couldn't. She was downhearted and each time she closed her eyes she could see Philippe, but dismissed the idea of anything more happening between them. It was what it was. He had been the one that had solved her problem with Larry and he hadn't made a song and dance about it. To go to the chateau could be embarrassing, and she felt she would regret it. She was lonely, but she would only admit that to herself.

Her thoughts were interrupted by her parents and Nancy coming into the salon. 'We thought we would pop in and wish you luck love. The place looks amazing. I love the Parisian mural on the wall. That must have cost a fortune,' her mum commented.

Patsy stared at it. She'd had it done yesterday by a young man from the nearby college, who fancied himself as an artist. Now she looked at it, she realised it had been an absent-minded spur-of-the-moment thing.

'Not sure about the white horse standing on its rear legs over there though. Granted, the blue sky behind it looks very dramatic, but what's with all of the artistry?' Her father laughed, while Nancy ran to her and hugged her.

'Why not?' Patsy smiled and blushed, burying her head in Nancy's hair. 'It gives the customers something to look at and comment on while they're having their hair done.'

Hiding her blushes, Patsy was pleased when the first of her clients turned up. It was one of her oldest customers who she seemed to have known forever, and so Patsy slipped on her tabard and helped the elderly lady with her Zimmer frame to one of the basins to wash her hair.

A couple of minutes later, Fin entered on his crutches. 'Just thought I would come and give you some moral support Patsy.'

'Me or Janine?' Patsy laughed as she shampooed the lady's hair. 'Actually, Janine, would you take over from me here, as I'm going to give Fin a well-needed trim.'

Patsy sat Fin in a chair at the far side of the salon once his hair had been washed.

Puzzled, Fin lowered his voice, frowning as he looked at Patsy in the long mirror. 'You're weird Patsy. How come you still wash and cut people's hair? You're Patsy Diamond – the boss lady!'

'It's who I am, Fin. Never forget where you came from. I enjoy it, I always have. Anyway, what do you care? You're getting a free haircut,' she laughed.

'Fair point I suppose. Never really saw it like that before.' Fin winced as he watched Patsy cut away at his hair. He could see his shoulder-length locks falling to the floor around him. 'How short are we going, Patsy?'

'Don't worry, there will be hair on top, to give you that air of authority. Anyway, what's happening between you and Janine?' she whispered, thankful that the radio was on in the background.

Fin flashed a glance at Patsy in the mirror. 'Why? What has she said?'

'Only that she likes you. What's the problem Fin, don't you like her? Is that it?'

'I'm not fooling myself Patsy. I've got nothing to offer her. I've been nowhere apart from prison. It's a nice thought, but I'm leaving it.'

Seeing his solemn face, Patsy grinned. 'You're wrong, Fin, you have a lot to offer. You have a job and you're more streetwise than most people I know. You know lots of things.' Seeing Fin shrug, she knew he was feeling depressed about the situation. 'It's up to you to come out of the shade Fin and do it properly. Take her somewhere nice, dress smart, put a suit on. You're as good as anyone Fin,' Patsy stressed, 'and you're already halfway there because she really likes you.'

'I've been thinking about that Patsy. You and Victoria suggesting I change my name has got me thinking. I'm making money as your operations manager.' He grinned.

'What? I don't remember giving you that title.' Patsy laughed and slapped his head playfully. Others turned and looked at them both skylarking at the end of the salon, but they ignored them and carried on with their own conversation.

Sitting up straight and proud, Fin smiled. 'I thought of that one by myself. I don't claim benefits any more so I needed a job title. I oversee the mobile shops, and that is what I have put on the paperwork. Operations Manager.'

Patsy sat down in the chair beside him. 'I'm shocked Fin. You're going straight?'

'Well, I wouldn't say that, Patsy. The money isn't exactly straight, but it's time I became more than a useless waster and house burglar. I'm in my thirties, what have I got to show for it?'

Patsy now realised the seriousness of the conversation. Fin was wearing his heart on his sleeve and telling her all of his innermost thoughts without having to look at her head on. Patsy stood up and continued putting the layers in his hair. 'So, Operations Manager Fin, what is your plan of action?'

'I am about to change my name and that is a fresh start. I have a load of money stashed away but can't spend it. I have a reputation in Glasgow, so I have decided to move...'

Stunned, Patsy said nothing. This was a totally different Fin to the one she had met in her flat over a year ago. He had become a man and grown up. 'I've spoken to Tiny, and I think he could sort the Glasgow operational manager duties. I think I might move to London. I could help Bernie and keep a close eye on things here. I could even travel between the two, overseeing both areas. I could get a bank account, a proper flat or something, and leave my past behind. Fin Diamond is born and William Finnigan is dead and buried. Maybe then, Janine would respect me.' He blushed.

Patsy was silent for a moment; she hadn't expected this bombshell when she'd started cutting his hair. Squeezing his shoulders, Patsy smiled. 'Whatever you decide Fin. You have sorted it out and for that I am happy; you've saved me the trouble. I agree, maybe it's time you left that boy behind and spread your wings. As long as everyone is happy and things run smoothly. That is all I ask.'

'We're partners in crime Patsy, always will be. I will always be on your right side and Sheila on the left, with Victoria and Maggie in the middle. We're in this together and things will run better than ever. I can commute; I can buy a car. I have the cash Patsy... thanks to you.'

Patsy couldn't help grinning. Fin really did have a business brain. If he had concentrated at school, he would have ended up at Oxford University!

Putting down the hair dryer, Patsy tapped Fin on the shoulder. 'Well, what do you think of your hair?'

Fin, who had been too busy talking to pay attention to what she was doing, looked up into the mirror. His hair was shorter, but

ng on top with a side parting. The front fringe seemed to flop on
s forehead and as he swept it aside, Patsy knew she had accom-
ished her goal. As she looked in the mirror, she saw Nick
iamond staring back at her. She had cut his hair exactly as she
d cut Nick's in the past. Victoria had been right, and Patsy
uldn't resist just trying Nick's hairstyle on him. He looked a
anged man already.

'I like it actually, Patsy; it suits me.' Stroking his hand through
s newly cut layers, Fin nodded and gave it the thumbs up.

'Well, Operation Manager,' Patsy laughed, 'you can go and pay
er there.'

'I want a receipt though, Patsy. I can claim it on my tax!' He
ughed and ducked before she could slap the back of his head.

22

DECISION TIME

Standing in the church, Patsy looked ahead and saw Larry's coffi
Looking around the sparsely filled church, she saw Wendy wi
Paul and held up her hand to acknowledge them.

Sheila stood beside her. 'Not many here,' she whispere
'Who's that woman at the front?'

'That's his sister Jenny. She is the one that called me and ga
me the time and date for the funeral.'

'Have they asked you if you're going to the wake or som
thing?' Sheila asked.

'No, nothing as yet, but I wouldn't go anyway.' Patsy did h
best not to smile but couldn't help it. She was pleased she did
matter any more and she'd had no input in the funeral. She w
just a guest.

'Let's just get this over with.' After the short ceremony and
few songs chosen by Jenny and Paul, the curtains closed on Larr
coffin.

'Good riddance to bad rubbish,' Sheila muttered under h
breath. 'Come on lassie, let's go and leave them to it.'

Just as they were about to leave, Wendy walked up to Pat

and Sheila. 'Thank you for coming Patsy. Do you want to come for a drink? We're going back to Jenny's house.'

Patsy declined gracefully. 'If you don't mind, I just want some time to myself,' she lied. As an afterthought, Patsy stopped Wendy before she walked away. 'Is there any news from the police?'

'Nothing, love. Personally, I don't think we'll hear anything.' Wendy's face was as dry as her own. Each of them knew the real Larry.

Inside, Patsy was skipping. Larry and his secret would be gone forever.

Patsy and Sheila made their way to the car.

'Well, I don't know about you Patsy, but I could do with a drink to get the bitter taste out of my mouth.' Sheila opened the car door and got in.

Patsy took one last look at the church and the people coming out of it. That was just another chapter of her life closed.

She mused, 'By the way Sheila, that holiday you suggested. I can't go for another week or so, so why don't you do something on your own? I have had to give in to my parents. They're taking to take Nancy to Greece; it was all booked without them telling me.' Patsy raised one eyebrow and gave Sheila a knowing look.

'What about next month? We can have a look at the chateau. It should be all up and running by then. You might as well look at your going concern Patsy. It's your property and your money.'

'It's a deal.' Patsy laughed.

* * *

'Excuse me, I am looking for Patsy Diamond. I believe she lives here above the community centre?' The tall dark headed man addressed the gathering of people as they came out of the community centre. His taxi still had the engine running and he daren't walk away from it in case it left without him.

'Yes, this is Mrs Patsy's place.' Leandra spied the man curiously. His well-cut grey suit fitted him to perfection. His shoulder-length wavy black hair framed his handsome face and his solid, muscly frame towered above her. Puzzled, Leandra stepped forward; she could see it definitely wasn't a policeman. She knew most of the police in the area anyway; they frequented her brothel regularly. But this tanned handsome man made her suspicious; he had to be a work colleague of Patsy's.

'She has gone away with her daughter, but I can get a message to her if you want. What is your name please?'

'Sorry mademoiselle, I am Philippe Carreaux.' The nod of his head almost represented a bow, which made Leandra blush somewhat. Puzzled, he looked at Leandra. 'She is on holiday with her daughter?' Philippe frowned; he didn't recall her mentioning her daughter.

When she nodded, he thanked her, shook her hand, and got back into the taxi.

Sitting back against the seat, Philippe let out a huge sigh. He hadn't seen Patsy in over six weeks. At last, he had summoned up the courage to come to Scotland, only to find she wasn't here. That was a fait accompli, he decided.

'Back to the airport please,' he instructed the driver.

* * *

'I love this part of France Sheila; it's lovely to see the girls all running around in the sunshine. I swear they have all got tans already and it's good for Nancy to have ready-made sisters in Sharon and Penny.' Patsy smiled as she sat outside on the terrace drinking a glass of lemonade.

'My girls are your family Patsy and Nancy is mine.' Sheila lifted her sunglasses. 'Have you seen him? You disappeared earlier so I presumed you had a slow drive past the stables.'

'I gave in to my impulses and visited but he wasn't there. Anyway, it's been nearly two months. I am a distant memory by now...' Downhearted, Patsy adjusted her sunglasses and picked up her lemonade while watching Nancy and Sheila's two girls running around and playing. 'I had a message from Maggie today; she said some man was sniffing around the community centre looking for me. Leandra spoke to him, she wasn't sure if he was French or Irish. I can't think who it was, but apparently he seemed to know me. Maggie says that Leandra hadn't seen him before and he looked well out of place in his sharp suit. I wonder who it could have been? I hope it's not trouble.'

'Did he give a name?'

Patsy's smile was weak. 'Maggie couldn't remember it, and Leandra hadn't been sure, so I'm sure we'll find out when we get back, but it definitely wasn't police. Let's face it, if they can't tell the difference between French or Irish, he was probably Spanish!' Patsy laughed.

Sheila burst out laughing and lay back further on her chair to let the sun tan her chest and face. 'Me and Angus have set the date. We're getting married on Bonfire Night. Might as well go out with a bang, eh?' Sheila laughed.

'Oh Sheila, that's lovely. I do hope that yours will be the first wedding at the chateau. That is unless Angus is deeply religious and wants a church wedding.'

Thrilled, Sheila put her glass down. 'Oh my goodness Patsy, that would be great! But I presume there's all kinds of paperwork to fill in if you want to get married in a foreign country?'

'Not too much; people do it all the time. Let me pay for Angus's parents and any family to come and Paul can do your wedding.' Patsy grinned. She could see the delight in Sheila's face. She was surprised it had never crossed her mind.

'Bonfire Night in Paris and getting married to my Angus. Oh Patsy love I couldn't be happier. It sounds so romantic and we're on our honeymoon at the same time. Thank you, Patsy. Really, I mean that. Thank you.'

'Oh shut up you daft cow,' Patsy laughed. 'Paul has sent us a salad and stuff for lunch and it all looks very nice, but to be honest, I feel quite sickly. I might just have some crusty bread to line my stomach.'

Concerned, Sheila leaned forward. 'That's not like you Patsy, have you eaten something that doesn't agree with you?'

Patsy didn't meet her eye. 'Maybe it's just the sun; you don't get a lot of it in Scotland. I might just be a bit tired too.'

Sheila wasn't convinced, then suddenly, her eyes widened. 'When are you going to tell me Patsy? Is that why you came here?'

'Tell you what? I don't know what you mean.' Patsy blushed.

'You're pregnant. You haven't had a drink since we've been here and you're picking at your food. My guess is those little French tadpoles have hit the back of the net.' Sheila laughed. 'Oh well, that's blown my news out of the water. But never forget,' Sheila warned with a wagging finger, 'I can see through that poker face Patsy. I know you too well.'

'You're right, but I'm suspicious. It took me years to get pregnant with Nick. I'm worried in case I'm wrong. I did think of telling Philippe, but he's not here and he would probably think I was trying to trap him.' Patsy shrugged. 'Anyway, what's your news?'

Sheila gave a sly grin. 'I'm pregnant too. Me and Angus are having a baby. God, I hope it doesn't have his beard!' Sheila burst out laughing.

Shocked, Patsy stood up and hugged Sheila. 'That's marvel-

us news. We're pregnant together.' Neither of them could
elieve it. 'Say nothing to anyone else, Sheila; I want to know
verything is okay first. I also want to tell Victoria when we're on
ur own. She is still my mother-in-law from Nick. I want her to
ear it from me first.'

'Oh for goodness' sake Patsy. She will be as chuffed as
inepence if she thinks you're having a baby. If you think she's
oing to judge you or something, forget it. Why should you feel
uilty? Nick was leaving you Patsy; sorry to state the obvious, but
e was and he was having a baby with another woman. A baby, I
night add, that is living with Victoria and she is bringing up in
ie absence of both parents.'

Frowning slightly, Patsy reached out her hand to squeeze
heila's. 'Still, not a word yet; it's not three months yet and I'm
uperstitious.'

Sheila made a sign of a zip across her mouth. 'Don't look so
vorried Patsy, everything will be fine. Enjoy it this time; we'll get
it together and moan about the size of our ankles and bursting
ladders! Yours will probably be born in a stable near his
avourite horse.' Sheila laughed. 'But you have to tell him Patsy.
'hat Milieu lot will know in time, and he's not stupid. I'm sure he
an add up.'

'I will tell him, but I don't want anything from him.' Patsy
oked downcast.

'You love him, don't you? I could tell that from the beginning.
d say you're well matched too; he's a strong man, and you need a
rong man, because you're a strong woman Patsy. Angus will
robably faint, but I'm glad I am giving him one of his own. He
eserves that.'

* * *

Wearing a red shift dress with a matching black-and-red bole
jacket and shoes, Patsy walked into the restaurant at the chatea
Paul was beaming. His huge bulk with his white apron wrappe
around him walked towards her from the kitchen.

'Mrs Diamond, thank you for coming.'

Glancing at the other assistant chefs in the kitchen, she cou
see them chopping and preparing all kinds of things as pots an
pans boiled away. Sheila, who was wearing a black trouser su
held the children's hands and kept them away from the kitche
appliances. 'Good luck Paul, you've done a magnificent job,' sł
called over as she steered the children out of the way.

'We have people staying tonight, Sheila. Guests at last!' Pa
clapped his hands together gleefully.

Patsy wandered around the restaurant with its huge silv
candlesticks as centrepieces on the fresh, white Egyptian line
tablecloths. Trailing her hand along the linen, she looked aroun
Her mind wandered back to when she had visited the chateau fo
the first time. How much it had changed, and that was all down t
Paul and his brothers. They had all worked hard and she made
mental note to give Paul a bonus for all of his hard work.

Leaving the restaurant, Patsy walked towards the long hallwa
with its winding staircase. Instinctively, she walked up it. Sł
marvelled at how clean and polished everything was. As sł
walked along the corridors, she looked at the names on tł
bedroom doors. They were all written in gilt-edged gold. It wa
very luxurious. Opening the door to one of the bedrooms, sł
walked in. It wasn't a bedroom at all, more like a mini flat. It had
chaise lounge, ornate vases and gold taps on the sunken bath. Tł
four-poster bed was enormous and made even bigger by the larg
thick duvet that covered it. Patsy looked around in awe. She ha
stayed in many swanky places in her time, but this took som
beating.

As she turned to leave, she looked up and saw Philippe standing in the doorway. Almost jumping out of her skin, Patsy staggered back. 'Oh my God, you made me jump! What are you doing here?'

'Looking for you. You're a hard lady to find.' He smiled as his eyes bore into hers. The chemistry between them was electric as they faced each other.

Patsy's heart was pounding. She had fantasised about how they would meet again and where many times. She had even practiced what she would say. 'Well, you have found me now.' Patsy blushed and dug her fingernails into the palm of her hands. He looked taller than she remembered, standing there in his tuxedo and bow tie. She breathed in his aftershave and could almost feel herself trembling.

Philippe took her hand and pulled her closer to him. Sweeping her hair from her face, he kissed her. Instantly Patsy melted in his arms and held on to him. All of her common sense went out of the window as she clung to him. Her hands reached into the inside of his jacket and roamed over his shirt covering his chest. Letting go of her, Philippe took off his jacket and let it fall to the floor. With his leg, he kicked the bedroom door shut. They didn't need words, their hunger for each other spoke volumes.

Lying in Phillipe's arms, Patsy entwined her fingers in the hairs on his chest. 'I've missed you,' she heard herself say without thinking.

'And I missed you, which is why I went to Scotland to find you. I don't know how, Patsy, but in those few short days you have bewitched me.'

Patsy sat up. 'You went to Scotland to find me?'

Philippe reached up and ran his hands through her hair. 'I did. I needed to see you. I have loved you since the day I pulled you out of that car. I dismissed it then, but you found me. I have always been a believer in fate, chérie. And I believe you are my fate.'

Philippe's loving sentiments melted her heart. He was saying everything she had only dreamed about.

Lying back in his arms, a smile crossed Patsy's mouth. Well, at least she knew who the visitor in Scotland was now, she thought to herself. And the very fact that Philippe had sought her out made her heart soar. 'Why me?' she asked pensively. She didn't want to get carried away with it all. She needed to know if this was real.

'I have known many women since my wife died of cancer. Each and every one of them wanted to clip my wings, but they like the money. I thanked all of them for their graciousness with a diamond bracelet and saw them on their way. I don't believe you would clip my wings Patsy, nor would I clip yours. We are cut from the same cloth you and me. I have my own business, you have your own business. I will not tread on your toes. I can advise, but I will not get involved.'

He smiled and kissed her forehead. 'I don't need your money Patsy and you don't need mine. I just like the way you made me feel. Like a man. Alive again. You didn't ask me for anything, you didn't know I had anything, and it didn't matter.'

Patsy thought about his words. 'It's you I have missed Philippe. I am ashamed to say it, I have never felt like this before. I have been a married woman and I didn't love my husband as much as I love you. There, I've said it.'

Getting out of bed, Philippe picked up his jacket off the floor and reached into the inside pocket. Taking out a box, he went back to bed and handed it to her. 'I have been carrying this for you. I didn't know when I would see you again, so I carried it with me whenever I went out.'

Patsy opened the box and looked at the ring inside. It wasn't anything like she had seen before. It was silver and had two back-to-back letter Ps for Philippe and Patsy. Each letter was diamond encrusted.

'Is this that Diamond bracelet you have thanked your other mistresses with Philippe?' Patsy asked while looking in the box. She was unsure of the sentiment.

'That's not a bracelet Patsy. See it as you wish, but I had it made for you and you alone.'

Patsy felt nervous; she wasn't sure if this was a proposal, or if she was being asked to be the viscount's mistress. Phillipe took the ring and placed it on her engagement finger on her left hand.

Not being able to take her eyes off the ring as it sparkled, she snuggled up closer to him. 'Are you asking me to marry you, Phillipe?' Patsy blurted out. She wasn't sure; he hadn't asked her. She wanted to get it right in her mind. 'What about your status? Am I just some bit of rough? And what about our mutual Milieu friends – would they agree with this?'

Philippe frowned and instantly went down on his knees. 'I would very much like it if you agreed to marry me. I love you, you make me feel whole again, like something has been missing in my life and it's taken a car crash to find you. My status, well, what does that matter? I marry whom I please. Can I get up now, or would you like me to do something else while I am on my knees with you stood naked before me?' He smiled and pulled her towards him. Feeling her own arousal, Patsy slid to the floor and consumed with passion, wrapped her legs firmly around him.

Reaching his hand across, he tweaked her nipple, and let his tongue roam over it, making her arch her back with desire.

Patsy slid her hand down the duvet and stroked him gently. Feeling his excitement rise, she straddled him. 'Now I am in the saddle, Philippe Carreaux.' She grinned. Sliding down upon him, she gasped. 'You are very blessed Philippe in that department,' she moaned as she writhed her hips upon him.

'I am the jockey around here,' he laughed and turned Patsy on her back. Their passion and hunger for each other overwhelmed them both as they clung to each other yet again, in ecstasy.

Panting heavily, and trying to gulp in air, Patsy lay back watching as Phillipe got out of bed and started dressing.

'I plan to see you tomorrow for a proper date. No ifs and buts. A proper time, a proper place. I will pick you up and I will meet your daughter and tomorrow evening you will meet mine. But while you share my bed, you share no one else's,' he warned.

'The same goes for me Philippe. I don't share. I've had a cheating partner and I don't want another one. Friends with benefits is one thing, the viscount's mistress is another. I am no mistress. We are equals.'

'I agree *chérie*. And if I didn't mean my words, I wouldn't say them. Believe me, the words do not come easy. You are Patsy Diamond. The queen of your own Diamond empire. Before you give me your answer Patsy, I want you to know I didn't have Larry murdered out of pity. It was selfishness. He wasn't having what I wanted so badly by fair means or foul. He needed taking out of the picture. I don't mind if you marry me or not, but I won't blackmail you into it. You come willingly or not at all. That needed saying, because you know the Milieu had something to do with Larry's death and that dreaded letter. Well, I wanted you to have it safely in your hands. It wasn't hard, he had it in his jacket pocket and when one of the men who had shot him, hired by myself of course, frisked him to check if he was dead or not, he found it.' Philippe paused, looking into Patsy's eyes. 'I wanted us to start by being honest with each other.' Taking her hand, he kissed the back of it tenderly. Philippe's nonchalance about Larry's death idn't shock Patsy, and Philippe was asking for no reward. He was ıst informing her. He wanted honesty between them.

'I know I can trust you. And to be honest if you hadn't done it, would have killed him myself. For the record I wasn't going to ıarry him. I had already made my mind up after I'd spoken to ou that I was going to call his bluff and take what came. I ouldn't share his bed after you. I want to be your wife, I want to e your lover and friend. I want to be honest and not make up xcuses for my absences, but I also want to put down roots, I'm ot sure where, maybe Scotland or London, and bring up my aughter. Do you understand?' Tears rolled down Patsy's face as ıe realised she had just given away her chance of happiness.

'What are roots Patsy? You talk of bricks and mortar. That is ot home. Home is where the heart is and my heart is with you, herever you are. Yours and Nancy's home is France. Make it your ɛtaway, your home. Breathe in the fresh air of the countryside. ɔu still have your apartment in Scotland for business and wher-ver you stay in London. She is your child and she will live with s, here in the sunshine. Put down your roots. Teach her to ride orses from my stables Patsy. If you marry me, we marry as equals ith respect. Sometimes, I feel respect is more important than •ve, although I do love you. I have told you already, I will not clip ɔur wings and you will not clip mine. I expect no questions Patsy, or will I question you. Go to Scotland, go to London, bring your mily here. That is the point of family Patsy? We surround ırselves with people we trust. Now you must go, you have a lot of ıinking to do, and I am staying here this evening so that my crest ill go above your restaurant doors. You see, I am making you oney already!' He grinned.

* * *

The following day, Philippe turned up at the cottage. His whi
shirt billowed out, showing the hairs on his chest, and he w
wearing his usual black riding trousers. Sheila looked out of tl
window. 'Oh my God lassie, Lancelot's here. Put your sunglass
on he's going to smile and those white teeth are blinding!' If n
Angus turned up wearing that shirt with lacy cuffs he'd lo
stupid, but Carrots looks like the fourth musketeer.'

Patsy was too happy to take offence at Sheila's quips, but sl
was also nervous. This was the moment of truth. She had to te
Philippe about the baby she carried. She wanted to do that befo
agreeing to marry him. She needed to see his face, be it disa
pointed or happy.

Casually, after dismounting his white horse, he sat in tl
kitchen and chatted with Sheila, Nancy and the girls. Spyir
Patsy, he stood up and put his arms around her. 'We're havir
dinner with my daughter this evening. She is looking forward
meeting you.'

'Phillipe, before this goes any further, I need to talk to yo
Nervously, she looked around the kitchen. 'Sheila take the gir
outside, would you?'

Doing as asked, she ushered the girls out and winked at Pat
and crossed her fingers for luck.

'I want to marry you Philippe, but there is something I have
tell you. I don't want to trap you and I want nothing from yo
but... I'm pregnant,' she said. She had resigned herself to h
rebuke and waited.

'Is that all that is stopping you from marrying me? Did yc
fear that I would turn my back on you?'

Patsy nodded. 'I want the truth between us and I won't give u
my baby for you Philippe.'

'Good, I don't want you to. That is my baby too you know,
viscount in the making, and I always like to seal a bargain. For tl

record Patsy, no one could trap me, not even you and believe me, women have tried. You overthink things and worry about things that haven't happened. Is that a yes then? Are you going to be my wife and the mother of my child?'

Tears of joy rolled down Patsy's face. 'Yes, that's a definite yes, Philippe.'

The door opened slightly and Sheila walked in. 'I take it all is well then?'

'Sheila say hello to the right honourable Patsy Diamond Carreaux.' Patsy laughed.

Confused, Sheila looked at them both. 'You're keeping the Diamond name?'

'She has to Sheila. This is her Diamond reign and that is how she is known. She is and always will forever be Patsy Diamond. Business first, then love. The forever diamond is the most sparkling and beautiful diamond of them all.'

Sheila was secretly pleased that Patsy would still be Patsy Diamond. 'Shouldn't you tell your Milieu laddies, especially that Manne bloke? Right misery guts him. Do they have to approve it or something? After all, you can't fart without their blessing.'

Pushing Patsy away from him, a serious look crossed his face and he stared at them both. 'I am the Milieu, ladies. Like my father and grandfathers before me. I am the head of the Milieu and that misery guts as you call him is my uncle.' He grinned.

Stunned, Patsy and Sheila looked at each other, their jaws almost dropping. Viscount Philippe was the Godfather of France and everything he surveyed, and now he had the forever diamond in his crown.

ACKNOWLEDGMENTS

Thanks to Avril for her support and to Boldwood Books for giving me the opportunity to let my imagination run wild. Many thanks to Emily Ruston, my patient editor, without whom I'd be lost.

MORE FROM GILLIAN GODDEN

We hope you enjoyed reading *Forever Diamond*. If you did, please leave a review.

If you'd like to gift a copy, this book is also available as an ebook, large print, hardback, digital audio download and audiobook CD.

Sign up to Gillian Godden's mailing list for news, competitions and updates on future books.

http://bit.ly/GillianGoddenNewsletter

Explore more gritty gangland fiction from Gillian Godden...

ABOUT THE AUTHOR

Gillian Godden is a Northern-born medical secretary for NHS England. She spent thirty years of her life in the East End of London, hearing stories about the local striptease pubs. Now in Yorkshire, she is an avid reader who lives with her dog, Susie.

Follow Gillian on social media:

facebook.com/gilliangoddenauthor

twitter.com/GGodden

PEAKY READERS

GANG LOYALTIES. DARK SECRETS.
BLOODY REVENGE.

A READER COMMUNITY FOR
GANGLAND CRIME THRILLER FANS!

DISCOVER PAGE-TURNING NOVELS
FROM YOUR FAVOURITE AUTHORS
AND MEET NEW FRIENDS.

Boldwood

Boldwood Books is an award-winning fiction publishing company seeking out the best stories from around the world.

Find out more at www.boldwoodbooks.com

Join our reader community for brilliant books, competitions and offers!

Follow us

@BoldwoodBooks

@BookandTonic

Sign up to our weekly deals newsletter

https://bit.ly/BoldwoodBNewsletter

Printed in Great Britain
by Amazon

45684218R00165